Watch over Me

Watch over Me

LUCY MONROE

BRAVA

KENSINGTON PUBLISHING CORP.

BRAVA BOOKS are published by

Kensington Publishing Corp.
119 West 40th Street
New York, NY 10018

All Kensington titles, imprints and distributed lines are available at special quantity discounts for bulk purchases for sales promotion, premiums, fund-raising, educational or institutional use.

Special book excerpts or customized printings can also be created to fit specific needs. For details, write or phone the office of the Kensington Special Sales Manager: Kensington Publishing Corp., 119 West 40th Street, New York, NY 10018. Attn. Special Sales Department. Phone: 1-800-221-2647.

Brava and the B logo are Reg. U.S. Pat. & TM Off.

ISBN-13: 978-1-61523-161-4

Printed in the United States of America

Chapter 1

"**D**eath is overrated, asshole."

Myk waited to see if the bastard he had pinned to the wall was going to heed the warning he'd whispered. It took a few seconds, but the massive body in front of him relaxed into a universal pose of submission.

"Good choice." Myk used the arm he had bent to the center of the would-be attacker's back to turn him around and face the woman.

He and his *friends* had been terrorizing the brunette in the alley. Unfortunately for them, the restaurant where Myk had an upcoming meeting backed up to the alley and he liked to case his environment.

The other man's cohorts littered the wet pavement of the alley. Myk hadn't killed any of them, but they wouldn't be waking up any time soon.

"I believe you owe the lady an apology." Myk thought his tone was conversational, but the guy flinched.

"Sorry."

Myk increased the pressure on the man's arm, just short of breaking it.

The man gasped. "We shouldn't have scared you like that," he said, sounding a hell of a lot more sincere.

The woman, who from her dress was probably a waitress for the restaurant, glared. "No duh, asshole."

Myk almost smiled. She was no pushover. She'd obviously been scared, but she'd been yelling invectives at the men tormenting her when Myk had arrived. "Did you want to call 911?"

"Already done." Anger radiated from the two words. "These jerks aren't getting away with what they've been doing."

"They've messed with you before?" Myk's muscles twitched, sending his fist into the belly of the last man standing.

The man grunted, knees buckling until the pain in his arm forced him to remain standing.

The angry brunette nodded. "And the other waitresses too."

"You'll press charges?" he asked. A lot of women wouldn't.

"Oh, yeah. My girl is on the force and she's going to enjoy nailing the hides of these lowlife bastards to the wall."

The sound of sirens could be heard now. The man Myk held immobile was blathering about having apologized between whimpers of pain. As if saying he was sorry could make it all better. Idiot.

"You look like your sister," a smooth, cultured male voice said from the darkness behind the restaurant.

With a quick flick of his wrist, Myk incapacitated the would-be attacker. Letting the man fall to the pavement, he turned toward where the voice had come from. "Whitmore?"

"In the flesh." But the man did not step out of the shadows.

Smart. But then that was to be expected from the director of the ultrasecret Goddard Project Agency.

Myk turned to the woman. "If the police want my statement, have them call this number." He handed her a business card with his cell phone number on it and nothing else.

"You're leaving?"

The sound of the sirens grew and a police car swept into the alley with squealing tires.

"I have a meeting."

"But—"

Myk didn't wait to hear what she would have said. He'd done what needed doing. The woman called out her thanks as Myk blended into the shadows, assuming his contact from TGP was following him.

They were a block away from the restaurant when Myk spoke again. "Where to now?"

"You like Vietnamese?"

"If the cook is from Vietnam, yeah."

"Take a right at the corner."

The Vietnamese restaurant turned out to be a hole in the wall, literally. No window on the street, just a door that opened into a dimly lit room with a handful of tables in the center and a smattering of booths around the edges. Andrew Whitmore led Myk to one in a dark corner.

Myk sat angled so that he could see both the restaurant and the swinging door leading into the kitchen. After the last eighteen months, the habit of taking the least vulnerable position was ingrained. He doubted it would ever leave him.

"Nice," he said, meaning the appropriateness of the restaurant for their meeting.

He was more comfortable in the shadows than the sunlight. Damn, that made him sound like a vampire, or something. And really? All he was—was an INS agent. At least he had been.

One who had been chosen for a deep-cover assignment in conjunction with the DEA because he'd been the *lucky* bastard to discover the connection between a particular slave run and a nasty drug cartel.

No, he'd never been able to content himself with just doing

his job as a border patrol agent, but had to follow his instincts to deeper and uglier things. He followed those instincts one too many times and got noticed by the guys in the suits.

It was only a matter of time after that before he'd had his first undercover assignment. That one had lasted only a few weeks, but it had led to information that warranted a long-term, deep-cover investigation. He'd gotten the promotion and the assignment that resulted in more than a year living amid people who were cruel, vindictive and amoral. Those were just the hirelings.

The leader of that particular cartel was a true sociopath whose death had not caused a single regret for Myk. No, Myk's nightmares came from an entirely different source.

Whitmore nodded, bringing Myk's thoughts back from a hell he wanted to stop visiting. "The food is good, but the privacy this place affords is even better, not that the other restaurant wouldn't have been just as good. However, I do not think we would have been able to meet uninterrupted after your altercation in the alley."

"It needed doing." He had been in the position where he *could* do something, so he had.

"You sound like your sister."

"Do I?" For some reason, that surprised him.

He knew Elle was, or had been, a federal agent. Yet he had never considered she might have been a whole lot different on the job than she was around the family. He should have.

He'd never threatened to kill one of his siblings . . . and meant it.

Clearly Elle had a different side to her as well.

"Yes, the physical family resemblance is apparent as well."

"If you say so." Personally, he didn't see it.

His brothers were both taller than his own six-foot-three and had the muscular builds of defensive linemen. His body might bulge with muscle, too, but it was a lot leaner. They all shared the same dark hair, though, including Elle. However, she had gray eyes, like Roman and their mother, while he had brown—the same as his oldest brother, Mat, their mother and their baby sister, Danusia.

But those superficial similarities aside, he'd never thought he had much in common with his family, either physically or under the surface.

After what he'd learned of Elle's job, he'd had to reevaluate that belief. But she still hadn't seen the kind of ugliness he'd lived with on a daily basis for the last year and a half. Even before going undercover, he'd seen stuff on border patrol that taught him to control a lot more than just his gag reflex.

Even so, when he'd first gone undercover, his marks disgusted him to the point of nausea on a daily basis. Men and women who would kill and torture for profit, who would use children for that same filthy profit. Not only selling them as slaves, but using them to carry drugs across borders. Inside body cavities, in their stomachs—whatever worked.

No one cared about the risks or pain inflicted on the children. No one but him, and he'd had to learn to turn it off. His emotions. His horror. His need to protect each child.

Oh, he'd done what he could, but ultimately? He'd done his job. He and the DEA agent assigned to the case had brought down the whole ring, their leader dying in the final showdown. Unfortunately, that truth hadn't mitigated the cost to the innocent.

Now, he was faced with another "found" assignment. He should be on vacation, relaxing on a warm beach somewhere far from child slavery rings, drug runners, and sadistic assholes who liked their jobs in both. But no, his family needed him.

"Elle is in deep shit." And she didn't have a clue.

"Your message requesting this meeting implied something of the sort."

"Yeah." Going through the files confiscated after the final

sting on his latest assignment, he'd discovered something that still had the power to send chills down his spine.

Some very bad people were interested in the work of Dr. Lana Ericson, Project Manager for Material Transformation at Environmental Technology Research and Design, a research lab in southern California. That in itself wouldn't have concerned Myk so much. He would have been more than willing to pass the information off to suits and let them deal with it.

But there was the small complication of his brother Mat working for the same company. Collateral damage could be a bitch. In addition, and at this point in time, more importantly, his sister Elle was the security consultant who had developed the new high-grade security measures for ETRD. To further complicate matters, she was also engaged to marry one of the company's project managers.

Both pieces of information had been in the file Myk had found—along with the notation that Elle was the initial target. In what and for what, he could only guess. All he had to go on was a copy of Dr. Ericson's research along with some notes she'd made in the margin.

Attached to the top of that stack of papers had been a cheerful yellow sticky note that incongruously said: *First target—Elle Gray.*

It was all he had to go on, but for Myk that was plenty. His family was in danger and that was unacceptable.

Elle had just found happiness after grieving the death of her first husband long enough to worry Myk. He wasn't sure she would ever get over it. Myk was not going to let anyone ruin that happiness.

Myk told Whitmore what he'd found. "I don't know whether they want Elle for the information she has on the security system—"

"Or if they intend to eliminate her and the threat she poses to any attempt they might make on gathering further intel and a usable formula," Whit said.

"Exactly."

"Did you call her?"

"Yes, but she thinks she's impervious." His little sister had coolly informed him that risks like the one he'd told her about came with her job and she took her own measures to circumvent them.

"She's a damn fine agent."

"She *was* an agent. Until you fired her." And good or not, no one was bulletproof.

Whitmore sighed, looking chagrined. "I didn't have a choice."

"Everyone has choices."

"True. And your sister made hers. She could have continued working for TGP."

"Out of the field."

"We all have to retire from fieldwork sooner or later."

"She's only twenty-eight. That's hardly the age for retirement."

"It all depends on what you want out of life."

"Are you saying you retired that early?"

A naked look of regret crossed Whitmore's features. "No." His expression going impassive with just a hint of warmth, the agency director put his hand out to shake. "Call me Whit."

Myk just looked at the gray-haired man with eyes that saw too much and revealed too little.

Whit smiled, not dropping his hand. "I have a feeling we're going to be working closely together."

"You were my last resort." No matter how happy Elle was now, Myk was pissed as hell at the man who had fired his little sister from her job. And he wouldn't have approached Andrew Whitmore for help if there had been any other choice.

Whit said, "The INS doesn't have a material concern in the matter."

"Right. No illegal aliens."

The DEA had been a little more willing to take ownership of the problem, but they'd made it clear that they couldn't give the situation top priority. It was a matter of resources and they just didn't have a team to assign to a situation that had not yet developed.

Hence his trip to Washington, D.C., and this meeting.

"Are you on a leave of absence?"

"No."

Surprise flitted across Whit's face. "I would have thought you'd want to be on the case."

"I have every intention of being the agent in charge." Which is why he'd quit his job with the INS.

Whit's brow lifted before a satisfied expression settled on his face. His hand extended further across the table. "Welcome to The Goddard Project, Mykola Chernichenko."

Myk shook the man's hand, making his pact with the devil's hindmost.

"Dr. Ericson."

Lana adjusted the angle on the microscope. Yes. Right there. Perfect. "Amazing."

"Lana."

She reached out blindly for the stylus to her handheld. *Got it*. She started taking notes on the screen without looking away from the microscope.

"*Dr. Ericson!!!*"

Lana jumped, bumping her cheekbone on the microscope's eyepiece before falling backward, hitting a wall that hadn't been there when she'd come in to work that morning.

Strong hands set her firmly on her feet as she realized the

wall was warm and made of flesh and muscle. Lots and lots of muscle.

Stumbling back a step, she looked up and then up some more. The dark-haired hottie in front of her was as tall as her colleague, Beau Ruston. Or close to it, anyway. She fumbled with her glasses, sliding them on her nose. They didn't help. Reading glasses for the computer, they only served to make her feel more disoriented.

She squinted, then remembered and pulled the glasses off again, letting them dangle by their chain around her neck. "Um, hello? Did I know you were visiting my lab?"

She was fairly certain she hadn't known. She forgot appointments sometimes. Okay, often, but she always remembered eventually. And this man hadn't made an appointment with her. She was sure of it. He didn't look like a scientist, either.

Not that all scientists were as unremarkable as she was in the looks department, but this man was another species entirely.

He looked dangerous and sexy. Enough so that he would definitely replace chemical formulas in her dreams at night. His black hair was a little too long and looked like he'd run his fingers through it, not a comb. That was just so bad boy. She had a secret weakness for bad boys.

Even bigger than the secret weakness she'd harbored for Beau Ruston before he'd met Elle.

She had posters of James Dean and Matt Dillon on the wall of her bedroom and had seen *Rebel without a Cause* a whopping thirty-six times.

Unlike James Dean, this yummy bad boy even had pierced ears. Only instead of sedate studs or small hoops, he had tiny black plugs. Only a bit bigger than a pair of studs, the plugs were recessed in his lobes. They had the Chinese kanji for strength etched on them in silver. Or pewter maybe. It wasn't shiny.

The earrings were hot. Just like him.

He looked like the kind of man who had a tattoo. Nothing colorful. Something black and meaningful. She wanted to see it. Too bad she couldn't just ask.

Interpersonal interaction had so many taboos. It wasn't like science, where you dug for answers without apology.

"Lana?"

The stranger had a strong jaw, too, squared and accented by a close-cropped beard that went under, not across, his chin. No mustache. His lips were set in a straight line, but they still looked like they'd be heaven to kiss.

Not that she'd kissed a lot of lips, but she was twenty-nine. Even a geeky scientist didn't make it to the shy side of thirty without a few kisses along the way. And other stuff. Not that the other stuff was all that spectacular. She'd always wondered if that was her fault or the men she'd chosen to partner.

It didn't take a shrink to identify the fact that Lana had trust issues. With her background, who wouldn't?

Still, people had been known to betray family, love, and country for sex. She wouldn't cross a busy street to get some. Or maybe she would, if this stranger was waiting on the other side.

The fact that she could measure the time since she'd last had sex in years rather than months, weeks, or *days*—which would be a true miracle—wasn't something she enjoyed dwelling on. She blamed it on her work.

However, every feminine instinct that was usually sublimated by her passion for her job was on red alert now.

"Dr. Ericson. *Lana.*"

She waved her hand at the noise buzzing in her ear, not wanting to look away from the tight black T-shirt that clung to a definite six-pack and leather jeans that molded to muscular thighs and an impressive package. She liked that word. *Package.*

It sounded so naughty and implied a man's member was some kind of present waiting for a woman to open. His was getting bigger by the second.

Oh my. She wanted to open that pressie. Considering the disappointment she'd had in the past from that particular type of gift, her desire surprised her. But then she'd never been this close to a living, breathing embodiment of her fantasies, either.

A very pointed throat-clearing happened near her ear.

She tried waving her hand again, but it was caught this time.

"No," she said firmly.

"Uh, Lana . . ."

She definitely *didn't* have an appointment with this guy.

One dark brow quirked, but he had yet to say anything.

"Dr. Ericson!"

Lana's head snapped up again and she saw that the stranger was accompanied by others. Her boss, Frank Ingram, and ETRD's security consultant, Elle Gray.

The tall, supermodel-beautiful woman was the one who'd grabbed Lana's hand. Was it fair that Elle could incapacitate a man twice her size, was probably as smart as Lana—well, close to—*and* was that amazing looking?

The only amazing thing about Lana was her brain.

Wincing at her thoughts as well as the small throb below her left eye from her run-in with the microscope, she said, "There was no need to shout, Frank."

Elle shook her head and laughed. "You were staring, Lana. Hard. At unmentionable places."

Oh, those pesky taboos again. Men got away with staring at breasts all the time, but a woman, particularly a geeky scientist, wasn't supposed to stare at a man's crotch. Still. "I was studying. It's what I do."

"You study men?" the stranger asked in a voice that made her thighs clench.

Wow.

If he could do that with his voice, what would he be able to do with other things? Maybe show her what all the fuss was about finally?

"I study everything."

Frank chuckled. It was an indulgent sound, one that she seemed to bring out in him more than the other scientists on ETRD's staff. "To the exclusion of noticing anything else around you. Hence the shouting."

She sighed, knowing her boss had a point. "I'm sorry, Frank." Meeting the dark brown depths of the stranger's eyes, she stifled a second sigh. "I also apologize if I made you uncomfortable."

She'd been told she did that sometimes. It was one of the many reasons she preferred her lab over social settings. Really, really preferred.

He adjusted his stance just a little. "Uncomfortable isn't the word I'd use."

Elle groaned. "Myk, you are so bad. *Baba* would slap you with the wooden spoon."

Things clicked together in Lana's extremely productive brain. "You two are related. He's your brother. Mykola, the one closest to you in age and an INS agent. You haven't seen him in over a year and you're hoping he gets along with Beau as well as Mat does."

Mykola turned a less-than-pleased look on his sister. "When did you get to be such a blabbermouth?"

Elle rolled her eyes. "Don't be an idiot. Lana remembers everything she hears, even in passing."

"And she puts it together like she does her formulas." Frank smiled proudly. "I bet she knows the name of my podiatrist."

"You don't have a podiatrist. There's nothing wrong with your feet, but have you considered seeing an allergist? I think you may have allergy-induced asthma brought on by something in Nisha's lab." She'd been meaning to mention that for a while, but had gotten sidetracked.

More than once.

It was the story of her life.

She'd never have a committed romantic relationship. No man would be able to tolerate the way her brain worked on a long-term basis, but she wasn't opposed to something less involved with the gorgeous bad boy in front of her.

"Lana!" Frank and Elle shouted in unison, both sounding equally scandalized.

Uh oh. "Which part did I say out loud?" she asked in resignation.

Elle gave her a look that hovered between pitying and hugely amused. "The part where you implied you wouldn't mind having sex with my *gorgeous bad boy* of a brother."

Chapter 2

Mykola leaned forward just a little. "What I'd like to know was the part you didn't say out loud."

Oh, he *was* a wicked, wicked man. Lana rarely got embarrassed because she was so used to doing embarrassing things, but this? Definitely mortifying.

She bent her head, sighed, and covered her eyes with her hand. "I need to get out of the lab more."

"Maybe I can help with that." Mykola's voice sounded like liquid sin.

She raised her head and frowned at him. "Clearly, I got the bad boy part right." She only wished he was serious.

He just shrugged.

"I'm telling *Baba*." But Elle's voice was amused, not threatening.

Mykola didn't smile, but he didn't glare at his sister, either. He just looked, well, he looked *unaffected*. Except where Lana wasn't supposed to be *looking*.

Was. Not. Supposed. To. Be. Looking.

Darn it.

She forced her gaze elsewhere, but if he was unaffected *there* then he was even more impressive than her first impression. Really, hugely.

"Do we have more security upgrades?" Lana asked, finally wondering why these people were in her lab.

"Not exactly."

Mykola's lips flatlined. "Some very bad people are interested in your work."

She was *still* looking at him. At least her eyes were settled on something above his waist. "Yes?"

"You don't seem surprised." His left brow quirked.

She'd never been able to do that. Good thing her desire to be the female version of Spock had not lasted past adolescence.

"Maybe because I'm not. I practice modern-day alchemy. Just as in times past, that sort of thing is going to attract both the idealist and the opportunist. Mr. Smith is the former, but I'd have to be naïve not to believe there were plenty of the latter." She also had personal experience that confirmed her belief, but she wasn't about to discuss that now.

Or ever.

Mykola glared. At her.

Weird. People didn't usually start glaring at her until they'd known her at least a couple of hours.

He crossed his arms, making his biceps bulge deliciously. "Maybe you should have considered that before you came up with a formula for turning lead into gold."

She dismissed that with a flick of her wrist. "The formula for that particular transformation has been around for quite a while, but it takes too much energy to make it a viable alternative."

"Your enzymes don't." There was that anger again. *Directed at her.*

Had she missed something? That wouldn't be anything new. Her brows drew together and she looked at Elle. Did the other woman know why her brother was mad at Lana? But no help there. Elle wasn't looking at Lana. Her gaze was set firmly on her brother and her eyes were filled with concern.

Lana stepped back toward her lab bench and started organizing her samples for the microscope while her brain struggled to figure out what heinous act Mykola thought she'd committed. "Um . . . my enzymes were developed to enhance the yield from edible or usable biological crops."

"Then why the hell did you put a side-note on your observations that said, and I quote: *lead into gold*?"

"Um . . . because that's exactly what it does? Or as good as. The enzymes take a dormant or already harvested plant and change it so that it will yield a crop. Once we have the enzymes working properly, they will make it possible to get a secondary crop from every planting, decreasing the stress on the resources needed to farm in areas that are suffering from drought or a naturally low supply of water, short growing season, et cetera."

She was very excited about this project. She had hopes to have a prototype enzyme ready for wide-scale testing within the year. Among other things, one of her most frustrating problems with the product, though, was the awful smell that emanated while the enzymes did their job. It had prompted Frank to ask if she was using decomposing bodies for fertilizer.

Eww . . . just eww. She'd bought gas masks for use by her and her staff and put an order in for a hermetically sealed door to be installed on her growing room. The order had been approved posthaste.

Those weren't options for use in acres of growing fields, however.

The soil exhaustion was an issue as well, though other biochemists worldwide were already working on that particular problem. And the use of her enzyme resulted in far less depletion of soil resources than an actual additional crop would.

Mykola looked unimpressed. "But can your enzyme be used to turn lead into gold?"

"Why would anyone want to?"

"*Please.*" Now the yummy man just sounded snarky. "You might not be in it for the profit, but that doesn't mean others won't want to capitalize on its potential. Those opportunists you were talking about."

"I am in it for the profit, that of improved lives and a decrease in worldwide starvation."

"That's not what I meant."

"I know."

She could swear the sound coming out of his throat was a growl. "Lady, has anyone ever told you that you're damn annoying?"

"Among other things." Her father's favorite question while she'd been growing up was, *Do you have to be such an f-ing pain in the ass?* Her mother was less antagonistic, but no more accepting. Her most frequent refrain was, *Just try to be normal, Lana.*

"It's not intentional, though." That didn't usually matter, but she always tried saying it. "What I meant was that turning lead into gold when you could turn it into platinum would be silly. Platinum is rarer and has far more practical uses than gold."

"So, the enzymes *could* work on metals, too?" Elle asked.

Lana shifted her attention to Elle. "I don't know. Maybe? If you got the genetic coding right. It's essentially the same process."

"Explain," Mykola demanded.

"You're kind of snarly, aren't you? And nosy. You read my notes."

"Yes."

She liked that he didn't deny it, or sound particularly bothered that she'd made the observation. "I'm easily distracted."

"I noticed."

"We both have annoying character flaws."

"I'll tolerate yours if you tolerate mine." He didn't sound

very tolerant. More like on the edge of losing control over the barely banked fury she still didn't understand.

"You're mad at me. Really angry."

"You put my sister at risk. That's not something I take lightly."

Elle protested and so did Frank, but Mykola ignored them. So did Lana. It wasn't their opinion she was interested in right now. It was his.

"How?" she asked.

She liked his familial loyalty. She'd never experienced it personally, but she admired it nonetheless. Her family had done nothing to find her, or get her back, when she'd disappeared seven years ago.

"You explain first, then I will."

"Explain what?"

"The enzymes and how they work." He hadn't even rolled his eyes at her, or sighed like he'd rather be anywhere but here talking to the blinky scientist. Despite his obvious anger, he sounded almost patient.

"Oh, right." That was easy. "As you already know, the transformation process is done with enzymes. They have genetically modified markers that convert the cellular signature of the plant."

"Essentially, they rewrite a plant's DNA," Elle clarified.

Lana nodded. "Right."

"And these enzymes could work on metals?"

"I don't know. I've never pursued it, but the process would be much the same. The enzymes would be modified so that they changed the crystal structure of the base metal. The lattice arrangement of metal is similar to the DNA strand of carbon-based life forms."

"You're saying you've never tried it?"

"Why would I? I'm interesting in ending world hunger, not undermining world financial markets."

"Undermining?"

"If you did the transformation on a large enough scale, financial markets would crash. Think about it. They are based on a balance of precious and common commodities. Imagine if platinum was suddenly more common than lead. Prices on the most precious metal in the world would plummet and so would millions of financial portfolios."

Frank grinned. "I told you her mind worked like a puzzle."

"More like a puzzle solver." Mykola's smile was nowhere in evidence. "*Shit.*"

"Now, it's your turn."

He nodded, apparently not having her problem with getting sidetracked. "Your notation caught the attention of some very dangerous people."

"Who?"

"The Vega Cartel."

"It's a South American drug cartel," Frank elucidated.

"Headed by one Anibal Vega," Myk said grimly. "He doesn't limit himself to the cartel, though. He's got his fingers in lots of pies like slavery, assassins, and stolen merchandise. The bastard believes himself to be a direct descendant of Tomas de Torquemada."

"The original inquisitor-general for the Spanish Inquisition?" Lana asked with a squeak she couldn't suppress. That was one heritage she'd keep hidden. Yuck.

"The one and only. Vega has been known to use his ancestor's torture techniques in testing the loyalty of his followers, or when extracting information from people of interest."

"That's disgusting." And horrifically scary.

Mykola's face had become an unreadable mask. "Agreed."

"And this man is interested in my enzymes?" Lana felt her gorge rise and had to fight to conceal her distress.

Mykola's eyes narrowed. "You had to be aware your enzyme would be of interest to people like Vega."

"I don't spend my time thinking about people like Vega at all."

"That doesn't make them go away, Lana. He's still out there, whether you think about him, or not."

"I am aware of that."

"Knock it off, Myk." Elle's tone could have frozen concrete. "You're scaring her."

Too late. Lana was past scared and on her way to terrified.

Mykola fixed his sister with his glare. "She needs to face the truth."

Lana was getting tired of his accusatory attitude. Frightened or not, she was no pushover. "What truth might that be? That my research could be misused? Scientists working on improved fertilizers and growth-yield hormones are also aware their research won't only be used to increase beneficial crops."

She got right into Mr. I-Know-Better-Than-Everyone-Else's face and did some glaring of her own. "If we allow the Vegas of the world to stop us, then they win—just like his ancestor won when all of the practicing Jews were evicted from Spain in 1492. More than five million children die every year from hunger-related causes. I'm looking for ways to bring that number down. God willing, it will one day be completely eradicated. I am definitely not going to stop doing what I'm doing because of the risk that someone like Anibal Vega might misuse my efforts."

Her enzymes were far less likely to be misused than a growth hormone or a new fertilizer. "I don't have enzymes developed for harvest duplication on drug crops, much less those that would work on transforming lead into platinum."

Not that a fact like that was likely to matter to the Vega Cartel. She had learned that those with a myopically self-centered view of the world weren't worried about little trivialities like reality. They believed that with the proper *inspiration* a scientist could create anything.

"Lana's working enzymes have taken three years to develop; they're still not ready for mass prototype testing." Frank's wrinkled nose reflected his uncertainty she'd ever be able to deal with the odor problem.

She nodded. "The exchange of energy and negative side effects are such that they aren't yet a practical solution for plant life, much less metals."

"Unfortunately for Elle, these people don't know that."

Elle? "Why Elle?"

"They've identified her as their first target."

"They probably think I'm in the way." Elle didn't sound particularly bothered by that fact.

In fact, she seemed pretty pleased about it.

Lana's lips quirked, but she was careful not to let the grin she felt inside show. She liked the other woman's attitude and lack of fear.

"You aren't indestructible," Mykola ground out between clenched teeth.

Elle gave a gorgeous runway smile. "I never claimed to be."

"But you're flattered they consider you such a threat," Lana guessed, unable to stop the grin this time.

The other woman shrugged, but Lana knew her supposition had been correct.

Mykola muttered something in Ukrainian. It sounded like he was calling his sister an idiot with a couple of swear words thrown in. Lana was sure of it when Elle gave her brother the glare of death and bit out something even more insulting to him in the same language.

"What are you two saying?" Frank demanded.

Lana shook her head at him. "You don't want to know."

Elle and Mykola gave up glaring daggers at one another and turned two equally intense gazes on her, one gray and one Hershey Kiss brown. Even his eyes were yummy. Darn it. Lana loved chocolate.

"Was that a lucky guess, or do you speak Ukrainian?" Mykola asked for them both.

She would have thought that was obvious. "Some of the best physicists in the world are Ukrainian."

"So?"

"I prefer my own translations of their work as well as talking to them in their native tongue." Her tone implied that most serious scientists would feel that way and that made her feel guilty for sounding like a snob. Not everyone had her facility for languages. "Mat and I have had some very productive discussions in Ukrainian about our work here. Sometimes the words just fit better."

Even though he was American born, Matej Chernichenko spoke Ukrainian both on a social and a scientific level fluently.

"You chat in Ukrainian with my big brother?" Mykola asked.

"Yes. He's brilliant. A bit gruff, but that seems to run in the family. At least among the males," she said the last bit under her breath but apparently perfectly audibly, if Elle's infectious laughter was anything to go by.

As much as Lana would prefer not to like the woman who had caught the interest of the only man she'd wanted in years, she found herself enjoying Elle's company more each time they interacted. Of course, the crush Lana had had on Dr. Beau Ruston was small, stale potatoes next to the sizzling fries that had been short-circuiting her brain ever since Mykola had sauntered into her lab.

Well, she couldn't be *sure* he'd *sauntered*. After all, her first awareness had been once he was already within touching distance, but she was fairly certain the bad boy intent on protecting his sister sauntered most places—rather than doing anything so mundane as mere walking.

Lana winked at Elle and then turned to Frank. "If that's all you need from me, I'd like to get back to my work."

What she really wanted to do was keep the sexy Mykola Chernichenko in her lab. Or better yet, take him home where she had privacy and a bed for a whole new type of research for her. Since neither was going to happen, she needed to stop daydreaming and get back to saving the world's starving children.

"That's it?" Mykola asked, his rich voice laced with shock and a little disdain. "I tell you that your project has put my sister at serious risk and you want to get back to your work?"

"Myk, that's enough. My job is what has put me at risk. Not Lana, or her projects."

"I don't agree." He didn't raise his voice, but it was filled with a passion of purpose Lana understood only too well.

She wished she could help him, but she didn't see what she could do to improve the situation.

Elle was looking far from amused now. "You don't have to."

"Tell these really dangerous people that the enzymes don't work on metal." Lana picked up her electronic tablet and stylus to jot down an idea.

"It doesn't work like that." Mykola put his hand over her tablet, filling her personal space. "They have no reason to believe us."

"Or accept that verdict, even if they do believe it," Lana acknowledged with an inner shudder, memories she'd buried surfacing in flashes that made her want to throw up.

"So, give them a reason."

Lana's head snapped around, and she stared at the newest visitor to her lab. It was Dr. Beau Ruston, her former heart-throb, Elle's current fiancé, and second in command here at ETRD.

He grinned, a look that as recently as that morning would have sent butterflies on a high-wire act in her stomach.

Right this second with tall, protective, and dangerous in her lab, it just caused her to smile in return. "Hello, Beau."

"Hey, Lana."

He punched Mykola on the shoulder. "You're the super-spook. It should be a piece of cake to convince the bad guys that Lana's experiments are a washout. Hell, more than half the projects we work on here at ETRD never see the light of day or large-scale prototype testing."

Beau moved right into Elle's personal space and it was like the air shifted around them, sealing them in a bubble the rest of the world couldn't touch.

Lana couldn't imagine having something like that with someone else. The level of absolute trust and commitment these two showed toward each other was something she'd never known in her life. Not from her family and certainly not with the few boyfriends that had taken up temporary residence in her orbit.

"As brilliant as your insight is, my love, this situation is not that simple." Elle's expression sobered. "We can't be sure they're looking at the mythical concept of base metal alchemy. The Vega Cartel's primary commodities are illegal substances. They may very well want the enzymes exactly for their intended purpose—to increase their cash crops."

"If it is, we don't have enzymes created for the type of plants they harvest, either."

"You mean the enzymes aren't universal?" Elle asked, sounding intrigued.

Lana shook her head. "Not even close. The enzyme developed for *Phaseolus vulgaris* wouldn't work on another type of bean crop, much less a different plant family altogether like *cannabis* or *Papaver somniferum.*"

One of the things she loved about her enzyme project was that it was plant specific. If the concept was going to be misused, it would require a different scientific team than her own to develop enzymes for growing more marijuana or opium poppies.

"But it could be developed," Mykola said.

"With as much likelihood of success as the enzymes we are currently working with, yes."

He gave her that glare again. The one that blamed her for the world's problems and all their ramifications.

"What would you have me do?" she asked him with exasperation. "Stop my experiments? That's not going to help. As you say, the word is already out." She smiled at Elle, when she felt like doing anything but. "I wish you'd been here to stop the leaks before my notes got copied, stolen, or whatever."

"Damn it." Sounding deeply surly again, Mykola spun away from her.

She felt the rejection but pushed it down where it couldn't hurt. The same place she kept her fear at bay.

"I'm not like you and Elle. My skills don't range to protecting others. I ask again, what do you want me to do?" Then a truly horrifying thought came to her. "*You want me to turn myself over to the cartel?*"

"No!" Elle and Beau said in forceful unison.

Mykola's glare did not soften. If anything, it got more pointed. "Of course not."

"Don't be ridiculous, Lana," was Frank's contribution.

She almost laughed. They all sounded so sincere—appalled that she would even make such a suggestion. Only, if the choice came down to it, she'd bet Mykola would trade her for the safety of his sister in a heartbeat. That Elle would not willingly go along with such a plan was immaterial.

Not everyone got a vote in situations like this. Not even the people most affected. Lana hadn't. Before. She'd been sold out for motives a lot less noble and compelling than the safety of a family member. Her research, her freedom, her *life* had been put on the auction block for five hundred lousy dollars and a handful of pills that wouldn't have lasted the length of time it had taken her captors to get her interred in her new home.

She was never going through that again if she could help it. Images of a hot, windowless lab with a steel door in northern Turkey threatened to take over her mind. She shoved them back with more concentration and determination than she gave anything besides her work.

Her libido doused like a candle flame under a hurricane wave, she turned away from them all, going back to the safe and familiar. "I believe that I've told you all that I can. If I can help with anything else, ask."

With that, she went back to her work.

She could have asked what they planned to do to protect her. Even if Mykola's sole concern was his sister, Elle and Frank saw Lana as a valuable resource for ETRD and presumably wouldn't want to lose her. She had no doubts that if not now, once Mr. Smith was made aware of the situation, plans would be made to keep her safe as well.

It didn't really matter, though. No one's personal security could be guaranteed. She would do her best to stay safe and if she was taken, she'd do what she had to in order to get away.

Just like she had the last time.

Chapter 3

"What the hell just happened?" Myk asked as he, Elle, Beau, and Frank walked down the nondescript gray hallway toward Elle's office.

For a company on the leading edge of environmental technology, the building's décor was less than inspiring. Who knew? Maybe gray walls and white labs were supposed to promote creative thinking to compensate?

Frank checked his watch and pulled the cell phone from the holster on his belt, clearly needing to make a call. "That's just Lana. Don't take it personally."

"It's hard to take her desire to have sex with me any other way."

Beau choked on a laugh. "She said that?"

"Myk! Stop it." Elle sounded serious. "Lana's social skills are a little unpolished. She spends too much time on her own. The only other person she talks to regularly is her lab assistant."

Frank chuckled. "I swear those two talk in some kind of code. Half the time I can't follow their conversation."

"So?" Myk shrugged.

"So . . . just don't make fun of her. You, either," Elle said to

Beau and then stopped at her door and passed her hand over the biometric lock. "She's a brilliant scientist and a caring person."

"Yeah, she cares so much, she dismissed us after I told her you were the primary target for bastards that would make slitting your throat seem like a favor."

Elle spun to face him, her glare familiar and yet more intense than it used to be. "*First* target. Not *primary*. Ultimately, to make whatever scheme they've got going work, these people are going to need Lana, not just her formulas. That makes her the primary target and don't think she's so lost in scientific theory she hasn't already figured that out."

Right. "Then why didn't she ask what we are going to do to protect her?"

"I'm sure she doesn't think you are interested in protecting her at all." Elle pushed the door to her office open and stepped inside.

Beau followed her. "Sounds like I missed some fun showing up late for your talk with our little alchemist."

"That's bullshit," Myk said to his sister, more annoyed than he should be by the accusation. "I'm lead agent on this case. Her safety is my responsibility."

"You didn't tell her that, though, did you?" Elle shook her head and sat down behind her desk, giving him a look that reminded him of their mother in full disapproval mode. "No, you made sure you told her that if anything happens to me that it's *her* fault."

Myk wasn't taking that back. He was furious that his sister was at risk from a drug cartel that made the slavery ring he took down look like school-yard bullies in comparison.

Elle sighed, her expression going somber. "Besides, I doubt she believes that she's safe, regardless of what measures are taken."

"Why?" Beau asked from his perch on the edge of Elle's desk.

"Do you know something we don't?" Frank asked thoughtfully, his phone open but inactive in his hand as he took one of the chairs facing Elle's desk.

Myk opted to stand.

"I'm sure Mr. Smith is aware of it," Elle said with some derision. "But he's already shown he shares information on a need-to-know basis and he decides who needs to know what."

"*What* does Mr. Smith know?" Myk asked, on the downhill slide to psychotically frustrated, a condition only the women in his family seemed to be able to elicit in him.

"Lana was a child prodigy."

"It figures," Myk muttered. The woman was even smarter than his sister, but he didn't see what that had to do with her perception of personal safety.

"Honey, that's not exactly a state secret," Beau said.

Elle hushed him with a look. Huh. So it worked on non-Chernichenko males as well. Must be the connection between them.

"She had a double PhD in applied physics and chemistry by the time she was twenty-one." Elle's admiration was clear in her tone. "Her doctoral thesis for her PhD in chemistry had applications for chemical warfare, though *she* was interested in improving water supplies without hugely expensive water-treatment facilities."

"And?" Frank prompted when Beau and Myk refused to do so.

Chernichenko women were notorious for dragging out a story. The men in the family had a policy of not encouraging them. Myk was glad to see Beau taking the same tack.

"And she was kidnapped by a radical faction of the Kurdish rebels a week after she defended her thesis to the doctoral committee. The rebels wanted her to create chemical weapons for them."

Several beats of stunned silence followed Elle's revelation.

That was one need-to-know fact Myk would never have guessed resided in the sexy scientist's history.

"Someone found out and got her released?" Beau asked.

Elle's gray eyes flashed. "She blew a hole in the wall of the cell equipped as a lab that they kept her in. The door was steel, set in a steel frame, but the walls were more vulnerable."

"Day-am," Beau's drawled.

Myk's reaction was less printable.

"Two soldiers died in the explosion and several others would have suffered permanent nerve damage from the gas she released to incapacitate them for her escape."

Myk shook his head in amazement. "She'd make a hell of a soldier."

"You think?" Elle didn't look convinced of that fact. "There's a reason she spends more time in her lab than she does at home and barely has a social life outside of ETRD."

Frank was frowning in thought. "She didn't start working for ETRD until she was twenty-four."

"She disappeared after the explosion. She didn't show back up on anyone's radar until six weeks before she started working here."

"Mr. Smith found her."

"Probably, but if he knows how she spent that year plus, he's never said."

"Year plus? How long did the Kurds have her incarcerated?"

"A little over eight months."

Myk's insides twisted in a way he'd thought he'd grown immune to. "They forced her to work for them."

"She's a pacifist who has dedicated her life to mitigating world hunger. What do you think?"

"Hell."

"That's exactly what I'm sure she lived in for those eight months."

"Mr. Smith never told me any of this." Frank closed his phone without making the call and put it back in its holster.

"Surprised?" Elle asked.

Frank's jaw locked. "No." He might not be surprised, but he was obviously pissed.

"And you think she believes I have no interest in protecting her from the Vega Cartel?"

Elle's look of sisterly censure was easier to read than *See Spot Run.* "You did a good job of selling it."

"I'm worried about you. Is that a crime?"

"No, but neither is trying to feed starving children."

Shit.

Myk spun on his heel and headed back to Lana's lab.

He found Lana back at her microscope. Muttering to herself, she took notes on an electronic tablet with one hand while staring with rapt attention at whatever she saw beneath the lens.

Just like before, she didn't appear to notice the arrival of someone new in the lab. Damn.

This was not good. Clearly she felt safe here, but she shouldn't—at least not to the extent that she became completely impervious to what was going on around her. It amazed him that she could, after the experience she'd had. No matter how good Elle's protection measures for ETRD were, nothing was foolproof.

He'd just dropped a bomb on Lana's sense of security. Or it should have been. However, despite her own knowledge to the contrary, Lana Ericson acted as if she was completely naïve to her potential risk. He trusted Elle when she said she thought Lana was too intelligent not to realize she was a target as well.

Which meant what?

Myk didn't have an answer for that. The woman should be a nervous wreck, but instead she was lost to the world around her while she worked on her project.

And as dangerous as that was, she charmed him.

Damn it.

"Do you always talk gibberish to yourself when you are alone in your lab?"

She stiffened. "It's not gibberish. It's formulas. For my project."

She'd heard him the first time he spoke, unlike when Frank and his sister had been trying to get the modern-day alchemist's attention earlier.

Interesting. "Ah."

"Did you need something?"

"For you to look at me to start with." He tugged on her ponytail of stick-straight strawberry-blond hair. It was soft as silk and he couldn't resist the urge to subtly caress it as he let go.

This woman was lethal to his self-control.

He forced himself to take a step backward as she turned to face him.

Soft gray eyes dusted with flecks of green stared at him in wary confusion. "Did you need something else?"

"Yes."

"What?" Her gaze skimmed over him like it had earlier, the heat as honest as it had been the first time, though the wariness remained.

Her reactions were so candid. So damn different from him. Because while his sex had thickened to the point of straining against the leather of his pants, his breathing and expression were carefully controlled.

No way would she know how she affected him unless she

looked directly at the only evidence. And even then, the snug leather did a good job of holding him in.

She didn't look. This time.

Elle's reaction earlier must have had an impact on the scientist's uninhibited behavior.

Too bad.

He thought he might just be able to come in his pants from the blatant and hot, yet innocent interest of the usually preoccupied scientist.

So maybe his control wasn't as good as it should be if he was having thoughts like that.

Back to work, Myk. "I'm not going to let them take you."

She shrugged, her lack of belief obvious.

He couldn't help it. He stepped forward, invading her personal space once again. She needed to trust him. He was the agent in charge. Her safety was his responsibility. "You're not going to end up in another prison cell lab. You have my word."

Her eyes widened, like his knowledge of her past surprised her. Then she wrapped her arms around voluptuous curves not completely hidden by her lab coat. "You can't make that kind of promise."

"Yes, I can." The need to touch the alluring scientist too strong to resist, he cupped her face. "I may not be a brilliant head-geek, but I'm damn good at what I do."

Her breathing hitched, causing the generous swell of her breasts to brush his elbows. He was going to go to Agency Hell for the thoughts he was having about this woman he was supposed to protect. But damn if he didn't want to rip the nondescript lab coat from her body and then peel away the clingy lime-green T-shirt with a picture of Winnie-the-Pooh, his hand caught in the honey jar, on the front.

Lana wasn't skinny like so many women in California. She

had real breasts, real hips, an indention at her waist that would be perfect for holding on to while she rode him, and thighs shaped like a woman's legs should look. Okay, so her khaki cargo capris, mostly hidden by the lab coat—that was looking more and more like wrapping paper on a present he really wanted to open—didn't give that kind of visual detail.

His mind's eye had no problem filling it in, though. He pictured her nipples a shade darker than her luscious, pink lips. Her nether lips were probably a shade or two darker than that even. And covered by pretty strawberry blond curls. Delicious.

And he wanted a taste. Of it all.

His favorite desert had always been strawberry shortcake.

Something of what he was thinking must have shown in his expression—so much for his game face—because the green in her eyes grew more prominent until they looked like shimmering emeralds.

He tilted his head, intending to get a small sample of the taste.

"I don't understand."

The words stopped his mouth from making contact and brought his raging impulses to a screeching halt. What in the *hell* was he doing?

She looked at him, her eyes too focused for how far gone he'd been feeling. "Why did you say I'm your responsibility?"

"Because you are."

"You say it, therefore it is?" Her mouth was still too close for his self-control.

"Yes." He moved back, but only a few inches. It was as if his body couldn't stand a bigger separation. He was so screwed. And not in a good way.

She cocked her head to one side, tugging her ponytail holder from her hair, and studied him. "Too bad."

"What's too bad?"

"That I'm a physicist, not an anthropologist." She dropped the elastic band on her bench.

Or probably intended to. It fell to the floor and he leaned over to pick it up. "Your brain doesn't work like other people's."

She frowned, sadness he didn't like seeing flitting through her expression as she braided her hair haphazardly. "I know."

"I'll probably regret asking, but why are you disappointed you aren't an anthropologist?"

She finger combed the braid from her hair, the strawberry blond silk so tempting, his fingers literally itched to reach out and touch. "I'm not disappointed, but if I were one, I'd have a perfect example of Cro-Magnon man to study."

Offense and amusement warred for supremacy. Amusement won and he laughed. "You think I'm prehistoric?"

"Well, you claim responsibility for me like some sort of caveman. *Me strong man, you weak girl scientist. Me protect you*," she said in a deep voice, intended to mock.

He laughed again, delighted by her. He hadn't been amused like this for a very long time. Probably not since the last time he'd been with his family before going under deep cover.

It felt good. "I'm responsible for you because I'm the agent in charge. A perfectly logical, not to mention *modern* reason for my point of view."

"Agent in charge?"

"On the case."

"Case? You're an INS agent . . . how is this sort of thing *your* case?"

"I quit the INS when I found out about the Vega Cartel's interest in Elle. I'm working for a different agency now."

Lana started looking for something, moving things around on her lab bench and ducking to look under it. "The one Elle was working for when she hired on as ETRD's security consultant?"

"No one is supposed to know about that."

She straightened, her gaze zeroing in on his hand, her look going triumphant. "Like any other company, ETRD has lots of gossip." She reached out and grabbed the ponytail holder from him.

"And you hear even when others think you aren't listening."

"A lot of times *I* think I'm not listening." She gave him a wry smile as she started pulling her hair together. Both arms rose to gather the silky strands high on the back of her head. The movement put her breasts in prominent relief as her lab coat separated.

He had to swallow back the growl that wanted to surface. Nothing could stop the pre-come leaking into his snug black briefs.

"You're listening now."

"Yes." She secured her hair and dropped her arms. "And what I hear is that you're claiming responsibility for my welfare because you are in charge of the case. But even if that's true—"

"I don't lie." Unless it was part of the job, anyway.

"Defensive much?"

"You said *if*."

"Fine. But *even though* you are agent in charge. I'm unclear as to in charge of what?"

"The case, I told you." Having a conversation with her was like trying to solve a crossword puzzle without any clues.

"What is your directive?"

His directive was to protect the USA's interests and prevent homebred technological designs from being stolen or used against the nation. Just as with his previous agency, the safety of individuals did not supersede the greater good. His personal attitude in the matter didn't necessarily match agency directives, though. His sister was involved and no way was he letting her get hurt, even if it meant accomplishing the greater good.

"That is classified."

"I see, but whatever it is has you believing you need to make a promise to me you most likely won't be able to keep?"

Oh, now that was a direct hit to his ego. And he wasn't taking it lying down. "I told you, I'm good at my job."

"I don't doubt it. So is Elle, but you're still here, making sure she's safe. If she can't protect herself, you must realize that you can't protect me with one-hundred-percent assurance either."

Having her repeat his own attitudes back at him was more than a little annoying. Had Elle introduced Lana to their mother? "You'll just have to trust me."

"The only thing you can truly trust is a proven chemical reaction, and only when conditions surrounding the reactions remain constant." She said it by rote, as if it was one of her formulas that she had memorized.

He stared at her. "You're serious, aren't you?"

"Yes."

"You don't trust people? At all?" She didn't come off as a cynic.

"I don't trust any person implicitly."

"Who do you trust—marginally?"

She didn't hesitate. "Mr. Smith."

Myk did not like hearing that. "What about my sister?"

"I trust her abilities to secure ETRD's secrets as much as is humanly possible."

"You don't trust her with your personal security?"

"My safety is not her responsibility."

"I doubt the other scientists at this facility would agree with you."

"That is because the overlap between our personal safety and the interests of the company and its secrets is such that it is easy to be deceived into believing the overlap is complete."

"But you don't see it that way."

"I see empirical facts. The truth that the overlap only extends so far is one of them."

"You seem so sweet and somewhat ditzy, but you've got an inner core of steel, don't you?" She'd have to in order to function like she did after what she'd been through.

"I'm made up of flesh and bone just like everyone else, well, except people who have had joint replacements and the like."

"You're very exact."

She frowned, that sadness he didn't like passing through her hazel eyes—more gold than green right now. "It's the only way I know how to be."

"I like it." He leaned back against the lab bench, crossing one leg over the other.

"You do?" The shock in her tone was unmistakable, as was the look of interest she gave his body in the more relaxed pose.

"Yes."

"You're one of a select few, then."

He narrowed his eyes, anger burbling where there should be nothing but detached interest. "Who doesn't like it?"

"A lot of people."

"Name one."

"My father."

"What about your mother?"

"You only said to name one."

"So, both your parents find that trait in you annoying?"

"They find pretty much everything about me annoying."

He didn't say she had to be wrong, even though he wished he could. He'd seen enough parents who didn't love their

children the way his own parents had loved him to acknowledge the possibility hers were the latter. "Then they've got no
taste."

Lana smiled wistfully. "You think?"

"I know." Just like he knew he was going to regret his next
action.

But some things were worth a few regrets later. He figured
what he was about to do was one of them.

Reaching out, he snagged her lab coat and reeled her in until
their bodies were only a breath apart. "I want to kiss you."

Shock widened her eyes. "You do?"

"Yes."

"Prove it."

He was laughing softly when he did. He had a feeling Lana
Ericson was not going to ever react the way he expected.

Damn.

Her lips tasted like berries and cream, so sweet and decadent. So soft. Deliciously pliable. The perfect bow-shaped
morsels molded to his like they'd been kissing for years. Only
the electricity zinging through his body, making him vibrate
with need, testified to how new this was.

He had just enough control left to keep his hands gripped
in her lab coat and not let them roam over the curvy body so
close to his own. But as the kiss progressed, his control broke
and he cupped her face, tilting it so he could get just the right
angle. He mapped her features with this thumbs, brushing
over her eyes and cheeks, hungry for the feel of other parts of
her body.

She made a whimpery little sound, her mouth parting just
a bit. He didn't take the kiss as deep as he wanted, but he did
allow the tip of his tongue to slip between her lips, taking in
a more intimate layer of her taste. Her tongue flicked against
his and then withdrew, her body giving a violent shudder.

Damn, if she responded like this to a kiss, what would she be like naked and tangled with him between the sheets? Or on top of a lab table? Or on the floor? Or up against a wall?

"Let her go!" A blow against his back and the screeched words derailed Myk's fantasy train.

He released Lana and spun to face his opponent.

Chapter 4

The small, redheaded, freckled man glared at Myk through thick glasses. His fists were raised in an aggressive, if wholly ineffectual stance. "I already pushed the panic button for security. You'd better get out of here before the guards show up."

"Casey, why did you call security?" Lana asked, sounding a little dazed.

"He was attacking you."

"I was kissing her."

"Lana doesn't kiss people."

"She did today."

"Lana?" The boy . . . man's voice wavered. "Were you kissing him voluntarily?"

"Yes, Casey."

Casey's face turned as red as his hair. "Oh."

"I'm sorry," Lana said.

"Why are you apologizing?" Myk asked, irritated.

"Because allowing you to kiss me in the lab wasn't a good choice. Casey had no way of knowing it was voluntary and now he's embarrassed because he overreacted."

"His adolescent reaction was hardly your fault."

"I'm not an adolescent! I'm twenty-four. I can drink legally and everything, even if I don't."

Lana moved forward and squeezed her assistant's shoulder. "It's okay, no harm done."

Just then a single security officer came into the lab, no weapon drawn. Myk was tempted to lay him out just to teach him a lesson. "You took so long to answer the distress call, I could have ransacked the lab and taken out both Dr. Ericson and her assistant before you got here," he growled.

Casey's green eyes went wide and he cringed.

The security officer gave Myk a flat stare. "I got here as quickly as I could."

"Why are you alone?" Myk demanded.

"I'll ask the questions here." The security officer took in the three occupants of the lab. "Who pushed the panic button?"

"Are you kidding me? Which one of us does not belong here?" Myk asked, his voice going lethally quiet.

He was going to have a serious talk with his sister.

"As far as I know, you all belong here. You can't get into the building without going through security, so you've all got clearance," the officer said triumphantly.

"And if I bypassed security measures?"

"Can't be done. Ms. Gray is the best."

His sister was going to shit a brick, or break one over her security team's collective heads, when she heard this one.

"So, you came ambling in, alone, based on the premise that no one who shouldn't be in the building *could* be in the building?"

"I rushed."

"Like a hundred-year-old tortoise. I saw."

"Listen, buddy."

"Casey, Bob, on the floor, your hands behind your head." Elle's voice was deadly and the two men went down without a breath of protest.

Elle turned to her brother. "What's going on?"

"What are you doing here?"

"The head of security called to let me know that one of the panic buttons had been pushed. He told me I needed to look into the wiring, that it was probably a faulty connection." Elle's eyes snapped with fury.

"Nothing wrong with the install, but your security force needs some retraining in how to react."

"Tell me."

"Casey came in here and found me kissing Lana. Apparently, that's such a shocking occurrence he assumed I was attacking her. He pushed the panic button and then he accosted me."

"Casey accosted you?" Elle asked with awe.

"I did," the redhead answered before Myk could. "Can I get off the floor now?"

"Yes."

Casey jumped up with surprising agility.

The guard started to get up, too, but Lana barked, "I didn't say you could move."

"Ms. Gray—"

"Shut it." Oh, his sister was *mad*.

Good. Her security team was a bunch of idiots. "He assumed there couldn't be anything really wrong because no one with malignant intent would be capable of bypassing your security measures to get into the building."

"Please tell me you're kidding."

"Not."

She swore in Ukrainian.

"Exactly."

"Bob, get your ass off the floor and come with me." Elle turned to go but stopped before leaving the lab. "Don't think I've forgotten Casey caught you kissing Lana."

Then she was gone, leaving a still-blushing Casey, an amused Lana, and a more than a little disgruntled Myk behind.

Myk frowned at Casey. "So, you're the assistant."

The redhead shrugged. "The senior assistant. Dr. Casey Billings. You the boyfriend?"

"No."

"But you were kissing Lana."

"So?"

"So . . . you *kissed* her."

"Maybe she kissed me."

"Nah."

Lana huffed out a disgruntled breath. "Hey, I think I might resent that remark."

"Still . . ." Casey gave Myk an expectant look.

"What?" Myk rolled his eyes. "Men and women kiss all the time. Perfect strangers even. Just go to a club and you'll see plenty of liplocks on the dance floor."

"What clubs?" the younger man asked eagerly.

It was Lana's turn to roll her eyes. "Don't encourage him," she said sternly to Myk. "And you . . . give it a rest." That was directed at Casey.

Casey sighed, sounding a lot more dejected than the circumstances warranted. "What if Lana thought it was more than a kiss? Do you think that's fair to her?"

Myk almost laughed at the redhead's dramatic angst, but managed to control the urge. For some reason, he didn't want to hurt the young genius's feelings. "Isn't that between Lana and myself?"

"I suppose." Casey let out another long sigh. "Not like I'm all that good at that relationship stuff myself." He turned to look at Lana. "I'm going to take some samples from test epsilon on the hybrid maize."

"Sounds good. I think I may have discovered something on the slides for test omega on the *Oryza sativa* enzyme this morning."

Suddenly, Casey's demeanor changed from diffident boy-man to enthusiastic scientist. "Yeah? Way cool." Or maybe, freakishly young scientist.

What followed had to be one of those discussions Frank said he thought happened in a private language, because Myk only picked up about every third word. It lasted only a few minutes and then Casey disappeared through one of the doors in the far wall of the lab.

The brief time the door was open allowed a noxious odor out and Myk grimaced, grateful his gag reflex was all but eradicated. "Man, that stinks. What is it?"

Lana sighed. "The by-product of the enzyme."

"You sure it's worth it?"

"We're hoping to fix it. Though it might be worth developing the enzyme for the cartel just to let them experience the side effects in this form."

Myk chuckled and shook his head. "They'd leave it to the poor laborers to tend and harvest. The guys at the top wouldn't care about something they wouldn't have to deal with personally."

"You're probably right." But she looked like she was plotting and Myk had a feeling that was dangerous.

"Don't get any ideas."

"Who, me?" she asked with the perfect cartoon look of innocence.

"Lady, I have a feeling you could be very dangerous if you put your mind to it."

"You have no idea." But she wasn't smiling when she said it and he knew she was no longer joking. She pushed a button on her computer and high-powered fans set in the walls just below ceiling level went on. "That will clear the air in a few seconds."

Myk nodded. "So, did you?"

"Did I what?"

"Read underlying messages in our kiss?" He didn't know

why he asked. In any other circumstance, with any other woman, he would have sooner had his testicles in a vise than willingly participate in what he considered touchy-feely conversations.

Lana seemed as surprised he had asked as he was. "Don't let Casey's melodrama get to you. He's got lousy taste in women and is still young enough to think dating is worth the effort."

"You're not exactly ancient."

"I guess not. Twenty-nine isn't all that old, but I've lived long enough to figure out dating and the whole male-female mating ritual isn't as interesting as my work."

He was going to respond, but she went on. "As for the kiss, I'm a scientist, not a psychologist. I don't read underlying messages into things."

Myk snorted. Yeah, right. "You're still a woman."

"Most of the time, I forget that."

That really bothered him—for no reason he could fathom— He shouldn't care what perceptions she had of her femininity, but it did. And he wasn't about to let it go unchallenged. "Funny, I haven't been able to think of much else since walking in here."

"You're an odd man, Mykola."

"Why do you say that?"

"Besides the fact that you go around kissing dumpy scientists with more brains than beauty and even less people skills?"

Was that really how she saw herself? "You're about as dumpy as a 1940s vamp, and I don't mean the bloodsucking variety, either." He grabbed her hand and pressed it against his outstandingly obvious erection. "Dumpy doesn't do this to me."

She gasped, but instead of pulling away, she squeezed. "You're big."

And he about damn near came right then. "I don't compare myself."

"Seriously? According to what I've read, all men do that."

"I'm not like other men."

"No, you aren't. You want me." She was clearly both puzzled and very pleased by that fact.

"Yes, I do." But there were more important issues at stake than his unslaked libido right now.

Having the hots for a principal in the case was a complication he did not need. Not when his sister's safety and the security of said principal was on the line. "Unfortunately, we can't always have what we want."

"Tell me about it." With a sigh, she sidestepped away from him. "I suppose it was too much to expect a live-action fulfillment of my favorite fantasy." She got a comical look of dismay on her face as soon as the words left her mouth.

"*Favorite fantasy*, huh?"

"Sometimes my mouth has no filter." She looked and sounded adorably disgruntled.

His lips quirked in a half-smile. "I noticed."

"It's hard not to."

"Do you say everything you think?"

"No." She sighed dejectedly. "Just most of it."

"You're painfully honest, aren't you?"

"I don't lie, if that's what you mean. And yes, the lack of a verbal filter can be painful for me at times. Very."

"That level of honesty is a unique trait. Most people lie, if only to themselves."

"That's a cynical view."

"One you don't share?" The woman who didn't trust anyone *implicitly*?

"No, I don't. I think there are a lot of people that are basically honest."

"Like Mr. Smith?" Derision he couldn't quite suppress laced his tone.

Fire lit her eyes. "He made me believe I could practice science again, that I could still make a difference. That I still mattered somewhere."

Wow, that was some hefty emotional gain. "You trust him, if no one else. Right?"

"There are other people I trust."

Not completely, though. She'd made that clear. That had to be lonely—and scary. He'd lived in the underbelly of humanity for over a year, but he would still trust his life with certain people. Any member of his family, his former partner, and a couple of the border agents he'd worked with. No amount of money, or any other incentive would make those people betray him.

"Who?" he couldn't help asking.

"Who do I trust?"

"Yes."

"Besides Mr. Smith?"

"Yes." He smiled, not at all irritated by her need to be exact.

"The people who helped me once I escaped the Kurdish prison lab."

"Who were they?"

"Some women."

"You won't give me their names?" Because she didn't trust him. That bothered him. It shouldn't, though.

He bit back a curse.

"You don't need their names. Isn't that how spies operate, on a need-to-know basis?"

"I'm not a spy. I'm an undercover federal agent."

"They're not the same thing?"

"Nope. A spook is charged with discovering other nation's

secrets. I'm responsible for keeping information out of the wrong hands."

She nodded as if she got the distinction. Knowing her, she did.

"Is there anyone in this country, besides your pain-in-the-ass employer, who isn't nearly as honest as you, by the way, whom you trust?"

"He's not a pain." She completely ignored his implication regarding Mr. Smith's lack of overt honesty.

"Depends on your perspective. Now, tell me."

"I'll bet you're good at interrogation."

Thinking of a past he was fast deciding he wanted to forget, he nodded. "One of the best."

"Casey."

"That's a given."

"Why?"

"You would have to trust him to be willing to entrust your precious work with him."

"True."

"Who else?"

She thought for a second. "I trust a couple of the women in my belly dancing troupe."

"*Belly dancing?*"

"You act like you've never heard of it."

"Oh, I've definitely heard of it . . . seen it even."

"It's amazing, isn't it? The dance?"

"That's one word for it."

"It's fantastic exercise, too, for both your mind and body."

"You belly dance." He was having a really rough time getting that information to take root in his brain. "You don't seem the type."

"What type would that be? The seductive femme fatale?" Her naturally smooth brow wrinkled in a censorious frown.

"*Please*, belly dancing is so much more than an entertainment form for lusty desert sheikhs. There are several sects that refuse to perform for men at all. It's an art form of the body. A way for women to celebrate being women, no matter what their shape or size. For some, it's even a training form with underpinnings of Middle Eastern martial arts."

"It's your antisocial nature that has me surprised, not your lack of feminine grace."

"I'm not antisocial. More . . ." She paused, as if thinking. "I guess socially awkward is the right phrase, but I enjoy belly dancing."

"You're serious."

"Of course."

"I want to watch you." Well, hell. Talk about having no filter.

"Now?" she squeaked, clearly shocked to her Mickey Mouse tennis shoes. The woman had a thing for Disney.

"No." Though the thought was tantalizing. He wondered if she'd use her lab coat as a veil. Damn. He was losing his mind and it was all the sexy scientist's fault. "You perform, don't you?"

"Sometimes. My troupe competes and I teach a class for neophyte dancers on Fridays. During the last ten minutes of class, either I or my apprentice performs for the students to give them a taste of the full dance. When they see what they are working toward, they are less likely to give up when some of the moves are difficult for them."

"Do you let men watch?" Could he watch this surprising woman shimmy for ten minutes without exploding? It was a concept he wouldn't mind exploring.

"There are usually men in the audience at competitions, but I've never had one show up at my class. The neophyte dancers bring in their sisters or female friends to watch sometimes, but no one has brought a spouse, boyfriend, or anything like that."

Reality burst his bubble of sexy fantasy as he considered the impact her extracurricular activities would have on his ability to keep her safe. "You let anyone who wants to watch?"

"Sure."

"How do you know they're with your students and not some perv just showing up to watch you dance?"

"It's pretty much an assumption I make. Besides, it's easy to see who has invited the visitors because they usually stand together."

Like that meant anything. "So any guy who wants to perv on your dancing could show up and stand around like he knew somebody and you'd never be the wiser."

"I told you, I've never had a male visitor to my class."

"There's a first time for everything."

"I guess, but why do you assume the first time would be someone with ulterior motives?"

"There are a lot of bad people in the world, Little Lana."

She rolled her eyes. "I'm hardly little."

"Compared to me you are." And she might be curvy, but she was no giant.

"Oh, right."

"Listen—"

"No, you listen. There may be a lot of bad people in the world, misguided people and just plain stupid people, but there are lots of good people, too."

How could she say that after what she'd been through?

"Even though you don't trust them."

"*Implicitly*. Just because I don't trust people with my life doesn't mean I don't trust in other ways." She was pretty defensive on that point. "I trust that there are good people out there."

"You're just not sure which ones they are."

"I presume good until I see a reason for doing otherwise."

"While still protecting yourself."

"That's natural, don't you think?"

"Yes, I do." He didn't argue further. He liked her stubbornly positive outlook, skewed as it was by her very real, very justified trust issues.

"Good." She turned and headed across the lab, stopping at a door in the opposite wall. She looked over her shoulder at him. "Coming?"

"Is it a growing room?"

"Yes."

He couldn't hide his grimace. "You got an extra gas mask?"

"You won't need one." She grinned, like she'd played a joke on him. "While the enzyme transformation is the primary project in our lab right now, Casey and I are working on a couple of other things as well."

"Stuff that doesn't smell like decomposing corpses?"

She laughed and opened the door, going inside without answering.

He followed. So far, so good. In fact, it smelled kind of nice. "Flowers?"

"*Lathyrus odoratus.* More commonly known as flowering sweet pea."

"What did it used to be? Dead moss or something?"

Her hazel eyes shining, she looked up from a cutting she was taking from one of the plants. "Actually, it's the soil we're transforming, not the plant."

"You're transforming the soil?"

"Well, elements in the soil, anyway." She smelled the yellow flower with a short stem, and then extended her hand for him to do the same. "It's not exactly rose essence, but it's not bad for a fertilizer."

The pleasant floral scent had a slight underlying odor, but nothing like the toxic smells that came from the growing room Casey had gone into. "That's fertilizer?"

She nodded, her face alight with joy in her accomplishment. "One of the problems facing food growers, particularly in developing countries and those without strong environmental laws, is the toxification of the soil and/or groundwater. Both the toxified soil and what we refer to as acid rain are the result of pollution. We need a way to clean up our groundwater and soils, not just the air."

"And that's what you hope to do with this flower?"

"It's a rapidly growing annual vine. Perfect for what we want to do. Casey and I genetically altered the *Lathyrus odoratus* to produce a yellow flower, something horticulturists have been unable to do with simple crossbreeding." She smelled her cutting again, a smile warming her already delicious features. "But the flower is unique for more than its color. It takes in two soil toxins through its root system, ammonium from factories improperly disposing of their waste and nitric acid found in rain because of atmospheric changes caused by pollution. Then, the plant binds the two and the result is a flower abundant with ammonium nitrate."

"Fertilizer." And a highly explosive compound used in low-level bomb making. He didn't think he'd mention that fact, though. He didn't want to hurt her feelings. "That's amazing."

"Thanks. We're closer to a large field test on this one than the enzymes."

"Well, the smell is definitely better."

She laughed. "I concur." She bent to take another cutting from a plant in one of the other beds under the growing lights.

"So, tell me about your belly dancing troupe." He smoothly segued back to the topic of interest.

"We practice in a locked facility and don't let anyone watch."

Lana gave him a look that said she knew exactly why he'd brought it up. "Our choreographer is highly protective of her routines."

"Good." Fantastic even.

Lana shook her head. "I have a feeling you are more paranoid than she is."

"I can guarantee it."

"Oh, brother."

"I'd really love to see you dance." The idea of those very feminine curves jiggling with purpose enticed him big-time. "But for the time being, you are going to need to find someone to take over your class and refrain from performing. Though I don't see a problem with you attending practice." Accompanied, of course.

"No."

Chapter 5

"Excuse me?" He could not have heard her right. Although the single, monosyllabic word was hard to misconstrue.

She crossed her arms, giving him a look that said her positive view of life wasn't the only thing she was stubborn about. "Don't look at me like you're shocked the geeky scientist had the temerity to say *no* to you."

Damn it, he *was* surprised, though. Not that he'd call her a geeky scientist, more like a hot, "he wanted to touch her until she screamed out his name" one. He wasn't used to *anyone* telling him no, however, no matter how delectable. Even the dregs of humanity listened to him. They seemed to be able to sense that he didn't threaten, he acted.

Suzy Sunshine here, however, appeared immune to his anti-charm. He'd try logic. It had been known to work with his sisters and mom a time or two. Nothing worked with his *baba* when she got an idea stuck in her head. "I promised to protect you, but you have to do your part, Lana."

Far from looking convinced, her expression turned mulish. "Do you have a concrete reason to believe that *I* am at risk *at present*?"

"Other than the fact your project has been targeted by the Vega Cartel?"

"Yes."

"That was a rhetorical question. You weren't supposed to answer, but realize that I have a very legitimate reason for believing you are at risk. Namely that whole 'being targeted by the really bad guys who don't respect human life and consider torture part of their regular job description' thing."

"My project was targeted, not me. Unless those notes you saw mentioned someone besides your sister."

"No." He admitted that frustrating truth through clenched teeth.

"So, for all you know, I'm not a target at all."

"If they want your project, they are going to want you." He realized how very true that was after hearing her explanation of the enzymes.

"Maybe."

"There are no maybes. Your enzymes don't work on any plants but the ones they were created to enhance, much less metals. As soon as the cartel realizes that, you'll be their number-one target if you aren't already."

"You said you thought Elle was their number-one target."

"She corrected me and she was right."

"Should I tell her you said so?"

"I'd consider it a favor if you didn't."

"I'll think about it." Lana bagged her cuttings.

"Elle's their first target, probably because they see her as a roadblock to getting what they want. Your enzymes or you. Most likely both."

"That's speculation on your part."

"I'm good at this kind of guessing. You're going to have to trust my instincts on this one."

"I'm not going to start living like a prisoner. Been there. Done that."

He could understand her attitude, but he couldn't accept it. "Giving up teaching a dance class is not the same as getting locked in a prison lab."

"No, it's not, but it's also not living my life to its fullest. Which is something I promised myself I would do, after Mr. Smith convinced me to come back to environmental research and development."

"Listen to me, Lana—"

"No, you listen to me." She got right into his face. "I was incarcerated for eight months by the Kurdish rebels, and that was horrible."

"I know."

"No, you don't. You can't. You probably admire what I did to get away."

"I do."

"I don't. I hated it. I still wake up at least once a week from nightmares, the smell of burning cordite in my nostrils and the sound of screams from falling men in my ears."

Shit. He reached out for her, but she twisted and moved her body to avoid his touch. "The horror didn't end when I got away. I made it back to the United States, but I was still in prison. My fears were the bars and they held me more securely than any four walls and a steel door could have."

"I'm sorry."

"Don't be. I made it out of that prison, too. I'm not going back in."

"I'm not trying to make you. I'm trying to keep you safe so you can continue to live outside of that prison for a long, long time to come."

Ideally, she and Elle would go to a safe house until the issue had been resolved. He didn't see that happening, however. Not for his sister, who would probably shoot him if he suggested it, and certainly not for Lana. Protective custody had to be a last resort for a woman who had been through what she had.

"By curtailing the very activities that prove the absence of those bars in my life now."

Damn it. "Lana, we have no way of knowing where they will strike or how quickly. We need to keep you safe until the threat is neutralized."

"That could take days, weeks, months, years even."

"I'm too good at my job for that."

"You're even more arrogant than your siblings."

"I thought you liked Mat and Elle."

"I do, but their confidence levels are definitely higher than the average person."

"That doesn't make them arrogant, just aware of their own strengths."

"You sound just like them."

"And you sound like a woman who doesn't want to admit when she's in danger."

Lana sighed. "I admit the danger exists."

"Good."

"But not that it's immediate."

"Damn, it, Lana!"

"Don't curse at me, Mykola. This situation could be a long-term issue for the Vega Cartel. It could be something they are only mildly interested in, or even something they will never actually pursue. Regardless, you're assuming they'll come after me, but you don't have any evidence pointing in that direction."

Was she being deliberately obtuse? "They had your notes!"

"For all you know, they have notes on other scientists' projects as well."

He wanted to deny the possibility, but the only reason he had the information he did was that the Vega Cartel had shared those particular notes with the organization he'd brought down. "I don't have enough information to speculate on that."

"And you don't have enough information to draw the conclusion that I'm in such grave danger I need to start living like I'm in prison again, either."

"They named my sister their first target. Which means they have plans, most likely immediate plans. If they didn't, they would just wait for her to move on to her next project. After all, she's not an employee of ETRD, she's a consultant."

"That still doesn't mean I'm at risk."

"They named her their *first* target, not their last!"

"I'm not going back into prison." She crossed her arms and set her mouth stubbornly. "I'm not."

"You don't have to live like you are in prison," he ground out the reminder.

"Really? What would you call putting my life and the things that are important to me on hold *indefinitely*?"

"Smart." The need to touch her again was growing with every word.

She was not reacting rationally and he didn't want to, either. Call him primal, but he wanted to kiss her into submission. His gut told him it would never work, but it would be damn fun trying.

"One thing you cannot call me is stupid."

"I wouldn't dream of doing so, but that doesn't mean you can't do something dumb. We're all capable of random acts of idiocy."

"Even you?"

"Especially me."

"Like what?"

"Like this."

He reached her in two long strides and pulled her into his arms. She gasped in shock, but didn't struggle.

Not even a little.

He was smiling inside as his mouth claimed hers.

She tasted just as sweet as she had the first time, but now he knew what to expect and he wanted more. Tilting her head back, he brushed his thumb against the corner of her lips while his mouth pressed against hers with intent. She got the hint and her lips parted, giving him access to an even sweeter version of the berries and cream spiced by sexy girl scientist flavor unique to Lana.

Damn. She was delicious. He'd been hooked after the first taste, but now he was facing true addiction. Enslavement. He would never need to eat again if he could just go on kissing this woman. She was exquisite.

Warm and silky, her tongue slid against his. She returned his kiss, tasting him with as much obvious enjoyment as he was experiencing.

And rocked his control to the core.

He thrust his tongue against hers before twirling it around the tip and then thrusting again. He had a deep need to conquer her mouth and to be conquered in return. So, he wasn't the least disappointed when she countered his thrust with one of her own, starting a duel that lasted several long seconds while their bodies moved closer together until her fleshy curves were pressed against him.

He broke his mouth away only far enough to demand against her lips, "Lose the lab coat."

She didn't argue, shimmying out of the scientist garb as she enthusiastically dove back into the kiss. Pushing her tongue into his mouth, she fought for supremacy. He allowed her to explore his mouth just as he'd done hers, mostly because his hands were busy exploring the curves now covered in nothing but a snug fitting Winnie the Pooh T-shirt. She was wearing a bra; he could feel the straps when his palms skimmed her shoulders, but the fabric was lightweight enough it might as well have not been there.

He could feel the heat of her body through her clothes. Either her temperature was spiked with arousal, or she had an abnormally high ambient temperature. He was guessing the former because he felt like his own blood had grown volcanically hot. And he knew it was because she inflamed his senses to the point of spontaneous combustion.

He traced the lines of her barely there bra, cupping the encased mounds and wishing both the T-shirt and bra to Hades. Her breasts were large and round, so perfect, he had visions of coming between them, leaving her decorated with a string of liquid pearls. His cock throbbed in his leather jeans, aching for just such a release. Her nipples pebbled under his fingertips. Unable to help himself and unwilling to even try, he lightly pinched them, reveling in their increased turgidity. He rolled them between his thumbs and forefingers, loving the way the flesh responded to being abraded through the layers of fabric—becoming adamantine, their diamond-like hardness calling to his base desires.

He so wanted to take her into his mouth and suck on flesh both hard and soft and oh so succulent. Her mouth was so delectable; the rest of her body was bound to be scrumptious.

She made a feral sound of her own as he continued to chafe her stiffened nipples. Her arms came around his neck and she forcefully pressed her body into his. He wasn't surprised when a sound of frustration from her mouth vibrated against his lips.

He knew the feeling—the need—driving her. To get the kind of satisfaction they both craved, they would have to be naked.

And no matter how far gone his libido was, he wasn't

about to have sex with her for the first time in one of her growing rooms. Even if it did smell of sweet pea rather than a gas-mask-worthy stink. Hell, considering the type of security systems his sister favored, Myk doubted he would *ever* be willing to get naked in *any* room at ETRD.

He wasn't into exhibition.

Which didn't mean he had to stop kissing her. And that was a good thing. Because she tasted necessary.

Like his next breath necessary.

Like catching the bad guys necessary.

Like survival necessary.

She seemed to agree as her lips molded to his and she accepted his tongue back into her mouth, where he set a rhythm like the one he wanted to create with their bodies. Her hips swiveled against his, telling him she was thinking along the same lines.

Damn. She was a good fit for him.

He reached down and cupped the perfect spheres of her bottom. Deliciously fleshy. He caressed her through her capris, cupping the enticing globes and lifting her body until their sexes were in alignment through their clothes.

She squeaked against his mouth, her shock stilling her tongue momentarily.

Without breaking the kiss, he opened his eyes to meet hers. Was it too much?

Her eyes were open, but even if her body had stiffened with surprise, the hazel depths of her eyes glittered green-gold with desire.

He withdrew from her mouth with every intention of returning. "What?"

"I'm too heavy."

He said a word that made her flinch and slammed his mouth back onto hers. Her eyes fluttered shut and he let his close as well. Better to savor her.

Women and their misconceptions about their bodies. He would have thought that his sexy little scientist would be the last woman to buy into Hollywood's fallacy that thin to the point of emaciation was sexy. Wasn't she busy trying to feed the starving masses of the world? Why in the world would she think she needed to look like them to be attractive?

Hell, her belief she was too heavy was a slight on his masculinity as well and damned if he'd take that lying down . . . or standing up and kissing as the case may be.

He set about showing her just how much *not* too heavy she was for him to do what he wanted. Using his grip on her delectable bottom, he held her still for pelvic thrusts that were both intensely pleasurable for him and proof that she was anything but unwieldy in his arms.

His dick was like to explode, but he wasn't about to stop.

Hell, if he came in his pants, he'd chalk it up to her sexiness and not his own lack of control.

From the way she was moaning and thrusting her tongue against his, he'd say he wasn't the only one in danger of climaxing from the intense kissing.

He broke the kiss. "You are not too heavy." He accentuated each word with a thrust of his hips. "Understood?"

She threw her head back, letting out a keening cry of need. "*Yes.*"

Damn, he wanted to see her come. But this was not the place. He changed his hold on her so that one arm curved around her hips. He used his other hand to bring her head back up so their lips could meet again.

C-4 exploded behind his eyelids as their mouths collided once again.

"Oh, jeez. Get a room, I mean one with a bed. You two . . . This just isn't right, Dr. Ericson. This is like watching my parents kiss, but way more intense. It's kind of sexy, but *ew*, too."

Shit. It was the assistant. Again. At least this time, he wasn't trying to bash Myk's head in.

Lana went absolutely rigid in his arms, but it took her a flattering number of seconds to break her lips from his. "Hello, Casey. Am I to assume you are finished taking samples?"

"Yes, boss. You're not going to believe what I found on the *Oryza sativa* plants."

Lana sighed, her light golden freckles drowned by the crimson blush on her cheeks. She met Myk's gaze. "You can let me down now."

"Are we agreed you are not too heavy?"

She rolled her eyes. "I can't believe you're still on that."

"You slighted my manhood."

"It looked to me like she was trying to pay homage to it, not slight it, but that's just me. I've probably got less real-world experience than even Dr. Ericson when it comes to sex."

"Casey?" Myk asked.

"Yeah?"

"Shut up."

"Oh, uh, sure." A couple of seconds of silence followed during which Myk lowered Lana so that she was standing once again. "But I mean, do you usually take offense at a woman rubbing off on you?"

Groaning, Lana covered her face with both her hands.

Myk got control of an unexpected urge to laugh before turning to face the young male scientist. "My offense was taken when she said I was too weak to hold her up."

"That's odd."

"That I took offense?"

"No, that Lana would accuse you of being weak. You are well above average height for a male of this era, very clearly in good shape, and too young to have muscle definition loss from aging."

"You call her Lana and Dr. Ericson both. Why?"

"He calls me Dr. Ericson when he is angry with me, embarrassed about something, or in an uncomfortable situation."

"Were you angry to find your boss kissing another man?" Myk asked.

"Not at all. Though, the *ew* factor, so not something I want to deal with on a regular basis, you know?"

"We won't be making out in the lab regularly." Lana sounded very sure about that fact.

Casey didn't look nearly as convinced, but surprisingly he kept his opinion to himself.

Myk dipped his head toward the other man. "Thank you for not trying to cosh me again."

"I only did that before because I thought you were attacking her." Casey was now blushing even more brightly than Lana.

Myk raised a single brow at the younger man. "Now you know she's a normal woman like any other."

"No." Casey shook his head for emphasis.

"No?"

"Lana is smarter than ninety-nine-point-five percent of all other women. She's not normal."

Lana groaned and Myk stifled another laugh. He knew Casey didn't mean to be insulting. "And you? Is your I.Q. in the stratosphere, too?"

Casey just shrugged.

"Casey is very bright. The idea for the genetically altered *Lathyrus odoratus* was his."

Myk would call that more than *very bright*, but then he wasn't one of the head geeks in his family. "So, you two have been working together for a while?"

"Since Casey's doctoral dissertation." Lana shrugged back into her lab coat and moved so she was facing both Myk and Casey.

"Was he another child prodigy?" Myk asked.

"*He* is right here. Sheesh. I thought only parents, doctors, and teachers talked about a person as if they weren't there." Casey did disgruntled very well.

"You've been looking into my background?" Lana demanded before Myk had a chance to respond to her assistant.

"It's my job."

"I suppose." She smiled at Casey. "I'll let Casey answer your question about him, since he *is* here."

"Thank you, boss." Casey's direct gaze met Myk's. "Yes, I was what you term a child prodigy, but instead of thinking I was some kind of freak like Lana's did, my parents were really proud of me."

Myk slid a sideways look at Lana, but she didn't seem offended or upset by Casey's comment. "Aren't they still proud of you?" he asked Casey.

"They're dead."

"Casey's parents were killed by a drunk driver going the wrong way on the freeway two years ago."

"I'm sorry," Myk said to Casey.

The young scientist nodded at him. "Thanks. It still hurts, you know?"

"I can imagine." He and his family were close. Myk couldn't fathom losing both his parents in one harsh blow like that.

"I'm surprised you didn't know that already," Lana said.

Myk frowned. "I haven't had a chance to do all the background research I would have liked. I came directly to ETRD after getting the prelim stuff out of the way for me to work for my new boss."

"The Goddard Project?" Casey asked.

"Damn, does everyone in this facility know who Elle used to work for?" Maybe the agency's policy of taking compromised agents out of the field wasn't so draconian after all. Even other federal agencies weren't supposed to know TGP existed, much less who might work for it.

He could see that his career with the agency was going to be a short one because he was going to be exposed simply by association with his sister. He could come up with a clever cover, but chances were, no one was going to buy it. Not at ETRD, anyway. The employees here weren't your average Joe Shmoe off the street.

Their ability to do inductive and deductive reasoning scenarios far outclassed the average citizen. Everyone but the security detail. That group of dimwits had a rude awakening coming to them. Now that Elle knew how complacent they were, even after the attempts that had been made on ETRD's projects in the past, she would take measures to rectify the problem.

He didn't envy them. Not one bit.

Chapter 6

Lana sipped at the caramel mocha latte that Casey had talked her into getting after Myk left their lab muttering under his breath about dimwits and blown covers. She and her assistant had come to their favorite independent coffee shop only a few minutes' drive from ETRD. The African tribal décor was a genuine tribute to the Kenyan family that ran the shop.

The grandfather greeted customers across the counter while his son made the drinks and his grandson kept the restaurant neat and clean.

"Now that's coffee," Casey said with a happy sigh after taking a sip of his triple-shot espresso, no syrup or milk added. He leaned back into the brown leather sofa he sat on.

Lana kicked off her Mickey Mouse tennis shoes and tucked her sock-clad feet under her on the oversized chair she'd taken kitty-corner to Casey's spot on the couch. "You might as well hook yourself up to a caffeine drip and be done with it."

"I'm not a caffeine junkie just because I don't defile the purity of my coffee with enough milk and sugar to make a confectioner proud."

"First, it's not called defilement, it's called enhancement. Second, you're an addict because you require a triple-shot espresso before lunch."

"Does that make you a sex fiend for having not one, but two hot kisses with our resident security expert's brother *before lunch*?"

"I can't be certain, since it isn't my area of expertise, but I can surmise that it would take more than a couple of kisses following a year plus of celibacy to label me a sex fiend." Lana gave Casey her best haughty look before taking a sip of her yummy coffee confection.

"Wow, you're worse off in that department than I am."

She glared, but Casey just looked pityingly at her. "I am not worse off. Sex is hardly the be-all, end-all of the human existence. I'm perfectly content with my life. I have a job I love, good friends, and my belly dancing."

"You only see your friends at work."

"I'm seeing you now and we aren't at work."

"It's during work hours. Same thing."

"If you say so. I do not need a sex life to have a good one."

"You can say that after the way you were humping Mr. Tall, Dark, Dangerous, and Just a Little Bit Scary?"

Lana could feel the blush she'd finally gotten rid of returning. "He's not scary."

"If *you* say so." Casey took a sip of his coffee and an expression of bliss suffused his face. "What is he doing here anyway? I don't see Ms. Gray needing reinforcements."

"Our secondary crop enzymes have come to the attention of the Vega Cartel. Apparently they have targeted Elle Gray because of their interest in the enzymes."

Casey's eyes rounded. "You mean the Queen of Badass is in danger?"

"Don't call her that."

"It's what everyone calls her."

"It's disrespectful."

"I doubt she'd mind. In fact, I bet she knows about it and likes it."

"She has a perfectly good name. Use it."

"Yes, mother." Casey cocked his head to one side, clearly thinking. Then he asked, "Why Ms. Gray?"

"She's in the way of them getting the enzymes maybe? Security was good before she came."

"But not good enough. Now it's phenomenal."

"Exactly."

"You think they plan to kidnap her and torture her until she tells them how to circumvent the security measures she put in place?"

For the second time that morning, memories threatened to overwhelm Lana. It took all she had to shove the images back into the dark closet of her mind she'd relegated them to. "I hope not."

"She can handle herself if they do."

"You think so? She's amazing at her job, but she's not impervious to hurt. No one is."

"The same could be said of you."

"What?" Did he know about her past? She trusted Casey, but she'd never told him about what had happened to her.

"No one, not even brilliant lady scientists with amazingly brilliant assistants, is impervious to sexual desire. It'll bring you to your knees if you don't watch out. Which technically isn't such a bad thing, if you like giving oral sex, that is."

"Dr. Billings!"

"What?"

"You have less of a filter than I do. Which most would say is impossible. And don't think I didn't notice how you called me merely brilliant while you are supposedly amazingly brilliant."

The redhead grinned, his white teeth gleaming in the coffee shop's warm lighting. "So, do you?"

"Do I what? Or should I even ask?"

"Like giving oral sex."

"You think this is an appropriate discussion between two scientific colleagues?"

"It's your own fault. I'm your best friend, not just your colleague. If you had developed more friends outside work, you wouldn't be stuck with me as your confidant."

"And I'm yours. What does that say about your social life?"

"That it's pathetic? So? Spill."

She didn't make him repeat the question. "I never have in the past."

"You think that could change with Myk?"

"I think that I'm considering reevaluating my stance on the whole sex issue and once again trying to find out what all the fuss is about." And wasn't that a shocker? She hadn't wanted anything but her hand and her BOB for a very long time.

"Makes sense. You are a scientist, after all, and empirical research is in the job description."

"That argument might hold more water if I was a psychologist or anthropologist, or even a sex therapist—don't you think?"

"I think you'd make the world's worst sex therapist and that you should go for it with the guy you can't seem to keep your lips off of."

"Thanks a lot. You want to know what I think?"

"What?"

"You should worry about your own sex life."

"Or lack thereof," Casey said glumly.

"Get dumped again?"

"Nah. I did the dumping this time."

"Why?"

"She was seeing other guys."

"Did she promise exclusivity?"

Casey sighed. "Not per se."

"If not per se, then how?"

"She kissed me."

"Ahh . . ." That explained some of Casey's reaction that morning.

"A kiss is an intimate act," Casey said with vehemence he usually reserved for his work. "If it didn't mean anything to her, she should have said something."

"Casey, hon, I think a lot of women today kiss without putting significant social or relational meaning behind it."

"Maybe I should have been born in a different time."

"And live without a computer? I don't think so."

Casey laughed, like she'd meant him to, but Lana felt bad for him. His problem wasn't that he'd been born to live out his life in the twenty-first century. It was that he was a geek. A nerd. Amazingly brilliant, just like he'd said. But sadly lacking savvy in interpersonal relationships. He was more naïve than she'd been before her first serious boyfriend had sold her out to Kurdish rebels who wanted their own stockpile of chemical weapons.

"Have you tried dating someone from work?"

"No."

"Have you thought about it?"

"Do I have to answer that?"

"You have! Who?"

He remained stubbornly mute.

"Come on, Casey. You owe me a secret for digging into mine. Spill."

"I think Nisha is incredible, but she'd never be interested in someone like me."

Nisha Garjana was eight years Casey's senior, but didn't look it. Like many women of her genetic predisposition, she would maintain her youthful, exotic beauty for decades to come.

"Have you asked her out?"

"No!" Casey look scandalized. "I couldn't."

"You could. In fact, I think you should. She's not seeing anyone right now. She finds intelligence highly attractive, and I think she's lonely."

"She told you that?"

Lana just looked at her assistant until he nodded, looking a little sheepish. "I get it. It's just more of the information your brain catalogs about the people who populate your environment."

"So, you know it's true."

"But what if she thinks I'm a baby?"

"The trend for older women to date younger men is growing."

"Really?"

"Would I lie to you?"

"No more than you would lie to yourself."

"Your point?"

"If it wasn't crass, I'd make you a five-hundred-dollar bet that you and Myk are going to end up doing the nasty before the double Chernichenko wedding."

"Elle, Beau, Chantal, and Mat are getting married next Saturday," she said with shock. She wasn't surprised Casey thought she and Mykola were going to have sex, but that he thought it would happen so soon. And that he was so certain, he'd be willing to make such a large bet on it.

Although, she'd known Myk less than an hour when he kissed her the first time, a kiss was a far cry from penetrative sex. Or, at least, that had always been her experience. With Myk? She'd been on the verge of climaxing and she'd never even gotten her pants off.

Still, she wasn't jumping into bed with a man she barely knew. "You're on."

Casey grinned, so smug it made her teeth hurt. "It looks like I'll be getting that new game system before I planned."

She shook her head before he pulled her into a discussion of everything that had happened in the lab before he arrived that morning.

When Casey had pulled every detail about the Vega Cartel situation out of her, he drained his espresso cup with one final grim pull on the dark brown liquid. "Man, that is heavy."

"You sound like a sixties beatnik."

"I told you I should have been born in a different era."

"I'm glad you were born in this one."

"Thanks, boss."

"Though maybe you should stop watching movies made in the 1960s."

"I've been on a kick lately."

"I noticed. It's better than when you were in your John Wayne phase."

"I don't do a good impression of the Duke, do I?"

"It never really worked for me, no."

"I found a library in Orange County that has a collection of the first-ever talkies."

"Maybe I should buy you the *Star Wars* series."

"No, thanks. That whole doughnuts on the sides of Princess Leia's head makes me laugh out loud and I can't take the movies seriously."

"You are a strange man for a geek, you know that don't you?"

"No stranger than my belly dancing boss."

"You've got a point."

She reached across the table and grabbed his hand. "I'm not convinced the situation is as dire as Mykola intimates, but I want you to be careful. Okay?"

"You think they'll try to get me?"

"You know as much about the enzymes as I do."

"That's an overstatement, but I could see how the uninformed might assume it to be the case."

"So, you'll watch out for yourself? Maybe stop visiting the clubs for a while."

Casey gave her *the look*. "It sounds to me like you want me to take the advice you're fighting to ignore."

Lana pulled her hand away and looked down, guiltily breaking eye contact. "It's different for me."

"Why? Because you've got some training in Middle Eastern hand-to-hand defensive combat?"

"It helps." Though she wasn't so naïve she believed she could save herself from truly determined kidnappers. She just had a fighting chance now, not like before when she'd been clueless how to fight back. "Besides, if you are going to ask Nisha out, you aren't going to need to be going to the clubs."

"I'll make a deal with you. If she says yes, I'll stop clubbing, but if she says no, you go clubbing with me. You can protect both of us."

Casey's uninformed attitude that they were safe bothered Lana, but she liked it better than unadulterated fear. "You've got a deal."

Steaming, Lana slammed her front door shut before spinning to lock it.

She wasn't sure what irritated her the most. The security officer who arrived in her lab and informed her it was time to go home, or the knowledge that Mykola had arranged it. She'd argued that she wasn't done working, but the security guard had remained obdurate, not budging from his hovering position until she had shut down her computer, packed a satchel of work to take home with her, and agreed to leave the building.

Then? The man had had the effrontery to follow her home.

He'd saluted her from his car when she'd unlocked the front door of her secured building. She'd been so irritated, she hadn't even had her usual smile for the female security guard at the front desk.

Tina was four months pregnant and tended to take things personally. Lana sighed. She would have to make sure she stopped to say hi at the desk the next time the other woman was on duty.

The phone rang as Lana spread her work out on the coffee table in front of the television, watching a rerun of *Buffy* with the volume set on low. It was probably Mykola calling to tell her what other plans he had to ensure her safety and future need for counseling on anger management. Ready to yell, she grabbed the phone only to almost swallow her tongue when a familiar if infrequently heard voice came across the line.

"Mr. Smith?"

"Hello, Dr. Ericson. How are you?"

"Frustrated."

"With Agent Chernichenko?"

She didn't bother to ask how he could guess. Presumably Mr. Smith knew a little something about Elle's brother. "Yes."

"You know he wants only to keep you safe?"

"I would say that was a secondary consideration to keeping Elle from trouble, sir."

"I get the impression that Agent Chernichenko takes all his considerations seriously, secondary or otherwise."

"No doubt."

"Have you given further thought to his desire for you to give up teaching belly dance for the time being?"

"No."

A bark of laughter sounded over the phone line.

She sighed. "There's no use dissembling, sir. I'm not going back into prison."

"I believe, my dear Dr. Ericson, that is exactly what the agent is hoping to avoid."

"There is more than one kind of prison, sir."

"I am aware."

Silence reigned for a full minute.

Finally, Lana sighed. "I'm scared to give up the freedom I've fought so hard to attain."

"You will not go back to living that half-life I enticed you away from." He might as well have said rescued from, but that was Mr. Smith, giving the people he believed in the benefit of the doubt.

"You sound so sure."

"That is because I am."

"Then you have more confidence in me than I have in myself."

"I have complete confidence in you."

"I'll think about it. Giving up the class for the time being."

"That is all I can ask."

It wasn't. He could order her to do it. He had to know she'd submit out of loyalty and respect. But that wasn't Mr. Smith's way.

Myk stood in the men's room cubicle and fought the urge to retch. He refused to let his sister see him like this. Or anyone else for that matter.

But damn it to hell and back. The Vega Cartel bastards had tried to kill his little sister this morning. The fact that they had not succeeded in no way mitigated Myk's fury, or his fear.

His sister had been marked by a cartel *jefe* for death.

She was supposed to get married in less than a week. And he couldn't be sure he would be able to keep her alive long enough to make it to her honeymoon. Not with her refusing to go to a safe house. He'd expected her denial when he made the suggestion, but the reality was too fricken hard to deal with.

He'd thought he could handle this case with an objective view. No way in hell.

Some part of him had to have been banking on the fact the cartel had been interested in taking Elle, not taking her out. Kidnapping an agent as well trained and deadly as his sister would have been a whole lot harder, but a well-aimed sniper's bullet could kill the best agent in the world in a matter of seconds.

The Vega Cartel wanted Elle dead. The only reason she wasn't was because her assassin had tried to make it look like an accident. Next time, they might not be so lucky.

And that made Myk angry enough to kill on his own. He slammed his fist against the wall of the bathroom stall.

It didn't leave a dent, but damn, his hand hurt. He cursed.

"The stalls are made with titanium walls."

Myk let his forehead drop against the wall in front of him at the sound of Beau Ruston's voice. What was he supposed to say to the man who was supposed to become his brother by marriage in a matter of days?

He put his game face on and exited the stall. "Titanium walls?"

"Yep." Beau was leaning against the bank of sinks.

"You worried about graffiti?"

"We're a company made up of scientists. They take notes anywhere. You should have seen the stall walls before Elle insisted on their replacement."

Myk washed his hands. He might have been in the stall for reasons other than its usual usage, but the place was still a bathroom. "Definite security hazard."

"Yes, and your sister was smart enough to see that." Beau turned his body slightly so he faced Myk.

"Her intelligence isn't going to keep her alive against a sniper rifle."

Eyes a shade lighter brown than his own but every bit as unreadable gazed back at Myk. "I agree."

"So, talk her into a safe house."

"You got any suggestions on how to do that?"

"The future husband love-guilt card didn't work?"

"No more than the concerned older brother love-guilt card did."

"She's stubborn."

"Pertinacious headed toward cantankerous. I've decided she gets that from your grandmother."

"*Baba* would refuse the safe house, too."

"Probably. Life wasn't always safe in her little corner of the Ukraine before she came to the States. She survived."

"You think Elle can will away an assassin's bullet?"

"I think that as long as the cartel thinks Elle's unaware of the danger, they'll stick with the arranged accident scenario."

"That will make it harder to succeed."

"Yes." Beau's jaw went taut. "But not impossible. Elle believes that if she disappears, it will tip the cartel off that she's on to them. She thinks it will make it harder to bring them down before they get their hands on Lana."

"No one is getting their hands on Lana. Or Elle."

"I want to believe you." For one short moment, the terror living inside Beau for the woman he loved showed clearly on his face.

"Then believe me. You think we can get Elle to disappear if she's convinced it won't compromise the case?"

"I think we'd have a fighting chance."

"Then, I guess we'll have to get that fighting chance."

"You have any ideas how?"

"One. I need to make a couple of calls to set it up."

Beau nodded. Then he took a deep breath and let it out slowly. "Thank you."

"You don't have to thank me. She's my sister."

"I'm leaning toward the belief that you're a hell of a brother to have."

"Here's hoping."

They shook hands and Beau left.

Myk made his calls.

On his way back to Elle's office, Myk considered how best to present his plan to Elle. His phone calls had borne fruit. Now he just had to get his sister's buy-in. He couldn't even pretend to himself he looked forward to that conversation. He had a secret weapon, though, and wasn't afraid to use it.

Mostly.

Elle lived by the motto that paybacks were a bitch and she'd proven time and again growing up that little sister, or not, she held her own just fine with her three older brothers.

Reflecting on that less-than-palatable truth, Myk looked up to find Lana rapidly approaching him from the other end of the corridor.

His dick took immediate notice. A whole lot more disturbing, however, was the way his lips curved into an involuntary smile at the sight of her.

The hard-won control he had over his every emotion was about to go to hell in a handbasket, too, but not because the sight of the gorgeous double-doctoral recipient elicited a renewal of his fury. She evoked a few strong feelings all right, but none of them had anything to do with being angry.

Every one of them could be linked to the salacious desire he felt toward her. A desire that had kicked him in the gut when he'd walked into her lab yesterday morning and had been wreaking havoc with his body and thoughts ever since. He'd needed focus the night before to review files he hadn't had a chance to look at before arriving in California, to get a feel for the major players, to do any of the myriad of things related to the case. But his thoughts had been scattered. Memories of their kisses frequently intruded to shatter any semblance of linear thinking on his part.

He could remember every single nuance of her taste and the feel of her body against his. He'd found it a lot more challenging to remember particulars about her assistant or the lab for his notes. That had never happened to him before. He'd never wanted a woman so much she clouded his other impressions.

After struggling to organize thoughts that should have been easy to catalog, he'd accepted that the million-dollar question was: would his focus be more compromised by leaving his desires for the sexy scientist unfulfilled, or indulging in their mutual lust?

Which course of action would make doing his job and protecting his younger sister the hardest?

He still did not have an answer.

Or maybe he did. The urge to press Lana against the nondescript gray wall and kiss her until they were both stupid with it grew stronger with each step nearer she took. He needed to drown his desire in her body so he could get back to his job with an unclouded brain.

With that realization, he looked more closely at the sexily intelligent scientist. Lana did not look like she'd spent the night contemplating sexy games with him. In fact, she looked more likely to take after him with a fire hose—after setting his shirttail on fire—if he wore a shirt that had a tail.

She stopped mere inches from him, her entire body radiating affront. "You can wipe that predatory look right off your face, Agent Chernichenko. There will be no more kisses."

"Really?" He so did not agree.

She glared. "Really."

"May I ask why?" Was she afraid to give in to the fantasies she'd voiced in her lab when she'd been looking at him like a year's worth of chocolate desserts and talking out loud?

"As if you don't already know." She crossed her arms and gave him a look that would have shriveled his balls if they weren't so full from sexual need. "Mr. Smith asked me to rationally consider your request. And I was willing to do that. I really was, but I will not be dictated to in regard to the time I leave for or from work."

"What are you talking about?" He hadn't put Lana on a schedule and wouldn't dream of doing so. It would make her comings and goings too predictable. Even a rookie agent would know better than to do that.

He was no rookie.

"You and your Gestapo-like security-guard watchdogs." She poked his chest for emphasis. "That's what."

Chapter 7

Myk grabbed Lana's finger and held it against his chest. Caressing the back of her hand with his pinky, he said, "I asked Elle to order a security detail to follow you home and escort you to work. Nonintrusive surveillance of that nature hardly justifies you likening them to the Gestapo."

"Nonintrusive?" Lana asked bitingly as she yanked her hand from his. "You call showing up in my lab and demanding I stop what I am doing, important work for my projects that does not suit well to a timetable I might add, so he could escort me home *nonintrusive*?"

Myk opened his mouth to answer, but she didn't give him the chance.

"And strong-arming his way past the security guard in my building in order to show up at my door when I was still dripping wet from the shower, only to sit in my living room, waiting impatiently while I finished getting ready, is not what I call nonintrusive. Do you see my hair?"

"Um . . . yes?" When a woman was in this mood, a man had to be very careful of his answers and even so, he was still statistically biased toward failure.

The picture she was painting was one he had every intention of taking turpentine to. Those idiot security guards would be lucky to still have their jobs when he was done with them.

"My hair is still wet. Would you like to venture a guess as to why?"

"Because you didn't dry it?"

"Because the security guard you instructed to follow me to work today had to relieve the night guard and had me feeling so guilty for my tardiness that I left the house without drying my hair, eating my breakfast, or reading my paper. I didn't even have my morning coffee!"

That explained the cranky she had going on. "I apologize. Apparently Elle was not specific enough with her instructions."

"Really? Because from where I'm standing, those guards had very specific instructions that resulted in nothing short of my *harassment*. I told you I'm not going back to living like a prisoner and I won't!"

If Myk himself wasn't so close to the edge because of his sister's brush with death earlier, he might have paid better attention to the signs of irrationality marking Lana's reaction. But he was still riding a fury bronc that was busting his ass. He chose to ignore any underlying issues to go straight for the jugular of the problem.

"You'll do what is necessary to keep you and Elle safe, Dr. Ericson, and if that means giving up your precious belly dancing for the time being, then, so be it. You will do nothing that will increase the chances of your being taken and my sister being killed." He didn't yell. He didn't loom over her to intimidate. He spoke in the quiet tone of voice he'd used to tell the drug lord in his last undercover assignment that Myk would shoot if the man did not drop his weapon.

The drug lord had ignored the warning and he had died.

Not that Myk had even the slightest interest in hurting Lana, but he'd slap her luscious ass into protective custody in a heartbeat if that's what it took to keep her and Elle safe.

Lana stared at him for several tense seconds and then asked, "What changed?"

"Nothing changed. I told you yesterday, we needed to make some alterations in your social schedule for the time being."

"Not that. Yesterday you said Elle had been targeted, but you weren't sure if it was for a kidnapping or an assassination. You're certain it's death now. So, what changed?"

Myk took a deep breath and stepped back. "Someone tried to run Elle off the road on the coastal highway on her way to work this morning. If she'd gone over, both she and Beau would be seriously injured, or dead."

"You're sure it was on purpose? California drivers are really aggressive."

"Elle is sure."

"Oh." Lana's entire countenance changed. She went from furiously indignant to compassionately worried in the space of a heartbeat. "Are they okay?"

"Yes. I won't even say she's shaken up, though Beau is pretty upset. Not about his own safety, but about hers."

"He loves her." Lana got a far-off look in her eye. "I thought he'd be like that if he really fell for a woman."

Something about the way she said it made Myk wonder if, at one time, Lana had wanted that woman to be her. Hell, she still might.

And didn't that idea just piss him off all over again. "So, you can see why I expect your cooperation in ensuring both your safety."

She sighed. "Yes."

"Good." But damn, that defeated look had to go.

"How long do you intend to box me in with what you consider to be safety measures?" The helplessness in Lana's voice bothered Myk as well.

"It is not my intention to box you in."

"Intention is not always the birth of deed."

"Trust me on this." He would set the security guards straight, too. "I might even be able to arrange something for your belly-dancing class."

Nothing about her countenance changed except that she looked away from him. Like she hadn't heard him, or discounted what he'd said completely. "Where were you headed when I stopped you to let you know how unhappy I am with the current situation?"

Definitely still unhappy. Myk didn't have to be an expert at body language and voice tonal qualities to get that. Or to take note of the underlying sadness tinged by fear.

He wanted to promise—again—that he was going to protect her, but he didn't want to hear her denial that he could. He might do something entirely inappropriate in response. Something that would have her comparing him to Cro-Magnon man again.

"To Elle's office."

"To discuss the security measures for our safety?"

"Yes."

"I'm coming."

"There's no need. I can stop by your lab to give you a report on what measures will affect you." It was not SOP to bring civilians in on the professional consult. Elle was an exception because of her background. Myk didn't mind Beau being there because he was counting on the other man helping to convince Elle to go along with Myk's plan.

He welcomed suggestions from his sister on how best to protect Lana. At this point Elle knew more about Lana's habits and daily schedule than he did. She also knew more about ETRD and the security already in place there.

Lana's jaw set stubbornly, which, rather than annoying him, just turned Myk on. "On the contrary. There is every need.

This is my life you're making decisions about. I have a right to hear what those decisions are, *before* they happen, like my guard detail last night and this morning."

"If the guards had done their jobs correctly, you would not have been aware of them."

"I prefer to be aware, if it's all the same to you."

"You're sexy when you're snarky, you know that?"

"I'm not aware of being sexy in any mood, so no."

"You're serious?"

"Personal sexual appeal has not been high on my list of topics to study, Mykola, and you can stop changing the subject."

"At least you are calling me by my first name again. Though you are the only one besides my mother and grandmother who use it. Even my dad calls me Myk."

"I like it."

"Thank you." He made no effort to resist the urge to reach out and brush one fingertip down her cheek. "I bet you thought about how appealing you are when you were crushing on Beau."

"Beau is my coworker and your sister's fiancé."

"That doesn't mean you didn't find him hot."

"If I did, I don't any longer."

"You sure about that?"

"Is this pertinent to your case?"

"It's pertinent to me."

"So you expect me to answer you?"

"Yep."

She was downright adorable when irritated. "Yes. At one time, I found Beau attractive."

"I'm surprised you admitted it."

"I have no filter, remember? I would probably blurt it out at some point. That is if you spend enough time around me to hear what comes out of my mouth when I'm thinking out loud. Which you probably won't, so I guess I could have kept my embarrassing secret."

"Nothing embarrassing about a former crush. And yes, I definitely plan to be around enough to learn all your secrets."

"Oh. I'm not sure if I like that, or not."

"I am sure I like your honesty."

"You aren't going to sidetrack me with compliments. I intend to crash your meeting with Elle whether you want me there, or not."

"You're an aggressive little thing for a scientist."

Lana just glared at him. And damned if that didn't turn him on, too. Was there anything this woman could do that would douse rather than fan his libido?

Smart enough to know when he was beat, he said, "Fine. Come with me."

Beau was in Elle's office when Lana followed Mykola inside. Frank was there as well, but while Beau and Elle had clearly been having a heated discussion, Frank was focused on his PDA. Nothing unusual there. The head of ETRD could get as lost in his e-mail and balance sheets as any of his scientists did their projects.

Mykola gave him a significant look that his sister did not miss despite her clear preoccupation with her fiancé. "It was Frank or Mr. Smith via conference speakerphone. I chose Frank."

"I don't blame you."

Frank made a sound of dissent.

Mykola shrugged. "No offense, but I'm not in the habit of conferring with civilians in regard to my job."

"I understand," Frank said, "but the situation at ETRD is a unique one."

"Because of Mr. Smith." Mykola always said ETRD's bene-factor's name with that particular sneer in his voice.

Lana wanted to know why.

"We'll talk later," Mykola said to her, confirming that she had once again spoken her thoughts aloud.

Elle was back to looking as amused as she had the day before in Lana's lab, but she focused her attention on her brother. "Because of what Mr. Smith knows and chooses to share with his company president."

"Fine. Frank can stay."

"Thank you ever so much," Frank intoned dryly.

"I've got a plan," Mykola announced as he seated Lana in one of the chairs facing Elle's desk with all the panache of a courtier.

Lana would have smiled at the gallantry, but was too suspicious about what that plan might entail and found herself frowning instead. Elle's expression mirrored Lana's. Knowing she wasn't alone in her distrust of Mykola's potential plans made Lana feel just a little better.

Beau, on the other hand, emanated relief and eagerness to hear what Mykola had to say. His PDA now forgotten and held loosely in his hand, Frank appeared interested as well. No doubt, had Mr. Smith been present via conference call, he would have been waiting with bated breath, too.

"Let's hear it," Elle demanded when Mykola dragged the silence out.

Myk radiated pure satisfaction. "The Vega Cartel wants you out of the way."

"That's a given."

"So, we give them what they want." He perched himself on the chair arm of Lana's seat with an attitude that all was right with his world.

Only the tension in his limbs so close to her gave away the

fact that he wasn't quite as relaxed about this conversation as he pretended to be.

"I am not faking my own death less than a week before my wedding." Oh, wow. Elle had that deadly quiet voice down pat, just like her brother.

"Credit me with some creativity here, sis."

"You flunked art. And music appreciation."

"In grade school. That doesn't count. And I didn't flunk. I got Cs. Just because I didn't like finger painting and learning how to read music doesn't mean I can't be creative."

"So, reveal this *creative* plan of yours." Elle could do sarcasm really well when she wanted; it fairly dripped from each word.

Lana almost pitied Mykola. Almost. He'd still set the guard dogs on her.

"We agree that we do not want to endanger the case?"

"Duh." Oh, direct sarcasm. Very nicely done, Elle.

Lana let a small smile tug at her lips.

"Your death would do that, wouldn't it?"

"Yes, but I have no intention of dying."

"Your ability to drive better than most NASCAR racers isn't going to save you from a bullet."

"The Vega Cartel is not going to risk alerting ETRD to their interest in one of its scientists. Their assassin is going to continue to look for ways to kill me and make it look like an accident."

"You could at least sound a little concerned about that fact," Beau snarled.

Elle whipped her head around and stared at him in shock. "Of course I'm concerned. You could have been killed this morning. If you'd been riding with anyone else, you would have been."

"It's not me I'm worried about."

"It is for me."

"Good," Mykola said, effectively cutting off an escalation of the argument. "Elle, wouldn't you agree that the hit on you is putting your fiancé at risk?"

"I'll watch out for him. I'm here this time." Elle's expression look set in concrete.

Mykola looked saddened. "Yes, you are. And you are a formidable opponent, but I think we all agree that minimizing the danger is the best course of action."

Elle looked at Beau and their gazes held for several seconds before she turned her attention back to her brother. "How do you propose to do that?"

"We get you out of ETRD and then out of the country."

Elle opened her mouth to argue, but Beau squeezed her shoulder. "Let your brother explain before you start ripping his idea to shreds."

Ellen closed her mouth and nodded.

Mykola said, "Thank you. What I propose is this: you were planning to end your consult for ETRD's security this week, so we make it official. You leave and ETRD 'hires' me as their new head of security."

"What about our current head of security?" Frank asked.

"He'll be in Oregon at the Black Eagle paramilitary training facility for the next eight weeks," Elle said grudgingly, as if supporting her brother's plan in any way went against the grain. "You can name Myk the head of security in the interim. I had someone else in mind, but this is a better setup for his investigation."

"Oregon?" Frank asked faintly. "Paramilitary training?"

"Not exactly. As a favor to me, Nitro and Josie Black Eagle have agreed to devise a training program specifically tailored to the security personnel for ETRD right away. It's a new service our recently combined security companies will be offering in the future. Nitro and Josie are willing to use ETRD's security officers as the program's guinea pigs."

"Lucky ETRD security guards." Mykola wasn't such a novice at sarcasm himself.

Elle got a distinctly wicked twinkle in her eye. "They won't be making the kind of mistake they did in Lana's lab yesterday again."

"So, you're sending the head of security?" Frank asked.

"He'll be in the first batch of trainees."

"How long does training take?"

"Two weeks. The current head of security will stay for the entire rotation of all our personnel, but he will be helping with the training in the later rotations."

Frank paled a little. "How many will be gone at a time?"

"A full detail. The rest of the personnel will have their schedules adjusted to compensate for each missing detail."

"I assume you've got something in place to replace the detail gone at training," Mykola said. "This is not a good time for you to be running on a skeleton security crew."

Elle didn't even have to say *duh* this time. She just looked it. "I've arranged for Brett Adams and his wife Claire, a total computer wizard, to come with a detail of employees from our security company. There will be at least one of our own on duty here at ETRD twenty-four/seven until the rest of the security force have been trained by Josie and Nitro. I was going to recommend Hotwire, I mean Brett, for the interim security position."

"You've done a lot of arranging without consulting me," Frank said mildly.

"I was going to recommend it to you and Mr. Smith as a follow-on to my security consult. However, the reaction to Dr. Billings pushing the panic button in the Materials Transformation lab yesterday showed me that the security guards at ETRD need some significant retraining if they are going to be effective. I felt the current situation justified taking immediate action."

Frank looked very unhappy. "I thought we had a strong force. They were all hired because of their previous experience."

"Which only goes to show how necessary this new service is for a lot of companies, not just your own."

"You're adjusting to civilian capitalism nicely, Elle," Mykola teased.

Elle smiled. "In fact, I am. I'm serving my country still, but in the private sector. I never realized how much my services were needed before, but Beau has helped me to see that ETRD is just one of many companies at risk because their security measures aren't up to standard with the criminal element."

"Good for Beau." Mykola said it under his breath, but Lana heard.

And it made her smile. It was so obvious how much each of these Chernichenkos cared about the happiness of the others.

"Okay, so we make it look like I've replaced my head of security temporarily with Myk," Frank said in a clear effort to get a grasp on the situation.

Mykola nodded. "Right. As planned, Elle leaves."

"I wasn't going to leave. Not now that we've found out ETRD's technological developments are once again at risk."

"That's not your problem, Elle."

"Of course it is."

"The case is mine."

"I'm still the security consultant for ETRD."

"Your consult is over. Like you said, you were going to recommend the training as a follow-up to your job here. Your primary responsibility right now is to stay alive."

"And I'm supposed to do that by quitting my job. I can see where that is going to be very helpful, assuming the Vega Cartel has a mole here, which they don't, because my measures are foolproof."

"No measures are foolproof when people can still be bought, Elle. You know that."

"I've personally gone over every file on the current security guards and while they may not have the background or training I'd like, none of them have anything that would indicate they are security risks."

"Someone gave the Vega Cartel your notes."

"It was probably the dirty security guard who sold copies of Beau's project."

"You can't be sure of that."

Elle went silent, her expression mutinous, but apparently she agreed with her brother's assessment. Interesting. Lana found the Chernichenkos and how they interacted fascinating. Too bad Matej wasn't here. Then again, Elle would probably dig her heels into petrified rock if she was facing off against two of her brothers.

"Getting back to my plan," Mykola said. "You don't just leave ETRD, but you go stay with the folks until the wedding. No one would think anything of you doing that. It certainly wouldn't clue the cartel in on the fact that we know about their attempt on your life."

Elle said nothing, but her expression said she was thinking plenty.

Mykola's tension increased, but it didn't sound in his voice. "After the wedding you go off on your publicly announced honeymoon."

"No way." Elle sat back in her chair and crossed her arms. "We're keeping that a secret."

"Whatever trip you and Beau have planned can wait for your first anniversary. For right now, you are going to announce plans to go on a four-week African safari." Mykola sounded very pleased with his plan.

"African safari?" Elle and Beau asked in shocked unison.

Lana thought it sounded fascinating and wouldn't mind such

a honeymoon herself, if she ever got married. Not a hunting safari, of course, but a trip into the wilds of Africa would be amazing.

"I get it. We pretend to go away while remaining here in secret so I can help you with the case." Elle smiled at that idea.

Beau, however, had a severe glare going on.

Mykola just shook his head. "Wrong. You go on the safari."

"Wouldn't that just make it easier for the cartel to kill her?" Beau asked.

"You're assuming their assassin will follow her. Once she's out of the way, they have no reason to follow through on the kill."

Beau looked less than convinced. "You hope. You can't be sure of that. If they do follow, how is she supposed to protect herself when she's completely out of her normal environment?"

"She's not supposed to. The guides for this particular safari outfit are former military. In fact, while they will take you both on a genuine safari, their company is only a cover for what they really do."

Beau smiled, appearing delighted. "They're mercenaries?"

"You got Roman into this?" Elle asked in a raised voice.

"Who is Roman?" Frank asked.

Lana could answer that. "Elle's second-oldest brother. He's military Special Forces, though I've never heard which branch. He doesn't come around the family often, but they all love him. Neither Mat nor Elle were expecting him to make it for their double wedding."

Mykola smiled at Lana, like he was impressed with her observation ability, like he didn't think it made her some kind of freak. "He's coming. In fact, he'll be in town tonight, along with a select squad of his elite soldiers. They will be handling security at the folks' place."

"Where you expect me to stay until the wedding?" Elle asked in a voice that said *not in this life*.

"Yes."

"No way."

Beau looked ready to explode. He dropped to his haunches and spun her office chair around so they were face-to-face behind her desk. "Damn it, Elle. I love your strength. I even find your stubbornness sexy, but we're getting married on Saturday. I'd like us both to be alive to make that possible."

"I can't live with my parents while you're at the condo." Elle reached out and cupped Beau's face. "For all we know, you'd end up collateral damage."

"If that's what's bothering you, I'll stay with your parents, too, but I think Myk has come up with a damn fine plan. Let him keep you safe, *please*."

"We won't be sharing a bed. *Baba* won't allow it."

Beau leaned forward and kissed Elle, nothing scorching, but incredibly intense for all that. "We'll just have to get creative, sugar. Do this for me. I'm begging you."

"I can't just leave while Myk cleans up my messes after me," Elle said the words in a quiet, subdued voice, but Lana had no problem hearing them.

She was sure no one else had, either. She could feel the distressed vibe coming off Mykola, and Frank just looked flummoxed.

"If you don't mind me saying so, Elle, this isn't your mess. You've done a fantastic job upgrading security at ETRD, but if you stayed until every wrinkle was ironed out, you'd never leave."

"That would make you an employee of Mr. Smith, not a consultant for him," Frank interjected.

Lana wasn't sure why that was a factor, but she would take all the help she could get.

Lana had no reason to believe the other woman would listen to her, but she had to try to make Elle see reason. "You no longer work for TGP. Mykola is the agent in charge on this case. That makes *your* safety and protection of the enzyme technology his responsibility. You owe it to yourself and to Beau to let your brother do his job while you fulfill your promise to marry my friend and colleague. A man I have never heard beg in all the years we've worked together, by the way."

Elle was listening, Lana could tell, but the other woman's gaze was fixed firmly on the man she loved. She didn't say anything, but she was no longer arguing and that had to be a plus.

"Thanks, Lana." Mykola gave her a one-armed hug, pulling her body into contact with his.

It made her feel surprisingly safe and not so surprisingly tingly.

The man was amazingly sexy.

"Don't thank me for telling the truth. Elle is taking responsibility for something that isn't hers to take. She didn't create the enzyme. She did implement an amazing security system, but as a consultant. Not an ongoing employee of ETRD. If this issue had not arisen, tomorrow would have been her last day here. I think for her and Beau's sakes it still should be."

Chapter 8

"How did you know that Elle was leaving tomorrow?" Frank demanded. "I suppose you put two and two together since Myk announced she planned to leave this week."

Everyone else in the room just gave Frank a look while Lana felt herself squirm. Sometimes, she felt like a voyeur, even though she never consciously spied on people or their conversations. It was just that so much got said around her because people thought she wasn't paying attention. And really, she didn't mean to. She couldn't help it.

"You know, that brings up an interesting question," Frank said musingly. "Why did the Vega Cartel make an attempt on Elle's and Beau's lives this morning when she planned to vacate her position tomorrow?"

"Because they didn't know she had those plans. Besides Lana, who else at ETRD knew Elle's contract was ending?" Mykola asked.

"No one. I hadn't announced it to the security team because I didn't want them getting complacent in my company," Elle said. "Frank and you were the only two people who knew."

"I didn't tell anyone, not even Mr. Smith," Frank said.

Elle nodded. "As far as anyone else was concerned, my consulting contract was running indefinitely. I hadn't even told Beau I was finished. I planned to surprise him by taking some time off after we got back from our honeymoon as well." She smiled at her husband-to-be. "I thought we could go to Texas and visit your family again."

"They're flying out for the wedding."

"But we'll be busy with all our other guests. This would have given us some time to be with them alone."

"You're assuming Beau can get time off from ETRD," Frank said.

"He's never taken any personal vacation days—he's got months accumulated. You and Mr. Smith will just have to deal," Elle said firmly as she turned to face the rest of them again.

"This means you no longer work for ETRD?" Beau asked.

"Yes, I suppose it does."

Beau was grinning as he lifted Elle from her chair, sat down, and pulled her into his lap. "That all sounds good to me, sugar. But the first four weeks of that vacation time is going to be spent on safari in Africa."

"What about *our* honeymoon plans?"

"Your brother's idea of taking the trip to celebrate our first anniversary works for me. How about you?"

Everyone waited for Elle's answer.

She smiled at Beau. "I can get tunnel vision when it comes to work, but Lana and Myk are right. I don't belong on this case and staying alive so we can have a long life together is my top priority right now."

"So, are we going to stay with your folks until the wedding?"

"Yes." Elle gave Mykola a squinty-eyed look. "Don't get used to me agreeing with you."

"Heaven forbid."

Everyone laughed, except Lana.

Mykola noticed. "What's the matter, doc?"

Other than the fact that now that Elle Gray was going to be out of the picture, nothing stood between Lana and the position of primary target for the Vega Cartel? Not that she'd mention that concern. After all, it wasn't as if she would have done anything to change it. She didn't want Elle at risk because of Lana's scientific research. The other woman had so much more to her life worth fighting for than Lana did.

Elle had been arguing with her brother over where she could take her honeymoon—a once-in-a-lifetime trip signifying the start of a new phase of Elle's life. And Lana had been arguing with Mykola over whether or not she could teach a neophyte belly-dancing class another instructor could easily take over.

How pathetic was it that Lana had nothing more than her belly-dancing classes to lose? Maybe she wasn't as far out of that self-made prison that Mr. Smith had found her living in than she thought. If it weren't for her work at ETRD, she'd say she hadn't come out of it at all.

"Technically, though I have a double PhD, I am not a doctor." For once, she'd managed not to blurt everything she'd been thinking and had in fact, even managed a bit of misdirection.

"If you say so . . . *doc.*"

The twit. Or not. The nickname was kind of cute and she'd never had one before. Sometimes, Casey called her boss, but technically she was his boss, so that wasn't really a nickname. "You may call me *doc* if you wish."

"Thank you. I will. Now, spill it."

"Spill what?"

"Whatever put that look of fear in your eyes a second ago."

"What about the Gestapo guards?" It was her second attempt at misdirection in as many minutes. She was impressed with herself.

This time it worked.

"What Gestapo guards?" Elle demanded.

Mykola repeated Lana's earlier complaints about the guards' high-handedness. He *had* been listening. Elle was furious, giving credence to Mykola's assertion that the guards had not been instructed to behave the way that they had.

Elle called the two guards in question into her office, along with the shift's lead security officer—a woman. Frank introduced Mykola as the new acting head of security and announced that after that night, Elle Gray's security consulting work for ETRD would be done.

Mykola took over from there. Glaring at the two guards and their team lead, he asked, "You are aware what a covert security tail is, aren't you?"

The two guards shot sideways looks at their shift leader before nodding.

Looking smug, Beau said with a singsong Texas twang, "Wouldn't want to be you," as he exited the room. Frank just shook his head and followed the other man out, giving his tacit approval of whatever was to follow.

"They were supposed to be covert, not just nonintrusive?" Lana asked, stunned by the guards' complete lack of effort to be either.

Mykola replied, "Yes."

"The guard last night, um, Perkins," she said, reading the man's name tag, "waved at me before driving away and the guard this morning, that would be . . ." She took another peak at nametags. "Nelson . . . insisted on being admitted to my building." Even she knew those activities couldn't be considered part of the broadest definition of covert.

Elle said an ugly word in Ukrainian. She glared at the hapless guards. "Explain."

"I wanted Dr. Ericson to know I was leaving," Perkins said, looking nervous.

Nelson looked far less belligerent than he had when he knocked on her door that morning, but his words still came out defensive. "It was my responsibility to see to her safety. I couldn't do that from the car."

"It was your responsibility to follow orders," Elle gritted.

"I don't see what the harm was. This was a simple training exercise," the team lead said. Her name tag read Ramirez. "My officers did as they were instructed."

So, that was how Elle had explained the instructions without alerting the security guards to the fact that Lana might be in real danger.

"No. In fact, they did not." Mykola had that deadly quiet thing going on with his voice again. "They were not covert, nor were they nonintrusive. They insisted on Dr. Ericson leaving her lab before she was ready and coming into the office before her usual time as well."

"Security guards may not have PhDs, but they do have their own lives," the shift lead sneered. "Expecting them to wait around past their own scheduled work hours at the whim of a coworker is not appropriate."

The room went totally silent. Elle made an aborted move for the telephone and then looked at Mykola. "As the new acting head of security, this is your call."

"The permanent head of security is still in the building. Call him in. We'll give him a chance to make the right choice. If he mishandles this situation, he has no business in his position, and I expect you to tell Mr. Smith and Frank that as one of your final recommendations."

Elle nodded and made the call. Silence reigned for the two

and a half minutes it took the older man to arrive. During that time Ramirez managed a very convincing air of boredom, while the two guards both sweated it out—literally.

When Elle told the security chief in precise tones exactly what had been said in her office, he rubbed his forehead. After turning to face his shift lead, he said, "No one said our officers had to wait past the end of their shift to see Dr. Ericson home. One of the swing-shift team could have been assigned the training opportunity once it was ascertained that Dr. Ericson was not finished in her lab."

"Once the officer was assigned his duty, it had to be completed," Ramirez argued.

"The duty was not a particular officer's, but rather that of our department, Ramirez."

"It was a training exercise!"

"And that is pertinent because?"

"Because you're acting like Dr. Ericson was really in danger."

"And if she was?"

"Was she?" Ramirez demanded to know.

"That's not the point. The point is that your officers did a piss-poor job."

"I deserve to know if one of my people is being put in danger in the line of duty," Ramirez said obdurately.

"It shouldn't make a difference as to how well they do their jobs."

"Were they in danger?" Ramirez prodded.

"I told you that the assignment was a test for security measures Mr. Smith asked Ms. Gray to consider implementing and I don't appreciate your implications otherwise," the head of security replied. "The last thing this company needs is more rumors for the already busy mill."

Ramirez gave a derogatory huff. "Frank Ingram would be

better off raising salaries for the employees that put their lives on the line for this company rather than putting more resources into pampering Mr. Smith's precious scientists."

"That's not a decision for you to make," Mykola said.

"Nor is your comment appreciated," the security chief said, ice in his voice.

"Who the heck are you to be making such a comment to me?" Ramirez demanded of Mykola while ignoring her permanent boss altogether.

"As of tomorrow, I'm going to be your boss."

"Unfortunately, that isn't the case." The head of security's tone had not warmed up a single degree. "Ms. Ramirez has been warned about her unacceptable attitude toward the scientific elite employed by ETRD."

"If they are so elite, why can't they see to their own security? Because they need grunts like us, that's why. A bunch of pansy asses, the lot of them."

"Ms. Ramirez, you are fired."

The team lead gasped and stared at her former boss. "You can't do that. *Tia* Maria will have your head."

"Your aunt is my wife's cousin, not my employer. I gave you a job, but you disregarded your duties and disrespected me and your position. You won't be getting a reference." The man inclined his head toward Elle. "If that is all, Ms. Gray, I'm going to walk this former employee off the property."

With a slightly bemused expression, Elle nodded. "Dismissed. You two may go as well."

The two guards gave visible signs of relief.

Elle smiled, but it did not reach her eyes. "Don't think you got off easy. You'll be in the first team sent for training at the Black Eagle training center in the Oregon Coastal Range. I'm a pussycat compared to Nitro and Josie Black Eagle in training mode. Myk will tell you and your team all about it tomorrow."

"Training?" Perkins asked.

Nelson looked like he'd swallowed a raw fish whole. "In Oregon?"

"Yes. It will be mandatory for all security personnel from this point forward."

"Pinkerton never expected offsite training," the older of the guards grumbled.

"Perhaps you would like to apply for a job with them?" Elle asked Nelson sweetly.

"No thank you, ma'am." The two guards rushed to get out of the office.

"Sounds good." Mykola turned his attention from Elle to Lana. "After that little fiasco, I think it would be best for me to see to your security personally."

"Now, why doesn't that surprise me?" Elle quipped.

"Because you would make the same call in my place?"

"Maybe not the exact same call. I prefer my partners to have more parts." Elle's grin was positively evil as she stood up to leave the room. "I'm going to finalize things with Frank and Beau, then I'll be back to pack up my office."

Mykola nodded as if some secret message had passed between the siblings. Lana couldn't begin to figure it out. She was too busy trying to decipher Elle's words. *Partners?* As in sex partners? It wasn't likely Mykola was interested in Lana for any other kind of partnership. Was she going to end up paying his sister five hundred dollars, too?

Mykola moved to sit in the chair beside Lana that Frank had vacated. Leaning on the arm of her chair had the benefit of being close to her, but he couldn't see her face from that angle. "Who do you owe five hundred dollars to and why would you think you had to pay my sister the same amount?"

He really enjoyed Lana's tendency to talk to herself out loud.

She looked like she wanted to sink through the floor. "I won't have to pay Elle. I didn't make a bet with her."

"You made a bet with someone else?" This just got more and more interesting."

"Yes," she grumbled.

"Who?"

"Is that any of your business?"

"No, but you're going to answer anyway, aren't you, doc? You can't help yourself." Man, she was fun to tease.

"You mean you think I'll mention it inadvertently."

He shrugged. They both knew the possibility was there. "You may as well be wholly advertent."

He grinned. Oh, yeah. He liked the idea of a completely open Lana. Of course, his mind had drifted from verbal honesty to accessible naked bodies, but he could hardly be faulted for the journey. She was the stuff his fantasies were made of. Sweet. Quirky. And oh, so sexy.

She expelled a huffy breath. "It was Dr. Billings."

"What did you and Casey bet on?" Myk wanted to laugh, but he didn't.

Lana sealed her lips like a small child refusing to speak.

He reached out and played his fingertip along the tight seam before letting his hand drop. "I'll just ask Casey. He'll tell me. I think I scare him."

"He bet me five hundred dollars that you and I would have sex." She looked away, her pretty pale skin going dusky. "Before Elle's wedding."

He knew he shouldn't, but he couldn't help himself. Myk burst out laughing.

Lana jumped from her chair. "I'm going back to my lab. If you want to send someone to follow me home, fine."

Myk leapt up and crossed the room to block the door before Lana had taken two steps. "The only one following you home will be me. As for the other, I wasn't laughing at you, sweetheart."

"I thought it was doc."

"Sweetheart suits you, too."

"No, it doesn't."

"Yes, it does. Only a woman with a sweet heart could have moved my sister's heart enough to get her to back down on the case today."

"She wasn't looking at the situation rationally."

"And you helped her see that without anyone losing a limb. I'm in awe."

"You're trying to make me feel better about laughing at me."

"I wasn't laughing at you. I was laughing at Casey's perspicacity." He gently turned Lana to face him.

Her body was stiff, but she didn't fight the movement. "His astute perception is hardly amusing."

"Sure it is, when you consider how clueless he probably is about his own dating life." That boy had geek down to a T.

"He's working on it."

"I'll offer a few tips." He tilted Lana's head up so he could see her face. "He deserves it."

"For guessing I wanted you so badly?" She didn't look as accepting of that fact as she had been the day before.

"For seeing that I wanted you even more."

Kissable lips formed a perfect circle while her pupils dilated. "Oh."

"Yes, oh."

"What about my belly dancing?" She tried moving sideways and away from him.

He blocked her exit with his other arm. "That's the third time you've tried that today."

"Tried what?" Her expression said she knew exactly what

he was talking about and wasn't too happy he'd figured it out.

"Changing the subject rather than answering a question."

She leaned back against the door, creating the only distance she could between them. "Technically, you didn't ask me a question just now."

Still, she didn't ask him to move away. Interesting.

"And *technically*, you didn't answer the one I asked earlier, but you will. Or I'll figure it out."

"You can't read my mind."

"Maybe I can. Maybe you realized just then that with Elle out of the way, the cartel would be free to focus on your enzymes and you."

The shocked recognition that lit her hazel depths told him all he needed to know. "I . . ."

He hated the fear he'd seen earlier and he refused to let her continue laboring under its weight. "But something you didn't consider is that I gave them a new target and that target isn't you."

Lana's eyes went cloudy with confusion and then cleared. "It's you! You took Elle's place as the one standing between the Vega Cartel and my enzymes."

"Yep. So, see, doc, you've got nothing to worry about."

"But I don't want you hurt, either!"

"I've just got one thing to say to those bastards. *Bring it on*."

"You and your sister are both insane! You're no more impervious to death than she is." In her agitation, Lana gesticulated with her hands.

There wasn't any room between them for that kind of behavior, so her hands ended up brushing against his torso.

He let himself fully appreciate the pleasure in that before replying. "Who says?"

"You aren't a superhero."

"I don't need to be." He moved forward so their bodies pressed against each other. Neither spoke for several seconds, but Lana's breathing grew labored.

And damn if he didn't like that proof of her desire. Every harsh breath brought her breasts into fuller contact with his chest. He couldn't wait to feel that particular phenomenon sans clothing—for both of them.

He leaned down until he was whispering in her ear. "I just need to be smarter than the cartel. I've already proven once that I've got the savvy."

She shivered in reaction to his breath in her ear even as a horrified sound escaped her. "If you don't watch out, your arrogance is going to get you killed."

"I'd rather watch you." He nuzzled into her neck, reveling in her scent.

She didn't wear perfume, but he could smell traces of the body wash she used. It smelled like peaches. Mixed with her personal fragrance, it was an intensely alluring combination.

"Belly dance?" she asked in a choked voice.

He couldn't keep the feral grin from his lips. Oh, yeah. But for his eyes only. He nuzzled her some more, dropping soft kisses against the sensitive skin just below her ear.

She shivered again, another desperate little sound escaping her. This one definitely of need.

He rubbed their cheeks together before lifting his head so he could look her in the eye when he spoke. As much as he wanted her, this was serious stuff. "I would prefer you gave up teaching right now, but if you're adamant, we'll work something out."

"Mr. Smith asked me to consider your request. Last night. When we talked on the phone. I told him . . ." Her eyes closed and her fingers kneaded his chest like a cat seeking the best spot to settle. He wouldn't mind her settling on him. "I told him, I would. I have."

"And?" He whispered the question into her ear and then couldn't suppress the urge to take a tiny taste, swiping his tongue over the soft flesh of her lobe.

"Oh. That feels good. Again. Do it again."

No way was he going to turn down that request. He did it again, this time taking the lobe between his teeth and biting very gently.

She made an inarticulate sound.

He needed to get the serious talk out of the way so they could finish this. "What did you decide, sweetheart?"

"Decide?"

"About teaching your class?"

"I'll stop. For a little while."

"Good."

"I thought . . ." She broke off, breathing heavily. "I thought you'd say that." Then she turned her face, her lips clearly seeking his.

He was moving so his lips could be found when a knock sounded at the door. "Myk, I'm back," Elle trilled through the door with enough teasing he knew his little sister guessed she'd be interrupting something.

Suppressing a growl, Myk pulled Lana away from the door and then released her.

Elle didn't wait for an invitation, but pushed the door open and walked in.

He valiantly controlled his urge to yell and said, "I thought you were going to be busy for a while."

"Frank is on a call to Mr. Smith and Beau is trying to keep something in his lab from exploding." Elle looked between him and Lana, but rather than smirking as he expected, she gave him a contrite look. "Sorry."

"No problem. This isn't the place."

"Sometimes, it doesn't matter."

Myk covered his ears and glared. "That was not some-thing I needed to hear from my baby sister." His frown inten-sified. "And I assumed no room in this building would be safe from security cameras."

"This one is. So is Frank's office."

"What about Beau and Mat?"

"They have the same random surveillance as everyone else. Favoritism would only cause problems down the road."

Myk agreed. "Mr. Smith knew about my request to Lana to give up her extracurricular teaching for the time being. How do you think he found out?"

"There's only one way he could have, unless Lana told him."

Lana shook her head, still looking a little embarrassed, but not ready to hide in a closet. "He called me about it. Last night."

Elle's brow furrowed. "Before Frank had even told Mr. Smith of your arrival." His sister went over to her computer and logged in with her thumbprint. "Frank didn't inform Mr. Smith about the threat against Lana's enzymes until today. Just now to be precise. He's telling Mr. Smith about Beau's extended leave of absence as well."

Myk didn't envy the older man. "That ought to be a fun conversation."

"With Mr. Smith, I have a feeling they always are."

Elle clicked her mouse and looked up from the computer. "The audio features of the security system are randomized, but Mr. Smith can access all logs."

"So, he overheard our conversation yesterday?"

"It's possible, but not probable." She clicked her mouse several times and then looked up again. "The audio function was not on in Lana's lab or growing rooms during the time you were there. Clearly he knew you were assigned to the case and correctly surmised the measures you would insist on taking to protect Lana from the cartel."

"Which means he learned about it elsewhere." Myk figured he knew just where, too, or rather who. "Whit, that bastard."

Elle sighed. "He's not a bastard, Myk. The Old Man and Mr. Smith have some kind of past."

"He could have warned me he was going to tell Smith about the case."

"I've given up trying to second-guess The Old Man on his intentions or motivations."

"It's a damn good thing he's not running the Vega Cartel."

Elle's silence acknowledged her agreement.

Chapter 9

Myk found Lana in her lab later that day. She'd made an excuse to leave Elle's office earlier within a couple of minutes of his sister's interruption of their third explosive kiss. Lana was currently immersed in her slides. She muttered to herself every few seconds and took notes on her electronic tablet without looking up from her microscope. Just like yesterday.

Unlike yesterday, however, her mutterings were not about her work. They were about him. Or at least he assumed the *too sexy for his own good, or hers, arrogant twit* was probably himself. Myk sure hoped Lana wasn't thinking sexy thoughts about anyone else right now.

He might have to kill someone.

"She gets like that sometimes."

Myk didn't turn to face Lana's assistant, but he acknowledged Casey with a wave of his hand while he continued to watch the beautiful scientist at work. "A lot of the time, if the past two days are anything to go by."

"That's true." Casey sighed. "I get like that sometimes, too."

Myk finally turned to look at the younger man. "And that bothers you?"

"Lana never dates. She doesn't have a life outside of ETRD." The redhead's expression was bleak. "I want one."

"She belly dances."

"If she was a lesbian, that might be heartening, but she spends all her off hours with other women."

"You don't want to be lonely."

"I'm already lonely. I try not to be. I've got good friends. Well, okay, I've got Lana and some of the lab techs here. But I want a special someone. Somebody who cares if I work late in the lab, or if I'm sick, or you know . . . anything."

"You said your family was proud of you."

"My parents. And they're gone. The people here are like a family, but Frank doesn't call to see if I'm feeling up to mowing the lawn on Saturdays."

"Do you have a lawn?"

"No, but I want one. I want to live a normal life."

Myk found himself feeling compassion for the young genius. "Even if you have a not-so-normal IQ."

"Right."

"You'll get it, Casey. One of these days."

"How can you be sure?"

"My family is made up of brainiacs. Don't let Elle's job fool you. She's as smart as the rest of them. Hell, even my Special Forces big brother has a degree in biochemistry. He was going pre-med but discovered talents in another area, I guess."

"But they're probably all gorgeous and confident like Ms. Gray."

Myk snorted at that description of his sister. It might be accurate, but come on. This was *his* sister Casey was idolizing. "She's special, all right," he said with sarcasm overlying his sincerity.

Casey didn't notice the sarcasm. "I'm not like that."

"Sure you are."

"You don't know me. How can you say that?" The kid looked so hopeful.

So, Myk looked him straight in the eye and told the truth. "Because Lana really cares about you and she doesn't get close to many people. That makes you special already."

Casey seemed to mull that over for several seconds and then nodded. "Thanks. I never looked at it that way before. Lana doesn't have a lot of friends because she rebuffs people. I forget that sometimes and think she accepts my friendship because she doesn't have any other options. But she does."

That knowledge seemed to make Casey really happy. "Uh . . . she told me I should ask this woman out. You know, that I'm interested in."

"Why don't you?"

"She's older than me. I don't care, but what if she does?"

"What if she doesn't?"

"She's so smart."

Oh, man. Seriously? Dr. Casey Billings, child prodigy, was worried about being brainy enough? "So are you."

"She's gorgeous."

"I've been told on good authority that the boy-next-door look really works for women."

"You have?"

"Yep."

"By who?"

"My former DEA partner. The man and you could have come from the same gene pool and before Elena roped him in, that man dated his way through half the female population of southern California."

"You're not just saying that? Making it up?"

"Scout's honor."

"Were you a Scout?"

"I was, as a matter of fact. An Eagle Scout."

"Wow. That's cool."

"It was then."

"You don't think so now?"

"There are a lot of years and even more experiences between the boy I was then and the man I am now."

"Lana likes you."

"I know."

"You like her, too."

"I do."

"You're honest. That's really cool."

"When I can be."

"It must be hard to have a deep core of honor and do undercover work."

The kid really was insightful. "You know a lot about me."

"I work with Lana. She thinks out loud."

"Is this woman you are interested in honest, too?"

Casey nodded vehemently. "Yes."

"Then if you ask her out and she says yes, you'll know she wants to go. If she says no and that it's because she doesn't date coworkers, you'll know she's being truthful."

"But I still won't have a date with her," Casey said glumly.

"No, but you'll know you have a chance."

"You mean I shouldn't just give up. Respect her boundaries?"

"There are boundaries and then there are obstacles you need to overcome."

"What's the difference?"

"A boundary is her telling you she doesn't like you that way and she doesn't want to see you. An obstacle is her believing you're a bad risk because you work with her or that you're too young. You just have to show her that she's wrong."

"Wow. You really know women."

"I really know how to go after what I want."

"My boss doesn't stand a chance, does she?"

"Nope."

"I prefer the term colleague. We collaborate, Casey. Even if I am technically your boss." Lana was eyeing them both with an expression Myk could not quite decipher.

Her countenance was no more readable when she opened the door to her apartment after he followed her home.

He'd snuck into her building, though it was admittedly a little more difficult than the average "secure" apartment building in the same price range. He wasn't surprised she'd chosen a secured community after what she'd been through, but he was impressed with her acumen in choosing this one.

He'd only had to knock once before she opened the door.

She gave him that unreadable look. "I thought you might come up. Though I was expecting to get a visitor call from the security desk downstairs."

"I wouldn't be worth my badge if I couldn't sneak past a one-person security desk." Even if said desk had a bank of video monitors receiving feeds from several cameras set around the building.

"I shopped around a long time with Mr. Smith's help before I found this building. It's got better security than most."

The mention of Mr. Smith yet again set Myk's hackles rising. "I agree, but nothing is foolproof. Not even my sister's systems."

"Because there's always someone you can buy off," Lana said, repeating his words from earlier.

"Exactly."

"Maybe you're wrong, maybe there isn't a single person on the security force at ETRD that could be convinced or coerced into betraying the company's secrets."

"If that was true, the Vega Cartel would not have your notes."

She sighed before leading him into her living room. "You have a point."

"Nice place." He wouldn't have thought a head geek like Lana was into interior design, but her home looked put together enough to have been done by a professional.

It was definitely her style, though. A trio of framed prints of black-and-white early versions of Mickey and Minnie Mouse graced the wall above the fireplace. The sofa, loveseat, and armchair were all Disney yellow. The throw pillows were black-and-white images of other Disney characters. The coffee table and end tables were glass tops on red enamel painted metal bases.

For all the bright color and the Disney theme, it wasn't cluttered with tchotchkes that would have made it feel over the top.

"Thank you."

He shrugged. "You don't like acknowledging there are basely selfish people in this world, do you?"

"Not working for the same company I am. Honestly? It's an unwelcome reminder that your life can be bought for five hundred dollars." She indicated he should take a seat. "Would you like a drink?"

"No, thanks. I'm good." He settled onto the sofa, which was surprisingly comfortable.

Even more surprising was that she took the other end rather than sitting away from him. She was not a woman who hid from her feelings. He liked that.

"Five hundred dollars? Are you talking about the bet you've got going with Casey? Which you are going to lose, by the way."

"Arrogant." She shook her head, but a smile tilted her lips. "No, I wasn't talking about Casey."

"What then?"

The ghost of a smile became a memory. "I was dating him."

"Who?" But he had a bad feeling.

"The boy who sold me out to the Kurdish rebels as the answer to their chemical warfare prayers."

Well, shit. "You were dating him?"

"A couple of times. We even had sex. It wasn't great. Maybe that's why he preferred five hundred dollars and a few pills of E over me."

She'd lost eight months of her life and endured horrors only she knew about for a lousy five hundred bucks. Wasn't that just like life? *Damn it, anyway.*

She shrugged, as if to say it wasn't that big of a deal. "I guess you would see that kind of thing a lot working for the INS. One person valuing another person's life in terms of a few dollars and/or drugs."

"Yes." Though he would never tell her about drug lords who considered children expendable in their efforts to make a few more dollars, or coyotes who would take not only the money but the lives of the people they promised safe passage across the border. "How do you know how much the Kurds paid for you?"

"Because I asked."

"Your captors?"

"No. My former boyfriend, after I got back in the States. I looked Artie up. I wanted to see his face when I told him what I'd gone through." She stopped talking, looking haunted.

"It didn't work out that way, did it?"

Lana shook her head. "I was going to regale him with every indignity, each moment of terror, each horror perpetrated against me to gain my cooperation in creating weapons I don't believe in." She hugged herself, her eyes developing a suspicious sheen. "I couldn't do it. I couldn't tell him about my ordeal because he didn't care. I could see it in his eyes. He didn't even try to lie when I asked what he'd gotten for information about me, for luring me to a place where it was easy to kidnap me."

"Was he wasted?" It was just a guess, but she'd said the man had accepted E as part of his payment. No way had he been setting himself up as a dealer with a few pills of Ecstasy, which meant they were for Artie's own use.

"Yes."

"Figures."

"Does it? I sure wasn't expecting it. He wasn't an addict when we were in school. At least I don't think he was. I certainly didn't know he did drugs, but when I went to see him? He hadn't bathed in days. His apartment was a sty. He couldn't focus. He could barely stand up. He was a mess. An ugly, pathetic mess whose once-intelligent brain wasn't capable of basic addition, much less dealing with the conundrum of a woman he thought he would never see again standing on his doorstep." The tears in her eyes spilled over and she dropped her chin, her hair falling like a curtain between them. "Even after everything I went through, I think I ended up better off than Artie. I wanted to hate him, but all I could do was pity him. Talk about pathetic."

Her shoulders shook, though her crying was silent.

Myk was terrible with a woman's tears, but he manned up. "Come here, sweetheart."

She shook her head. "I'll be fine in a minute."

To hell with that. He reached out and hauled her into his arms, careful not to hurt, but refusing to be denied.

Far from fighting being in his arms, Lana buried her face in his chest. "I really wanted to hate him, Myk."

"Just like you wanted to hate the men who died when you made your break for freedom."

"Yes," she whispered against his chest.

He tucked her more securely against him and rubbed the feminine line of her back. "I'm not a hugely religious guy, sweetheart, but Papa is a good Ukrainian Orthodox and he taught us that the Bible says to love your enemies. I think your ability to feel compassion for yours is a strength, not a weakness."

"But I killed those men." She looked up, her eyes filled with a pain he understood. "What does that say for my beliefs about war?"

"It says that you're no martyr. They had no right to take you prisoner, or torture you until you did what they wanted."

"I never said I was tortured."

"You didn't have to."

The sobs came then, interspersed between revelations that tore at his heart and fed the ball of fury against injustice inside him. So many innocents hurt because people with power pushed their agendas forward without thought for what or who they destroyed. Drug lords, slavers, corrupt leaders, they all made the world a damn mess. But then there were people like Lana.

A woman who felt sorry for the man who had betrayed her and mourned the men who had died in her bid for freedom.

"You make the world a better place," he whispered against her hair as she sobbed. He didn't know if she heard, but he had to say the words. She deserved them.

He let her cry it out, never once telling her to hush or let it go. Who knew if she'd ever talked this out with anyone? He felt nothing but honored that she'd chosen to open up to him.

Later, he retrieved his laptop and bags from his car while she slept the sleep of the exhausted on the sofa. He set his computer up on the dining room table, a retro table with a

Formica top and metal frame. The four chairs were covered in glitter red vinyl. The prints in here were in color, but were still Mickey and Minnie Mouse.

It was another cheerful room that he was doubly impressed Lana had been able to create after what she'd gone through in that Kurdish prison lab.

He was checking his e-mail when the cell phone buzzed against his hip.

He read the caller ID and grimaced before answering. "Myk here."

"Agent Chernichenko, how are things going?"

"I sent a report last night, Whitmore. I will be sending another one in a few minutes."

"I'm used to my agents calling in occasionally."

"I prefer e-mail, sir."

"You'd prefer to be working for just about anyone else."

Myk didn't bother to deny it.

Instead of being offended by Myk's silent agreement, Elle's former boss chuckled. "You're very loyal."

Again, that was self-evident, so Myk didn't see the need to add verbal agreement.

"I'd like to think your loyalties extend to The Goddard Project."

"If you didn't think they did, you shouldn't have hired me."

"If I didn't think they did, I wouldn't have."

"Did you call for a reason, Whitmore?"

"Is that any way to talk to your boss?"

"When my boss is wasting my time, it is."

"You've got a real chip on your shoulder."

"No, what I've got is a woman I refuse to lose to a stinking drug cartel. I need to spend my time working the case, not trading verbal barbs with my superior."

"You've got balls, I'll give you that."

"I'd rather you gave me confirmed locations on Anibal Vega and his lieutenant."

"You assume he won't delegate oversight of this job further down the food chain?"

"That's what my gut is telling me."

"Are your instincts as good as your sister's?"

"Better."

Whitmore laughed again, this time with a lot more humor. "Your sister would contest that."

"No doubt."

"Have you been in contact with Alan Hyatt?"

"The agency's research virtuoso?"

"Virtuoso. He'll like that one. Have you spoken to him?"

"I've e-mailed him and it looks like I've got an answer in my in-box."

"So, it's not personal that you don't call in? You really do prefer e-mail correspondence."

"No, it is. And yes, I do."

"Watch it, Myk. I respect cowboy agents with the balls to back up their attitude as much as the next man, but I won't allow a lack of respect from my agents."

"I may not like you, Whitmore, but you can damn bet I respect you, or I wouldn't be working for you."

"You needed an agency to back up your attempt to protect your sister."

"I could have gone independent."

"But you chose not to."

"Elle isn't the only one at risk here."

"Underneath all that bluster, you're an idealist, aren't you? You want to catch the bad guys and put them away, not just protect your sister."

"Lana's the idealist."

"The scientist on the alchemy project?"

"Yes."

"You're on a first-name basis with her?"

"I don't like to stand on ceremony."

"Smith said she might be a problem when it comes to curtailing outside activities to protect her."

"Did you tell Mr. Smith that I was here on a TGP case?" Myk asked instead of responding to Whitmore's comment.

"We spoke about it, yes. You and I agreed you would tell Elle and Frank the truth. I assumed Smith would be brought into the loop sooner than later."

"Regardless, you should have warned me you were going to contact Mr. Smith and what the nature of your conversation would be."

"I don't think so." Oooh, now his new boss sounded pissed.

But Myk was in the right. "I am the agent in charge on this case, which makes all contact with principals under my jurisdiction. While you are my boss, you are not working this case. Any contact you have with Mr. Smith, or anyone else connected to ETRD for that matter, needs to be reported to me. From this point forward, I want all communication with Mr. Smith run by me *before* you engage."

Several seconds of silence met Myk's words. Finally Whitmore sighed. "I don't like admitting it, but you're right. At least about my needing to report the conversation I had with Smith. I'll have an e-mail detailing it off to you within the hour. However, I have no intention of getting your approval prior to speaking to Smith, or anyone else."

"If you and Smith are old friends, that's your call, but I don't want you discussing the case with him."

"He owns ETRD. Of course I'm going to discuss the case with him."

"TGP isn't here in response to a request from him. That makes him a principal, not a liaison."

"The hell you say."

"Take a step back and consider for a second here, Whitmore. This is the third TGP case in little more than a year centered on the same company."

"What are you implying?"

"I'm not implying. I'm saying that Mr. Smith has access to all the technology at his brainchild as well as contacts we can't begin to guess at."

"You think he's a suspect?"

"I think he can't be ruled out just because he used to work with you."

"Smith would never sell his own people out that way."

"Right."

"He's going to laugh his ass off when I tell him you suspect him."

"You tell him and I'll instigate an internal audit of TGP."

"What the hell—"

"Don't mess with my case, sir. I won't take it lying down."

"I can reassign you with a few strokes to my keyboard."

"You can try."

"Damn it, I am your boss."

"You hired me to do a job. Let me do it."

Whitmore made a disgusted sound. "I thought some of my other agents were bad."

"I'm a pain in the ass. Ask anyone I've ever worked for, but I've never been fired. Think about it." Talking to his superior like this was a calculated risk, but it was one Myk had to take.

No one messed with him on an assignment.

"I refuse to consider Smith as a potential suspect. He's capable of pissing me off and I don't like how much he knows about my agency's activities, but he would never betray the people who work for him, or his country."

"You don't have to see him as a suspect, sir. That's my job.

All you have to do is keep your mouth shut when it comes to my case."

"He is not in league with scumbags like the Vega Cartel."

"I hope not, sir, but that's something I'll need empirical evidence to support, not your feelings."

"You trust your gut, I trust mine."

"Fair enough, but you still don't have leave to discuss my case with one of my suspects."

"Fine."

"You agree, sir?"

"I didn't get where I am by stepping on my agents' toes. You're lead on this case, I defer to your judgment. Even if I don't agree with it."

"Noted."

"I'll be looking forward to your report."

"Yes, sir."

"I trust it will be complete."

"I believe you will keep your word, sir."

"Good enough."

The call ended. Myk put his phone down onto the table as he clicked open the e-mail from Alan Hyatt. Virtuoso might be an understatement. Not only had Hyatt discovered that Anibal Vega and his lieutenant were currently visiting one of Vega's offices of operation in northwest Mexico, but he had also found a disturbing but illuminating connection.

Anibal Vega's wife had a very interesting brother-in-law. Ahmet Musa, a Turkish zealot, was known for his support of violent actions against his perceived enemies. And the list of the man's enemies was a long one, headed by the usual suspects, including every major Western political power.

This was so not good.

Not that Lana's enzymes could be used for warfare, unless Vega and Musa planned to stink their enemies to death. The news increased the scope of Myk's investigation by double. It was also information that was bound to upset Lana.

Myk didn't like that.

He considered holding it back from her. Did she need to hear about something that was only going to succeed in making her feel even less safe than she already did? It wasn't as if her knowing about the Vega-Musa connection was necessary to Myk's case. But damn it, she deserved to know that she was at risk from more than one direction.

The truth was, Vega could use anyone to bring Lana and/or her enzymes in. Which meant that she couldn't ignore the potential threat from a Midwestern American in a three-piece suit. So, again, there was no overt benefit in telling her.

Holding it back didn't feel right, though. Which was beyond ridiculous. Myk had never practiced full disclosure with civilians.

Wasn't that the root of Myk's latest beef with Whitmore? The fact that the other man wanted to tell Mr. Smith, *a civilian* and possible suspect, everything related to the case.

"Mr. Smith is a good man. He would never sell out ETRD." Lana's voice from right behind him shocked Myk.

He should have heard her approach.

He quickly closed the e-mail he had been reading and turned in his chair to face her. "I hope you're right."

Chapter 10

"I know I am." Lana bit her lip, looking adorably sleep tousled. "Why would you suspect ETRD's benefactor?"

"I don't." Not that Myk didn't wish he could think of one really solid reason to believe the mysterious Mr. Smith was involved.

However, Smith lacked discernable motive. And more to the point, Myk had a hard time believing that if Smith were involved in some way, anyone would have ever found out about the Vega Cartel's interest in Lana's enzyme. No matter how accidentally.

Her brow furrowed. "You told that person on the phone that Mr. Smith was a suspect."

"He is."

"That means you suspect him."

"No, it means I'm not ruling him out." A good agent was thorough. Smith just pissed him off on principle.

She finger combed her strawberry-blond hair, making an abortive move to contain it in another ponytail. She didn't have a scrunchy. "What about me, are you ruling me out?"

He didn't laugh, but the urge was there. "Yes."

"Why?"

"For one thing, if you were feeding the Vega Cartel information on your project, they would know it didn't really transform metals."

"We don't know for sure they're interested in a literal interpretation of my note. Doubling their drug crops would be almost as good as turning lead into gold."

"True, but even if that were the case, if you'd told them about the project, they would know you didn't have enzymes developed for their crops, either."

"I could be working on their enzymes on the side. In secret." She looked so sincere, he just wanted to kiss her.

He refrained. For the moment. "You aren't."

"I know. What I don't understand is how *you* can be so sure."

He scooted his chair back and then grabbed her wrist, tugging her toward him. She settled onto his lap with a minimum of fuss, but her expression was wary.

He kissed the furrows on her forehead and they smoothed away. "If you were involved, the cartel would have no reason to target Elle, would they?"

"Perhaps."

"Listen. In the field, you can't always get proof of what your gut is telling you, so you have to go with your instincts. Mine tell me that you are one of the world's true idealists."

"You trust me. *Implicitly*." She looked horrified by that possibility.

"That bothers you. A lot."

"I'm worried you're going to believe in the wrong person."

He stared at her and then shook his head. For a woman who had such an unjustified optimistic view of the world, she had major trust issues. "You're worried I won't do my job right."

"You're awfully trusting."

He laughed, the sound harsh even to his own ears. "I'm not."

"Well, no, you're right. I mean you seem to have this really cynical view of people. Even Mr. Smith is a suspect, but *you trust me*."

Why did she find that so hard to believe?

"Lana, you have been through hell and yet you maintain a view of the world that is staggeringly positive. You cried for the men who died when you broke out of the prison they put you in, even after they had tortured you."

"You can't know that."

"Are you saying you didn't?"

She frowned and looked down at her lap. "No."

"You still love your family though they don't accept you and didn't stand by when you needed them the most. I saw the pictures you have of them on the mantel of your fireplace, the birthday cards they sent you still sitting upright on display on top of your neatly dusted dresser even though your birthday was months ago." He listed his evidence before she had a chance to question his knowledge again. "You never turned your ex-boyfriend in for his collusion in your kidnapping. No way in hell would *you* ever willingly work with a drug cartel."

"You sound like you think all of those things are good."

"I so do."

"You don't think I'm a wimp?"

"You are stronger than any other woman I've ever known." How could she not see that? Lana had survived hell and not only lived to tell the tale, but *lived*—didn't just exist.

"No."

"Yes."

"What about Elle?"

"My sister is fantastic, but, sweetheart, you? Are amazing."

Lana shook her head.

Myk kissed her. It was a biological imperative he wasn't about to ignore. Her lips were sweet and soft and he was ready to take it deeper when his computer chimed the alarm to alert him he had a new e-mail from someone on his case list.

She lifted her head. "What was that?"

"I've got mail." He'd misquoted a romantic comedy his *baba* had thought was sweet and tried to get him to watch.

Lana grinned and winked, showing she got the small joke. "From a sexy woman interested in you?"

"The only sexy woman I'm interested in right now is sitting on my lap."

"Seriously?"

He cupped her cheek and looked into her hazel eyes, understanding how she could doubt. He was no player, but she wouldn't know that. "Seriously. I'm not a good candidate for long term, but I don't cheat. I won't be touching another woman as long as I'm sharing your bed. And I expect the same in return."

"One, I don't touch other women. I only swing one way."

He shook his head and found himself smiling again. It was becoming a habit. He wasn't sure he liked that. But her sense of humor got him every time. And her grin was too sweet not to enjoy.

She ticked a second finger. "Two, we aren't sharing a bed."

"Yet."

"Arrogant."

"Certain."

"Fine."

"Fine, you'll share my bed?"

"Fine, I won't be touching other men while we are touching each other." She sighed. "Not that you would have to worry about that anyway."

"There aren't a lot of bad boys working at ETRD, are there?"

"You remember what I said yesterday."

"Oh, yeah. But I took a look around your apartment while you were sleeping, too."

"I figured, you seeing my old birthday cards and all."

"I like your bedroom."

She examined her cuticles as if they were of incredible interest. "I do, too."

"You've got a serious thing for James Dean."

"He was a very sexy man."

"Should I get myself a leather coat?"

She met his gaze at that and gave him a wry smile. "I'm sure you already have one."

"Caught me."

"I like your leather pants even better than his jeans."

He liked her honesty. It was refreshing and it turned him on. "I like the way they breathe. They also give me a range of motion my jeans don't afford."

"Justify it however you like; you've got a definite bad-boy streak."

"And you find that sexy."

"Yes."

"To hell with e-mail."

Still holding her, he went to stand, but the alarm chimed again. He sighed. "I've just got to check this."

He was on a case. He couldn't let that get lost in the slaking of his libido.

"Of course." She made a move to get off his lap, but he held on with an arm across her hips. "I should get something started for dinner. I'm sure you're hungry."

"Maybe, a little."

"You could have gone and gotten yourself something while I slept."

"I wanted to wait for you."

"That was sweet."

"That's not a word usually associated with me."

Her eyes twinkled. "You sure about that?"

"Very."

She made another aborted move to get off his lap. "Dinner?"

"In just a minute." He tightened his arm around her.

He opened the first e-mail from Alan Hyatt with a click. It was a list of names. Some of them were a little odd, most of them were women, but he didn't understand their significance. The next e-mail was even shorter. One word. *Curious?* And a phone number.

He picked up the phone and dialed.

Hyatt picked up on the first ring. "So, you were curious."

"Of course. Why not just send the explanation with the list of names?"

"Wanted to talk to the newest TGP agent. We haven't met, but I heard from the Old Man that you think I'm a virtuoso."

Whitmore must have called Alan as soon as he hung up with Myk.

"Don't let it go to your head."

A bark of laughter sounded. "You are every bit as testy as Whit said you would be."

"I'm not as charming as my sister."

"Elle is like to bite a man's head off in certain moods."

"Like I said, I'm not as friendly as she is."

The laughter came again.

"You going to explain this list of women, or what?"

"It's not a list of women."

"What then?" He thought for a second. "Boats?"

"Barges, to be exact."

"Why did you send me a list of barges?"

"They've all gone missing in the last six months." Alan gave a second to let that sink in. "They were hauling scrap metal—stuff like pot metal, lead, and rusted iron. No precious metals. The barges were taken in international waters off the coast of China."

"The crews?"

"Considered missing at sea."

"Well, shit."

"My sentiments exactly. Ask me how many people have gone missing with the barges."

Myk's gut sank. "How many?"

"Thirty-three. Barges run with a skeletal crew, but that's thirty-three people that are most likely dead."

"*Upizdysh.*"

"Now that's a word I've never heard Elle use."

"You aren't likely to, either."

"What does it mean?"

"Something I won't say in mixed company."

"So, you *are* getting friendly with the scientist. Is she there?"

"What the hell? Did you and Whit gossip like a couple of teenage girls?"

"He's an unrepentant matchmaker. Sent me on the case where I met Jillian because he thought we'd be good for each other. I think the fact that I was the best agent for the job was just a side benefit."

"You're joking."

"No way. He sent Elle out to ETRD on purpose, too."

"You're screwing with my mind."

"Not. I'm from Texas originally. We don't lie to our friends."

"You and I are friends?"

"I'm hoping we will be."

"Elle has had a lot of good to say about you."

"She was a damn fine agent."

"She's still the best at what she does."

"Yep, and what she's doing now suits her better. She'd gotten too entrenched in the job."

"It's easy to do."

"Especially when you're hiding from feeling regular emotions."

"You do know her well."

"Better than the other agents, not as well as her fiancé."

"Beau will be glad to know that."

"No reason for him to suspect anything else."

"You coming down for the wedding?"

"As a matter of fact, Jillian and I will be in town the day after tomorrow."

"I look forward to meeting you."

"Same."

"You got anything else for me?"

"Not right now, no. You got my other e-mail?"

"The one about Musa?"

"That's the one. I'm chasing the paper trail right now, trying to determine if Vega has been funding Musa's activities."

"If he has been, it could put a whole different complexion on this case."

"You got that right. Though something serious is going down. They killed thirty-three people in the last six months."

"People are expendable to men like Anibal Vega."

"Yeah. You keep a close eye on that lady scientist."

"I plan to."

"See you in a couple of days."

"Right."

They ended the call.

Lana was looking at Myk with a saddened expression. "You said people are expendable to Vega." She worried her lower lip between her teeth. "They've killed people because of their interest in my enzymes, haven't they?"

"Over the last six months, barges of scrap metal have been disappearing. Along with their crews."

"What do you mean disappearing? Why hasn't there been anything on the news about it?"

"They were scrap metal barges, manned by skeleton crews."

"Not newsworthy."

"Even if they had been, the news may have been suppressed."

"What? Why?"

"They were taken in international waters near China. Initial investigations would have been under international news radar because that's the way a lot of governments work, but particularly that one."

"So the disappearances got ignored?"

"No, just not reported internationally. China has done preliminary investigations, but the metals aren't showing up anywhere, which is their best chance of finding the culprits."

"Because they're being stockpiled somewhere."

"Yes."

"Anibal Vega really is hoping to turn lead into platinum."

"Looks like it. Unless you can think of another reason to hijack barges filled with the world's discarded junk."

"The crews for the barges were never recovered? None of them?"

"No."

"But why? Couldn't they just drop them in another port?"

"And alert someone to what was going on?"

"That's horrible."

"Yes, it is."

"Mr. Smith would never be party to that."

They were back to Mr. Smith again. "I don't trust him."

"Why?"

"Other than the fact that he's a secretive freak who has never once met the president of his own company in person?"

Lana shifted. "So, he's eccentric. That doesn't make him dishonest. I've met him. Once."

"He didn't tell Frank you'd been kidnapped by Kurdish rebels and forced to work on options for chemical warfare."

"I know."

"Yet, you trust him almost implicitly."

"You think something about that fact means I shouldn't?"

"He lied to Frank."

"That wasn't a lie. He simply omitted facts I preferred to keep to myself." Lana's expression turned solemn. "I didn't want people looking at me funny. Or funnier than they already do. I didn't want to be the subject of speculation and pity."

"I understand that, but for your safety, ETRD security should have been apprised of the potential threat. That includes Frank."

"They aren't coming after me again." She said it stubbornly, like she wanted to believe it, but part of her didn't.

"I agree."

"But—"

"If the Kurd rebels who took you were interested in you still, they would have shown up before now, but that doesn't mean your skills aren't of interest to others. No security consultant, no matter how good, can prepare her team without key knowledge like the fact that your doctoral theses had unintended ramifications related to chemical warfare."

"I'm not a risk to ETRD."

"No, doc, you are not."

"So, why would anyone need to know?"

"Because working for ETRD is a risk to you."

"I chose to take that risk."

"That doesn't mean it shouldn't be minimized."

"Mr. Smith made sure it was."

"He should have told Elle."

"She wasn't really a security consultant and Mr. Smith knew it."

"Wrong. It might have been her cover, but Elle still had every intention of upgrading ETRD's security. Which, as you know, is exactly what she did do."

"It doesn't matter that Mr. Smith didn't tell her, though. She obviously found out on her own, or you wouldn't know about it."

"That's not the point."

"I thought my safety was the point."

"It is, and Mr. Smith holding back important information could have compromised it."

"He made sure I would never get lost again."

"What do you mean?"

"Let me up."

"I like you where you are."

"I want to show you something."

Myk grudgingly allowed Lana to stand. She tugged up the hem of her T-shirt, revealing a sexy strip of skin above the low-slung waist of her capri pants. Nestled right in the center was her belly button, her *pierced* belly button. Tinker Bell winked merrily at him from her dangling perch.

"The ring has a GPS locator on it. I can change charms, but I never change the ring itself."

"Mr. Smith has you Lojacked?" Myk asked in shock.

"Yes. If I ever disappear again, he'll be able to find me."

Provided her kidnappers didn't remove her belly button ring, but Smith had been smart. Chances were, the belly button ring was safe. First, it was unlikely kidnappers would be expecting a belly button ring on the scientist. Second, even if they saw it, it wasn't likely a GPS locator would be expected. There would be no reason to take it out.

"You don't mind him knowing where you are all the time?"

"It makes me feel safe." The way she said it kicked Myk right in the gut.

"I'm not going to let anyone take you."

"I know you will try."

"Count on it." He wanted to growl. Just like a damn bear. Having this woman doubt him while professing such absolute faith in the mysterious Smith, pissed Myk off. Royally. "You know he's responsible for my sister getting let go by her agency. He blew her cover."

"On purpose?"

"To Frank and Beau, yes."

"Her agency fired her because of that?"

"No. There were mitigating circumstances."

"I'm sure there were. Anyone can miscalculate, but Mr. Smith's intentions were good."

"You're so sure of him."

"He saved my sanity and gave me back my dream."

For that, Myk could almost persuade himself not to detest the other man.

Lana wasn't surprised when Myk refused to let her cook and insisted on ordering dinner in. He had the alpha male need to care for those around him. Add to that his apparent inexplicable desire to take care of her particularly and ordering dinner in after her earlier outburst was a foregone conclusion.

Of course, he instructed the Thai restaurant to leave their food with the guard downstairs.

Lana did the same thing when she ordered takeout.

She sighed, shifting restlessly in her chair. She was supposed to be interpreting data and had spread her papers out on the opposite side of the dining table from Myk.

He looked up from his computer where he had been typing furiously. "What's the matter? Are you missing something tonight you didn't tell me about?"

"That's likely, isn't it?" she asked with disgust at herself.

"Is that what that sigh was all about?" He got up and came around the table to squat beside her, his eyes burning with a sexy glint. "You're lamenting your lack of a social life? And here I thought I was enough for any woman."

She laughed; his conceit knew no bounds. "It could have been, but no. I just got another reminder that I wasn't as far from prison as I'd thought."

"Because I had the restaurant leave the food with the guard? We're still eating, Lana. Our choice of food. That's hardly prison."

"It doesn't bother me that you did that. It bothers me that I would have done the same thing. Last week. And the week before. Long before I knew about the Vega Cartel's interest in my enzymes."

He looked perplexed. "Why would the fact that you have a smart sense of personal safety bother you? If more people took such basic precautions, criminals wouldn't find it so easy to target their victims."

"You're a little biased in this regard."

"Maybe." He shrugged, then kissed her cheek. "I like you just fine the way you are, doc."

"Thank you."

He got up and went back to sit in front of his open computer. "Just consider one thing, Lana."

"What?"

"You're not the only home owner in this complex. I doubt a single one of them would consider living here indicative of a psychosis involving personal safety issues. And they would be right."

Myk went back to typing and Lana returned to her research, but her mind would not shut down. Finally, she laid her pen down and started talking.

Chapter 11

"When Mr. Smith found me, I was living in my parents' attic." Lana looked up to see if Myk was listening.

He was, his attention centered completely on her.

She took a deep breath and then forced words out that had been inside for too many years. "It was the only room in their house without windows. Even so, I had a single-room security system and I only left the house to go to work at the paper mill where my brother is a manager. I insisted on riding to and from work with him."

Why did she feel the need to tell Myk about that time? She had no answers for herself, just a burning need to share secrets no one except Mr. Smith knew. "I never went out. I didn't talk to anyone at work for fear they would turn out to be another betrayer. The thought of ordering takeout at all during that time would have nauseated me. I didn't trust anyone."

"You lived with your parents." Myk's dark Hershey eyes bore into hers. "You trusted your brother to get you to and from work safely."

"I *knew* they couldn't be trusted. They'd already bailed on me, so they couldn't hurt me anymore. In a twisted way, they were the safest people to be around because they couldn't let me down. I expected nothing from them."

"You trusted them not to betray you to someone else who might want to exploit your knowledge and intelligence."

"Believe it, or not, they were ashamed of both. I wasn't *normal* to them. There was no chance they were going to go around bragging about where I'd gone to school and what I'd studied."

"Elle said they didn't instigate a search for you when you disappeared."

"The university filed a missing persons report. My parents didn't feel it necessary to duplicate the effort."

"Why not?"

"They assumed I'd resurface without help. They thought I was too smart to let anything really bad happen to myself, so it had to be a voluntary disappearance."

"Have they been drinking the same water as the guards at ETRD?" Myk asked with undisguised anger laced with disgust.

She found herself smiling. A little. "Maybe."

"Idiots."

"More like they just didn't care enough to want answers."

"Criminally idiotic."

She surprised herself with a small laugh. "That's one way to put it."

"I bet they were pleased to have you working in the mill and rejecting your education."

"They were. The only thing that would have pleased them more would have been if I'd been willing to date, but that was something I refused to do."

"Understandable."

"They didn't think so."

"They were intimidated by your intelligence and suspicious of your education. You wanted a life they couldn't mentally grasp."

"They saw what happened to me as a means to bring me back into the fold they did understand. You know what *I* don't understand?"

"What?"

"I was really glad my brother liked his job at the mill, that he'd worked his way to a management position. Why couldn't they have been happy for my success, too?"

"They were afraid it would take you away from them."

She stared. "I never thought of it that way."

"You're a scientist. You told me already psychology isn't your strong suit."

"The subtext of human behavior isn't as easy to understand as y's reaction to x in the lab."

"Your parents' lack of follow-through in pushing for stronger measures to being taken in finding you is indicative that they had subconsciously accepted your loss before you ever went away to university."

"They should have cared. They should have worried about me."

"Yes, they should have. Their apathy to your safety cost them more than your choice for a different life ever would have."

"That's true. Once Mr. Smith convinced me to come to work for ETRD, I left and never looked back. They invite me to go 'home' every year for Christmas."

"You decline."

"I do."

"Understandable."

"I'm not sure it is."

"I can't believe Smith was the first person to offer you a job in your field."

"He wasn't. I refused my university's invitation to work in their research facility. I turned down job offers from half a dozen other scientific research facilities as well. I thought I could be safe if I didn't use my knowledge. If I lived the life my parents had anticipated for me before I turned into some kind of freak. Their words, not mine."

"What changed with Mr. Smith?"

"He made me see what I was doing."

"Living in a prison of your own making."

"Exactly. I couldn't let the people who had hurt me win like that."

"I'm glad he convinced you to come to work for ETRD, but he was motivated by self-interest, you know?"

"You think? There are other people in this country with my education."

"But none with your vision."

"That's what Mr. Smith said."

"I never questioned his smarts."

"You shouldn't."

"So, you never talk to your parents, or your brother?"

"Oh, we talk. Probably once a month, but I don't visit and I've never invited them to come out here. Once I woke up from the fugue I had been living in since getting back in the States, I realized how deeply I resented their lack of effort to find me. If they had insisted on a serious all-out search being done, maybe I would have been found. I don't think Artie would have been that difficult a witness to break."

"That I believe."

"You were right earlier. I do still love them. I always will and I've even forgiven them, but I'll never forget. I can't."

"I get that." Something in his expression told her he meant those words.

"You've got your own ghosts."

"Don't we all?"

"Some are more horrific than others."

"Agreed. The trick is to focus on the memories that aren't so bad."

"You mean like my time before I was kidnapped? I've tried that. It never works."

"No. I mean like the positive memories you have since then, even during the ordeal. There had to be moments that reminded you why it was good to be alive."

"I disguised experiments that were a precursor to what I'm doing now as chemical warfare development."

"Clever. Did you have any breakthroughs?"

She felt herself grinning. "Yes." They'd been worth the beating she'd gotten when her captors had caught on. "What about you?"

"My last case was filled with really rotten stuff, kids being sold and hurt. But I saved as many of them as I could and each one was a victory for the good guys."

The buzzer from the guard desk in the lobby sounded.

They ate their Thai food on the living room sofa while Lana's favorite Air Supply CD played in the background. Mykola had balked at her choice until she'd told him it was either that or Disney show tunes. She had the entire collection from every Disney movie and musical produced.

Having an eclectic ear, she had other types of music, too, but didn't bother telling him so. Why bother when the other CDs weren't what she wanted to listen to right now?

Mykola had been less than impressed and offered his MP3 player loaded with techno. While she wasn't averse to techno on occasion, like when Casey and she were working through the night on an experiment, she hadn't been in the mood tonight.

So, Air Supply. After all, it was *her* apartment and Mykola had admitted that in the right mood, he actually enjoyed the eighties band. Over dinner, he told Lana entertaining stories about his siblings from their childhood.

Still laughing over an anecdote about the time his mother caught Elle playing cops and robbers, Lana shook her head in disbelief. "You're kidding. You have to be. No way did she use your *baba*'s favorite wooden spoon from the old country as her gun. Even Elle isn't that daring."

"But she is that stubborn." Mykola had a wicked twinkle in his dark eyes.

"You dared her," Lana breathed in awe.

"You bet."

She shook her head. "You are so lucky to have survived childhood."

"Tell me about it. I was even crazy enough to play practical jokes on our oldest brother. No one else ever did."

"Roman. The military brother."

"That would be the one."

"He didn't have much of a sense of humor?"

"Nope. Papa used to say he was born with a serious expression that didn't crack until long after his first birthday."

"Wow."

"Now, there would be a study for your mythical anthropologist." Mykola ate a bite of his pad thai with gusto.

"My, huh?"

"The one you think would like to study me, Cro-Magnon man."

She laughed. "Are you saying Roman would make an even better subject?"

"For another scientist."

"Clearly. After all, I'm not an anthropologist."

"Besides, my brother isn't your type."

She finished chewing and swallowed her bite of spicy red curry before asking, "What type would that be?"

Chapter 12

Mykola waggled his brows. "I think you know."

"Bad boys?" She was never going to live it down now that he'd overheard her subconscious rambling and gone snooping in her bedroom.

"Not all bad boys."

"You think I've got a subgroup of particular interest?" She couldn't remember having this much fun with a man and this wasn't even a date. Not really.

Mykola wanted to have sex with her. Weird, but true. However, he was in her apartment now because he was intent on protecting her. She'd noticed the way he'd set up shop, and the fact that there was a strange black duffel on the floor of her bedroom. The man had every intention of staying over, whether he shared her bed or not.

He gave her a look that made her vaginal muscles clench spasmodically. "Yeah, I do."

"And what would that be?"

He set both their takeout containers with chopsticks on the coffee table. Then he leaned toward her, invading her personal space and giving her a whiff of his masculine scent over the Thai food. "The type that might dress and look the part, but when it comes to living, he's one of the good guys."

He was oh so right. "You mean men like you?"

"Your picture is still too broad, sweetheart." He leaned in and kissed the edge of her lips. Just a tease and she wanted more. "Guess again."

"We are talking about *my* preferences here?" She meant to sound mocking, but the words came out breathy and low.

"Oh, yeah."

"Then it wouldn't be a guess, would it?" She tried to focus on logic, but he was making it really hard. Impossible in fact.

He nibbled his way down her neck, his knowing lips drawing a response she was helpless to squelch. "There's only one bad boy in your preference bubble right now."

"Are you sure about that?" Oh, go her, coherent thought and a teasing comment to boot.

"Call me arrogant, but yes."

"*Yes*," she hissed the same time his lips latched on to where her shoulder joined her neck. Delight shivered through her while his tongue played over her skin. "That feels so good."

His only answer was his hand sliding under the hem of her T-shirt. Hot skin against hot skin. Callused fingers brushed smooth skin that never saw the light of day and rarely felt another's touch. It had been so long. Her body was not accustomed to any touch, much less that of a master in the art of sexual gratification.

If there was one thing she would willingly bank on right now, it was that fact. This man knew what he was doing. Man, did he know.

If sex had ever felt this good, it wouldn't have been so long since the last time she'd had it. Heck, she might have actually worked on making a relationship work. This was worth leaving the lab for.

Mykola's fingertips drew a pattern of desire on her midriff that sent shock waves to her core.

"I want this off. I want to touch. Now, Mykola." She scrabbled at the shirt that molded his muscular torso.

His head came up, his expression fierce with sexual need. "Whatever you want, doc."

The nickname wasn't exactly a romantic one, but spoken in that tone of voice, it made her thighs clench.

He ripped his dark shirt off over his head and tossed it aside, revealing a chest and abs that made her swallow against a suddenly dry throat. He was truly the stuff of fantasies. Especially her fantasies. A light dusting of black hair gave texture to his upper chest, but his skin showed through. He even had a tattoo over his heart—kanji characters she didn't recognize done in bold black slashes.

She traced the bisected shelf of his pectorals, brushing over the soft whorls of hair. "So strong."

"I work at it."

"I can tell." She let her fingertips trail down over his solidly defined six-pack. "So much muscle."

Big hands, every bit as strong as the other parts of him, settled around her waist. "You're soft. I like that."

"I should work out."

"You should be yourself." With that, he lifted her up, right onto his lap.

She faced him, her legs straddling his thighs, her bottom firmly settled on his adamantine quads. The diamond-hard surface of his lap should have been uncomfortable, but she had never felt so perfectly content. "You have a thing about me sitting on your lap."

"I like you there."

"I'm not too h—"

He cut her question off with a growl, and his lips pressed to hers. The kiss wasn't quite a punishment, but she felt his disapproval of her concern. Their mouths meshed for long, heated seconds.

When he tilted his head back, she didn't want the kiss to end and chased his lips with her own. He made an amused sound, but there was nothing funny about the way his mouth once again slanted over hers. This time, the kiss was feral, needy, and hot.

His tongue took the interior of her mouth like a warlord intent on conquering, but she wasn't ready to be conquered and she fought for equality in the kiss. He let her tongue slide into his mouth with no resistance, but she realized it was more a feint than a retreat. Suddenly, he was devouring her in a way that left her trembling and breathless against him.

She could do nothing when he pulled his lips from hers but gasp for the air she'd forgotten to breathe in amid the ferocity of the kiss.

"Like where you are?" he asked in a gravelly voice.

"Yes."

"Me, too."

"I'm glad."

"No more doubting."

She chuckled, impressed with how much he could convey with a few words and a scorching kiss. "Okay." She didn't fit the stereotype of the skinny scientist with glasses, much less Hollywood beauty.

And he didn't mind.

In fact, he liked it.

A lot.

For the first time outside her belly-dancing community, she felt comfortable with the body God had given her. The generous breasts, the curvy thighs, the waist that was more than a hand-span. Casey had told her once that she was vamp material. She'd thought he was nuts.

But maybe for Mykola, she could be. Just because she'd never experienced the fireworks and fantasies song lyricists rhapsodized about did not mean she had no idea what to do.

This time, she had a feeling she was really going to enjoy it. The fact that she vibrated with the need to touch told her that. She'd never wanted to explore another man's body so badly. Had never desired so deeply to give pleasure and to make that pleasure unforgettable.

She rose up into a sitting position again. Licking her lips, she surveyed his totally delectable torso. "Put your arms along the back of the sofa."

He quirked a brow in question.

"I told you, I want to touch."

"I'm all about the touching." With that he did as she'd instructed.

Having the embodiment of her favorite fantasies spread out for her like this was enough to make her lungs constrict in her chest. She had to force herself to breathe even as she could feel the dampness between her legs growing. "You're so sexy, Mykola."

"I'm glad you think so."

"Arrogant but not truly conceited?"

He shrugged, making all those delicious muscles ripple. His position should have made him look vulnerable, but he radiated sexual power.

"Keep your arms up."

"For a while."

She supposed that was a pretty good concession for a man used to taking charge. She had a thought. "You're not ticklish, are you?"

"No."

"Good." With that she began mapping the planes of his body with her fingertips.

She started with his neck, brushing down the strong column. He let his head fall back against the back of the couch. It was tall enough that his heavy-lidded gaze never broke from hers.

The expression in his dark chocolate eyes made her moan. One side of his mouth tilted, but no amusement shone on his features.

She brushed the soft bristles of his close-cropped beard. "I've never been attracted to a man with facial hair before."

"You filter your attractions through your fixation on James Dean."

"I'm not fixated."

"The framed posters on your bedroom walls say otherwise."

"They're art." And they had cost a bundle.

"They're eye candy for you."

"You don't look anything like James Dean, but you're sweeter eye candy than any man I've ever seen." For once she didn't care about her lack of filters. Hiding her infatuation with Mykola's looks would be like trying to ignore the smell her enzymes created when at work.

"It's the attitude."

"The bad-boy persona."

"Yep."

"You're sexier." She had never thought she'd be able to say that about a living man. Heck, maybe she had been fixated. But even if that were true, she sure wasn't anymore. The man who would dominate her sleeping and waking dreams now was Mykola Chernichenko. A living, breathing, special agent so very good at being in charge.

"You're damn fine yourself, doc."

She smiled, letting her hands slide down to rest over the small brown disks of his nipples. His big body jolted as she let her thumbs brush over the instantly hardened nubs.

He flexed his pecs. "Feels good."

"You feel amazing."

Her touch was drawn to the black slashes making up the kanji characters on his left pectoral. "What does this mean?"

"You don't know?"

"No."

"Warrior."

"Very appropriate."

"I thought so."

"When did you have it done?"

"After I pulled a gun on a coyote for the first time." He looked into her eyes and she had the feeling he was sharing a piece of his soul. "I wanted a reminder that sometimes a warrior has to use weapons to defend those under his protection."

"Coyote?"

"Men who prey on the dreams of others who want a better life. They take money promising safe passage over the border, but more often than not they're offering nothing more than a desperate death or introduction into what is at best indentured servitude."

"That's terrible."

"I think so, too. The border is a dangerous place. Too many who try to make it through the desert end up dying of dehydration, snakebite, and other natural hazards, but that is nothing compared to the dangers they face from two-legged predators."

"You tried to protect them."

"I did my job."

"Because you wanted to save people from such horrible fates."

"Funny you should realize that. Most people aren't so understanding of or impressed by the motives of INS agents."

"Everything about you impresses me."

Mykola raised his legs to force her body to slide forward until their crotches collided. "Even this?" He canted his hips up off the couch, pressing the hard length trapped behind leather into the wet heat hidden behind Lana's capris.

She rocked just a little, making them both groan. "Oh, yes."

"Take off your T-shirt." The command was rasping, but definitive.

She didn't even consider demurring. She wasn't worried about what Mykola would think. He'd made it clear she excited him just the way she was. She grabbed the hem of her shirt and slowly peeled it up her torso and then over her head before tossing it away as he'd done his. Her bra was a lime-green underwire of thin nylon that matched her panties and the color of her T-shirt.

"I want to touch," he demanded in a low, gravelly tone.

She nodded.

She wanted that too. Craved it.

He brought both arms off the back of the sofa, but instead of cupping her breasts like she expected, he framed her belly button with his hands. "Beautiful."

"I wear dangling jewels when I dance." Somehow, she didn't think of Tinker Bell as sexy.

"You know why men find belly button rings such a huge turn-on?"

"You mean the men that do?" She'd been with a scientist she'd met at a symposium shortly after coming to work for ETRD who had found her belly jewelry unimpressive.

"What man wouldn't?"

"Trust me, there are plenty."

"Whatever."

"So, what's so sexy about it to you?"

"It directs the eye to your belly and points downward, hinting at things below."

"Is that what men find sexy about earrings?" After all, they pointed down at a woman's breasts.

"Maybe."

"You're very primeval."

"So you've said."

"It's disconcertingly alluring." She was a modern woman of science. His primitive streak shouldn't be such a huge turn-on for her, but it was. It so was.

"Baby, you are the alluring one." His thumbs dipped lower, sliding just inside her waistband. He swished his thumbs side to side, side to side, side to side. Each brush back and forth ratcheted up her anticipation.

She bit her lip and sighed. Would he go lower? She wanted him to go lower. She needed him to go lower. The top of her pubis was extremely sensitive. She wanted to feel his touch there. He would know just how to caress her.

But instead of going down her body, his big hands moved back up her torso until they cupped her breasts as she had at first expected. He moaned, deep and low in his throat, just as if he was the one being touched. And really? She was doing nothing but kneading his chest reflexively as he explored her.

He took hold of her bra clasp, meeting her eyes. "May I?"

"*Yes.*"

He undid it, but did not pull back the thin nylon of her bra cups. Instead he leaned in and gave her a soft kiss. "Thank you."

"For what?"

"For sharing yourself with me."

Something inside her melted. Right into a puddle. If she didn't know better, she would have said it was the icy wall that had encased her heart since her boyfriend sold her out for a few hundred dollars and even fewer hours of mental escape. She let her forehead rest against Mykola's as they both panted through what felt like a profound moment.

Neither spoke. She couldn't. He probably had nothing else to say. After all, it wasn't a lifetime of his defenses in peril. She couldn't make herself regret that it was hers.

Finally, he pulled the lime-green fabric away, exposing her breasts one delicious centimeter at a time. Feeling the air against them made her already hardened peaks tingle and tighten further. The way their heads were angled down, she could see the blood-engorged nipples begging for attention. She knew he could, too.

But he didn't touch.

And she thought she'd go crazy waiting.

"Touch them," she pleaded.

He made a guttural noise but didn't speak.

She could feel the heat of his stare as surely as she could the warmth of his fingers as they brushed over her finely veined flesh at last. His touch was light, gentle. Unlike other men who groped her generous flesh like it was a sponge. Perfect.

Her breath hitched. "So good."

"Beautiful." He followed the line of fine freckles that decorated the top swell. "So damn gorgeous."

"Mykola." She couldn't say anything else. Couldn't think enough to form another word.

"Say it again."

Oh, wow. She didn't know a man's voice could sound like that. "*Mykola.*"

"I feel that in my cock."

She choked at the earthy sentiment, but it excited her, too.

"Damn, doc." He rolled her turgid peaks between his fingers and then squeezed them. "You turn me on."

Her? She was just sitting there. Letting him touch her until she thought she'd go insane with it.

"I can feel it," she managed to get out.

"Not like you are going to."

"I want that." So much. So much. *So much.*

She didn't realize she'd been chanting that litany out loud until he nuzzled her and said, "Shh, baby, I'm going to make you feel it all. I promise."

She whimpered. She couldn't help it. One thing she'd learned about the Chernichenkos, especially this one, was that they put a lot of stock in keeping their promises.

He slowly pushed her bra completely off her shoulders, caressing her arms as he did so. When it got caught at her elbows, he removed first one of her hands from his chest and slid the strap over her hand, and then the other. He brought both hands back to his skin and she slid them up to his shoulders, unable to stop the reflexive kneading she'd been engaged in before.

Then they were kissing again. She didn't know which of them moved first, but their lips fused and fireworks went off behind her eyelids. His hands were back on her breasts, rubbing, caressing, and arousing. He zeroed in on her nipples and the heat between her legs went volcanic. He did more than pinch and roll. He abraded them with the callused pads of his fingers, sending intense sensations straight to her core.

She moaned into the kiss, rubbing against him, pressing her apex against his hard bulge with an abandon she'd never shown.

He undid her pants with one hand while the other continued to torment her breasts and nipples. She tried to help him, but only got their fingers tangled.

"Let me," he demanded.

She nodded, though did not get much movement with her head because he was already back to kissing her.

She tried to undo the button on his leather jeans, but it was stubborn. Or she was fumble fingered. Either way, she had to settle for touching him through the leather of his pants. They molded to his large erection, allowing her to feel his shape if not his skin.

He groaned, bucking upward as he tugged her zipper down, already having gotten *her* button loose. His fingers delved into her panties, the back of one long digit sliding against her clitoris.

She screamed into his mouth at the electric contact.

He used his knuckle to stimulate her, not pressing too hard, but giving her something to push against. And push she did, rotating her hips as arcs of pleasure exploded through her body.

Her whole body felt sensitized, with the pleasure targeted toward that bundle of nerves he manipulated so perfectly. She felt a climax building faster than she would have thought possible. Then it was there, shattering once and for all her previous perception of sex.

This sex. Sex with Mykola was worth all the fuss. And then some.

She squeezed reflexively against the hardness under her palm, stroking it, wishing it was inside her.

His body went rigid under her and he groaned into her mouth, another sound that she'd never heard from a man before. It was so much more than a mere orgasm. He sounded like he was dying and happy with it. He gripped her hips and pressed up while pulling her against him, crushing their bodies together with near violent passion.

She experienced aftershocks that could have been measured on the Richter scale. After several seconds that felt infinite, he went still under her and they rested together.

Through it all, the kiss continued and his lips still molded hers, no less urgent after the peaks they'd both just reached. His tongue continued to plunder her mouth when he wasn't busy sucking her tongue into his.

Unbelievably, the level of her arousal never dropped completely and she was already spiraling toward renewal.

Breathing hard, he broke the kiss. "Bed. Now."

"Yes."

He stood up with her in his arms, adjusting his grip so that one arm created a shelf under her bottom and the other pressed against her back. Her desire ratcheted up another notch as she felt not only wanted but so incredibly cared for and safe.

She clasped her legs around him, latching her ankles against the small of his back. Her hands were busy caressing his face, reading the desire in his expression by touch. He carried her into her bedroom, sexual purpose emanating from him so intensely she trembled against him.

Not in maidenly fear, but absolute, overwhelming *want*.

They'd climaxed once, but apparently that had just been the appetizer.

She couldn't wait for the main course.

Chapter 13

Myk managed to get both himself and Lana naked in record time. Without ripping her sexy little lime-green panties.

He tossed the pile of pillows off the bed, including a stuffed Donald Duck. Disney's bad boy? Not in his world, but Lana's brain didn't work like other people's. He'd figured that out right away.

He yanked the fluffy down comforter back, revealing bright yellow sheets. Even under the influence of the harsh arousal making his body rigid with need, he found himself smiling at his surroundings. This woman was special.

He swept her up into his arms and laid her out like a banquet on the queen-size bed.

She cocked one shapely leg at an angle and let the other lay flat against the mattress while stretching her arms above her head. Her eyes followed his every move while she caught her bottom lip in her teeth. Could she be any more sensuous?

Except he would bet any amount of money that she wasn't trying.

She was so damn seductive, her voluptuous figure inviting him to share decadences she'd probably never even heard about.

Her entire body was flushed with satiated arousal, but the ruby-reddened tips of her breasts poked proudly forward, revealing her readiness for more.

Tempting him to taste.

Oh, yeah. He was so going to do that, but that wasn't all he intended to get oral with on her body.

If her nipples hadn't given her continuing desire away, the warm musk coming from between her legs would have. He inhaled a deep breath, taking in the sweet, almond scent of her postclimax aroma. He did love almonds. The fragrance of her sustained need was there, too, the smell of her musk confirming that her body was still secreting fluid along her vaginal walls.

His cock throbbed with the need to feel the slick tunnel close around him. That need warred with the one to taste that same wet heat. She was more than a banquet, she was a royal feast of multiple courses intended to last days. He couldn't decide which one to start with.

Irresistibly drawn, he crawled onto the bed. He lifted her straightened leg, pushing it and her bent one apart so that she was wholly open to him.

"Exquisite."

Her breath caught, but she said nothing in response. She widened her legs, just a little, though, as if inviting him to look his fill.

Day-um. What little blood was still in his brain rushed south.

In awe, he knelt there, inches from paradise, and breathed deeply of her feminine fragrance.

She reached for him, but he shook his head.

"Come here," she pleaded softly.

"Taste first."

Her eyes widened, but her hands tunneled into his hair, grabbing his head as he leaned forward to kiss her nether lips. Damn. They were soft. Plump. Moist. And delicious.

He had never tasted a woman so ideal for his palate. The bit of salty undertone only added to the piquancy of her flavor.

He knew from his file on her that she was clean, but he owed her the same assurance.

He lifted his head, met her dazed eyes. "I'm safe."

She opened her mouth, but no sound came out.

"You hear me, sweetheart?"

She gasped and nodded. "Me, too. Clean."

"I know."

"Then do it again."

He gave her a look he knew smoldered with the desire boiling through him. "I intend to."

And he did. Kissing and licking, tasting the very essence of her. So sweet. So good.

He pressed his tongue inside, nearly coming from how tightly the moisture-coated flesh gripped him. She was going to strangle his cock. Hell, yeah.

He drilled her with his tongue, lashing her sensitive flesh until she was mewling and thrusting her hips in tortured jerks.

That was his cue. It was time to tease her clitoris.

Pushing her thighs even farther apart, he nuzzled upward until his tongue tip barely touched the swollen nub. Her clitoris was small, almost hidden behind the hood of flesh that protected it, but damn she was sensitive. The merest swipe of his tongue made her shout and press upward hard against his restraining hands.

He flicked, nibbled, licked, and laved the bud of her pleasure, determined to drive her to the brink before claiming her body with his.

She was crying out, begging him for more when he finally couldn't take the need any longer himself. If he hadn't come once already, he would not have lasted this long.

He reared back, tearing from her grip on his hair. Condoms. She didn't have any. He'd looked. He only had a couple in his shaving kit, but that would have to do for tonight.

He dove for the duffel he'd left just inside the door to her bedroom earlier. He tore into it and then the shaving kit with no regard for what got tossed where. His fingers closed around a familiar foil packet and he had it torn open practically before he got it out of the bag. He rolled the condom over his engorged dick, stifling an unmanly whimper of need even that amount of stimulation caused.

He got back on the bed and settled between her legs again, this time with his cock head pressed against the entrance to her body.

"You ready for me?" He knew the answer, her body gave it away in myriad ways, but he wanted the words from her lips.

"More than." Her expression was fierce with arousal.

He slid home, his girth pressing open her swollen and incredibly tight flesh. She was so slick, nothing stopped his forward motion, but he was careful not to go too fast. He wanted her to feel all pleasure, no pain.

She took his entire length, the expression on her sweet face one of bliss.

"You are amazing." He had to say it.

He'd never had a sex partner who fit him so perfectly.

She just shook her head, her mouth making noises, but none of them distinguishable as words.

He wouldn't tolerate the attempt at a denial, though. He pulled out even more slowly than he'd pressed in. "Amazing. Beautiful. Sexy as hell."

"I . . ." Nothing else made it past her lips.

"Yes. *You.*"

He pushed inside again, this time picking up his pace just a little.

She gasped as he filled her, leveraging her hips off the bed and toward his invading flesh. "More!"

Another time, he would draw it out, but right now he needed as badly as she did. He finished his downward thrust and then pulled back, pushing forward again immediately. Within seconds, they were mating in earnest, their bodies slapping together, the heat generated between them furnace hot. He reached down between them, just barely touching the top of her clitoral hood with his thumb.

Her entire body jolted like she'd had an electric shock, and a keening cry sounded from her throat as the beautiful woman beneath him came for the second time. The cry was his name.

That knowledge penetrated as her inner muscles contracted around him with viselike intensity. Burying his face in her neck and breathing in her scent, he came, too.

He pulsed into the condom over and over again until he grew so sensitive he couldn't move inside her without feeling a mixture of pleasure and pain. He withdrew slowly and carefully before flopping onto his back, breathing like a horse after the Kentucky Derby.

She rolled over so she was lying half over him, her hand coming to rest on his chest. He managed to tangle their legs and twine their fingers together.

They lay like that for long minutes, neither speaking.

He couldn't.

She seemed content in the silence, so he didn't worry about it.

He was slipping into a light doze when she said, "We'll need to shower."

She was right. They were both covered in sweat and he had a used condom to deal with. "Don't want to move."

"Me, either."

"But . . ."

"We'll sleep better without sweat crusting on our bodies."

He agreed. In theory, anyway. It was still a few minutes before either of them moved and then it was as if by mutual agreement, they rolled in opposite directions and got off the bed.

"Shower together?" he asked. He didn't offer to take the guest bathroom, but figured the question was all the nod he had to give to civilized breeding.

"I've got a shower big enough for two."

"Shame not to put all that space to good use."

"I agree."

There were no awkward moments in the shower. They moved around one another, bathing each other and themselves as if they'd done it many times before. He touched her in places he hadn't yet, but was careful not to start something again.

She looked tired.

The ease with which they fit together freaked him out, but he hid his reaction.

They were cuddled together in the center of the bed, spooning even, when she asked, "Who or what is Musa?"

Shit. "Why do you ask?"

"You mentioned him on the phone, when you were talking to the other man from TGP." She nuzzled against the arm under her head.

"How do you know it was a man?"

"The tonal quality of his voice." She yawned. "I couldn't hear his words from the cell phone, but I could hear that his voice was too deep to be feminine."

"You really do hear everything that goes on around you, don't you?"

She went completely still. "I don't mean to."

He hugged her closer. "I believe you. Your brain is just too advanced for you not to."

"Do you think I'm a freak?"

"No, sweetheart. I told you earlier." He kissed the silky hair on top of her head. "I think you're amazing."

"That was sex talk."

It should have been. It wasn't. "I don't lie."

"Unless it's for the job."

"Right. Not for sex or anything else."

"I like knowing that."

"I like you." Well, hell. Why had he said that? It wasn't that it wasn't true, but women were bound to read stuff into comments like that that wasn't there. Stuff like a precursor to the other L-word.

"I like you, too, Mykola. Maybe that's one of the reasons the sex was so good."

"You didn't like your previous partners?"

"A couple of them. Don't ask why we had sex. I don't know. I was looking for a connection. I tried to like them. A couple I realized later didn't really like me. They found me annoying. Scratch that, eventually, they all found me annoying or intimidating. Either way, no relationship ever lasted."

A red flashing alarm went off in his brain. "This, us . . . this isn't a relationship." It was sex. Incredible sex, but not hearts and flowers.

"I know."

"You do?"

"My brain isn't just good for storing overheard bits of information and working out scientific theory, you know." She sighed, but he had no idea what that sound meant. "You're a really sensual guy. Sex is important to you and you won't go long without it. You find me attractive and enjoy my company. I feel the same about you. So, we had sex. Will probably have it again. There's nothing more to it."

They were all sentiments he was familiar with, but hearing her say them made him feel . . . itchy. He didn't like it, but he wasn't about to screw up by saying so. "That doesn't bother you?"

"No."

"No?"

"Nope." Unlike other women he'd known, Lana apparently felt no need to explain herself. "Tell me about Musa."

The change of topic was no more comfortable for Myk.

"I thought you were tired."

"I won't sleep until I know."

He just hoped she could sleep after. "He's a zealot."

"Political or religious?"

"Both." For Musa it was one and the same thing.

"A terrorist?"

"We don't know if he has terrorist ties."

"But he has ties to the Vega Cartel."

"How did you figure that?"

"His name wouldn't have come up in your conversation otherwise. Everything else was centered around your case."

"You really are scary smart."

"So I've been told."

He scooted a few inches away and rolled her on her back so he could see her face in the semidarkness. "I was just kidding about the scary part."

"Don't worry about it." She really did look tired, her eyes heavy-lidded with fatigue.

"I don't think you are a freak."

"I'm glad to hear that." She gave him a sleepy smile. "Now, what kind of ties does Musa have to the cartel?"

"Family."

"What kind of family?"

"Musa is married to one of Vega's wife's sisters."

"Serious tie, then."

"Yes."

"Anything beyond the family connection?"

"Alan is tracking the money trail, to see if any of Vega's leads to Musa."

"Can he find it if it does?"

"Yeah. He's scary smart, too. His researching skills are unlike anything I've ever encountered."

"Good thing he's on our side, then."

"Very."

She nodded and then turned on her side again, away from him. She plumped her pillow and then settled.

Assuming she meant to go to sleep now, he curled around her, nestling his semihard dick against the full curve of her ass. He didn't go fully flaccid around her, but despite her insistence on the late-night discussion, she was too tired for him to act on his dick's interest.

"Musa is a Turkish name."

Damn. "Yes, it is."

"I might know some people that could help Alan with his search."

"Really."

"The women who helped me escape the country after I got out of the prison lab."

"Why didn't you go directly to our embassy?"

"I wasn't feeling very trusting."

She'd been through an ordeal, but still something about her explanation raised a yellow flag for him. "Why?"

"The women who helped me told me that the rebels who took me had an inside man at the American embassy."

"Did you tell the State Department after you got home?"

"I didn't tell the State Department I'd been kidnapped. No one came looking for me. Not my family, not my country. But my government would have expected me to tolerate incarceration for my own good if I told them what happened to me."

"And you'd had enough of prisons."

"At least of other people's making. I hadn't figured out I was headed toward a personal prison yet." She sighed. "Besides, the women who helped me didn't tell me the name of the spy."

"How did they know about him?"

"They knew a lot of stuff I'm sure their own government and others wish they'd share."

"You think these women might help Alan?"

"If I ask them to. If I explain that I'm at risk again. They'll care."

The way she said the last two words made Myk's heart contract. "They aren't the only ones who care about keeping you safe."

Lana didn't answer and a minute or so later, her breathing told him she had gone to sleep.

Myk lay awake for a long time thinking about the conversation he and Lana had had in the dark.

Lana was reading the paper when Mykola came out of the bedroom, looking tousled and yummily tempting.

He stopped short when he saw her. "How long have you been up?"

"Since about three-thirty." She shrugged. She didn't need a lot of sleep. She just didn't have a lot of reserves when she actually got tired. Bedtime came and Lana was in bed. Full stop. Period. "I'd had that nap earlier and couldn't sleep any longer."

He frowned. "I didn't hear you moving around."

"I was quiet."

"You're showered. And dressed," he said accusingly.

"I used the shower in the guest room and I had clothes in the laundry nook I hadn't put away yet, so I didn't have to come back into the bedroom and wake you with my moving around."

He looked flummoxed.

She had a feeling she needed to get that expression off his face fast, or he was going to come up with an excuse to put someone else on her protection detail. "Your subconscious told you I wasn't a threat, so you slept through the noises I made. If I had been anyone else, you would have woken."

"I thought you said you weren't into psychology."

"It makes sense though, doesn't it?"

"I didn't hear you sneak up on me yesterday either."

"Further proof."

He looked grim. "I'm upgrading the security on your apartment today."

"Um . . . good idea?"

He frowned some more and grumbled something under his breath on the way to the coffeepot.

"Is this a bad time to tell you I called my friends in Turkey?"

He stopped pouring coffee for a split second, but then finished filling his mug. "What did they say?"

"Not a lot, but what they did know does not shine a favorable light on Musa."

"What exactly did they say?" He came around the half wall of cabinets that divided the kitchen from her small dining room.

Now came the hard part. "I can only tell you if you give me your word you'll keep the source of this information anonymous."

"I don't know the source, other than some women in Turkey."

"If you mention you got the information from Turkish women, it wouldn't take much to extrapolate who they are. There are few women with access to this kind of information. Wives of the men in power . . ."

"And the women who entertain those men in power." It looked like a lightbulb had just gone on in Mykola's brain. *"Belly dancers."*

"Yes."

"I have to mention the source of the information in my report."

"Then mention me."

"Whitmore is going to want to know who you got the intel from."

"We can't always have what we want."

"He's my boss."

"Whom you stand up to when it suits you." She'd heard that phone call yesterday and Mykola had proven that he did not intimidate easily.

In fact, he was pretty good at intimidating others.

"I don't like leaving important information out of my reports."

"I'm sure it's not the first time you've done it."

He grimaced. "No. It wouldn't be."

"Mr. Whitmore will understand you having to keep the source private."

"And if he doesn't?"

"Make him."

"And if I can't?"

Why was Mykola being so difficult? "Give me your word and I don't care how Mr. Whitmore feels about it."

"You trust me to keep my promise, even under pressure from my boss and perhaps others?"

"I do."

"Then, you have it."

Finally. She really didn't understand why men had to make things so complicated. "Thank you."

Mykola sat down across from her at the table. "Tell me what you learned."

"Ahmet Musa isn't a terrorist per se because he doesn't belong to any known factions, but his belief system is one that would lend itself to personal action."

"If he thought he could stick it to his enemies, he would?"

"Exactly. He can be cruel, has no remorse, and sees anyone outside his sphere as of little to no value."

"Did they know anything about his connection to Anibal Vega?"

"He is visited frequently by a rich and powerful man from South America. He calls the man brother, not by name."

"Anything else?"

"The last time they were together and called in dancers, they were full of themselves, even more than usual. Jubilant about something and very self-congratulatory."

"That puts a different complexion on the missing scrap metal."

"They aren't just interested in increasing their personal wealth."

"They want to crash an already fragile world economy."

"Yes."

"Turkey would be impacted, too."

"Musa thinks his government is weak and diluted by Western ideas."

"The man who would be king."

"Probably."

"Shit."

"It's not all that bad."

"How can you say that?" Mykola looked at her like she'd gone into the growing room for her enzymes one too many times without a gas mask. "These two sociopaths are planning a world financial coup."

"Their plans are worth less than the Absolut they finalized them over. The enzymes don't work to transform metals."

"They don't know that and even if they find out, they'll still want you to make them work." Wow, was he saying that her safety was as important to him as his directive to keep unstable or dangerous technologies out of the wrong hands?

"Maybe, but I can't. I've been thinking about it, doing some calculations in my head. The energy needed to catalyze the enzyme reaction would be more than current technology in that area, which is already prohibitive. Even if I could create an enzyme that would work for them, their plan would fail because it would cost them twice as much to create the platinum than it would to buy it."

Chapter 14

Mykola did not look appreciably relieved. "Their wealth may be immense, but it is not infinite. That's what it would take for them to succeed with a financial coup of the magnitude we think they are planning."

Instead of expressing relief, Mykola's features took on a worried frown. "How do you think men like Vega and Musa are going to react to that news?"

Oh. That's what had him concerned. Funnily enough, she didn't feel the angst he was showing. "About as well as my Kurdish captors when I refused to make the chemical weapons."

"You sound so damn calm."

"You aren't going to let them take me." She had to believe that even more than she had earlier when she'd gone through this discussion as a one-sided monologue in her head.

Mykola had been furious the day before when Lana evinced more faith in Mr. Smith than the TGP agent, but she'd needed time to see that he was truly one of the good guys. No matter what Mykola said to the contrary, he was the white knight, armor untarnished.

He loved his sister, but at no time had he entertained the notion of sacrificing Lana to the zealots as she'd at first suspected. His actions in putting himself in Elle's place between the cartel and Lana showed that, but his attitude consistently confirmed it.

"No, I'm not going to let them within ten feet of you."

"Then I don't see anything to get worried about."

"Nothing except the fact that I didn't hear you moving around for the last three hours."

"I didn't do that much moving." She indicated the paper in front of her. "I hardly ever get to read it front to back. I don't have the time."

He looked like he was going to say more, but just shook his head.

He took a long drink of his coffee before asking, "Anything interesting?"

"As a matter of fact, there is." She couldn't stifle a grin.

"What is it?" he asked in a wary tone.

"There's an announcement, a rather large one in fact, in the society column."

"About what?" The wariness was still very much evidenced in his voice.

"Your sister's wedding. Well, Mat and Chantal's is in there, too, but I don't think they're the reason Mr. Smith pulled strings with the media."

"Mr. Smith?" Mykola asked with the same tone he always used for her benefactor's name. It wasn't a complimentary one.

She gave him an admonishing frown. "I'm sure it was him. He got the paper to make a big announcement about the double wedding of two of ETRD's top scientists and the plans for their honeymoons."

"The African safari?"

"Yes, and the monthlong European tour Mat and Chantal are taking. The article makes it sound like they'll be city-hopping pretty much daily, but I know they intend to spend at least a week in the region Chantal is from. And it's made clear that Elle and Beau will be completely incommunicado for the month while in Africa."

Mykola looked pleased.

"Admit it."

"What?"

"Mr. Smith isn't all bad."

"The article is one more mark in his decency column," Mykola grudgingly conceded.

"What's the other one?"

"What he's done for you."

Lana was still reveling in the warm feeling she got from Mykola's remark earlier that morning when Casey floated into the lab.

Well, he walked, but he acted like he was floating. The expression on his face was nothing short of rapturous.

"You look happy," Lana said approvingly.

A beatific smile broke out on Casey's face. "She said yes."

"Nisha?" Lana couldn't believe her assistant had already asked the other scientist out.

"Who else?"

"I'm surprised you got up the nerve to ask her out already. I'm proud of you."

"It was talking to Myk."

Latent memory of the conversation she had overheard flickered through Lana's brain. "I'm glad he was able to give you some good advice."

"It was spectacular advice." Casey grabbed his lab coat from one of the hooks on the wall and put it on. "At first, Nisha said no. Because I'm too young and dating a coworker is risky."

"You convinced her otherwise?" Wow.

"Yes. I never would have even tried if Myk hadn't said what he did."

"His reminder that Nisha is an honest person?"

"Yes. I would have assumed she was making up excuses because she wasn't interested. Like a lot of women do." Casey's expression and tone said he'd had experience with those other women personally.

"Nisha isn't like most other women."

"No, she's not. I told her I didn't think age mattered when two people liked each other and shared a mutual attraction."

"She agreed?"

"Not at first, but I . . ." His voice trailed off and his cheeks turned rosy.

Lana felt her own eyes going positively round with shock. "What did you do?"

"I kissed her. It was wonderful."

"She must have felt the same."

"I think she did." Casey drew himself up, looking more confident than Lana had ever seen him. "I told her some risks were worth taking and I thought she was one of them."

"Oh, that was well done."

"She agreed, said yes to our date. I'm so happy."

"I think you should do the measurements on the *Lathyrus odoratus* this morning." There was no reason to ruin Casey's good mood with the smell from the enzyme growing rooms.

"Are you sure? That's not the usual division of labor."

"We're celebrating."

"You rock." He surprised her with a fierce hug. "As both a friend and a boss."

"Thanks, hon."

She wasn't at all surprised when she got a phone call later that morning from Nisha.

"I'd like to meet for lunch if you're free," the other female scientist said without preamble.

"I'm sure I can arrange that."

"Thank you."

* * *

Myk couldn't believe Lana was even asking him. "You can't go off-site for lunch without an escort."

"Nisha needs to talk about personal stuff. Having your glowering presence at the table isn't going to be conducive to our discussion."

"I don't glower."

"You do when you don't get your way. You don't think I should leave the safety of ETRD and if you do accompany me to lunch it will be grudgingly."

She had a point, but then so did he.

"As far as we can tell, these people have killed thirty-three people in the last six months, Lana. They aren't playing games. I don't want them taking you. I'm doing my best to keep you out of protective custody, but you can't take unnecessary risks."

Lana's hazel eyes narrowed. "Who wants to put me in protective custody?"

"Who doesn't? Elle left her two cents on my voice mail even though she doesn't know about the latest. Whitmore is practically apoplectic about the fact that you're still living in your apartment." Which really had surprised Myk when he'd talked to his boss that morning. Didn't the man get the concept of e-mail updates and reports? "Frank is so worried he salted his coffee rather than sugaring it when we talked this morning. Even Mr. Smith deigned to call me and suggest you going to a safe haven and Casey waylaid me in the hall to suggest I get you out of town for a while."

"Casey did that?"

"Yes."

"The little—"

"Friend? Very good friend? He cares about you, Lana. He doesn't want you hurt." None of them did.

She looked incensed. "He's at risk, too. He knows just as much about the material transformation projects as I do."

"We have no proof Vega or Musa are aware of that." But hell and damnation, he should have considered the possibility.

"You have no proof they are aware of me, only my enzymes."

"Damn it, Lana."

"Fine," she said in a tone that was anything but. "We'll get lunch delivered and eat in the courtyard. But you can't sit at our table and no glowering."

He couldn't believe how quickly she had capitulated and said so.

"I don't want to go into protective custody."

"Hell, sweetheart." He grabbed her and pulled her into an awkward hug. Awkward because she resisted, but she gave in and let him give the little comfort he could. "I'd like it better if you were more concerned with your safety," he couldn't help admitting.

"Of course I am, but watching over me is your job."

"You're right. It is." And he was inordinately pleased that she finally saw things that way.

She sighed, the sound muffled by his chest. "Mine is staying sane while crazy men once again target my research."

"I can help you with that."

"Let me guess." She looked up and met his gaze. "You consider sex stress-relief therapy."

He nodded solemnly. "It'll help keep your blood pressure steady."

"Not while we're making love, it won't." But she was smiling.

"After, though . . . you're golden." He tilted her head back just a tad more in preparation for the kiss he had every intention of giving her. "And the best part is that we can do it over and over again."

"You're crazy."

"I'm horny."

"You say it like that's my fault."

"Right now? Doc, it so is."

Her eyes darkened and her lips parted. He was lowering his head to kiss her when the sound of the lab door opening caught his attention. At least this time he hadn't been caught flatfooted.

He dropped his arms from Lana and tucked her behind him in one quick, smooth movement.

The blond man who walked in with a woman whose hair was the color of cooked carrots could be no other than Brett Adams and his wife Claire. Elle's description fit them both to a T.

Myk put his hand out. "You're early."

"Elle said you could use the help ASAP." Brett gave him an easy smile and shook his hand. "Brett Adams, but you figured that out already. This is my better half, Claire."

Myk shook her hand as well. "Nice to meet you both. This is Dr. Lana Erickson, the lead scientist on the project of interest to the Vega Cartel and Ahmet Musa."

The other three shook hands.

Claire asked, "Musa?"

Myk explained the Turkish connection.

"Thirty-three people?" Brett shook his head while his carrot-topped wife looked sick.

"Yes."

"The whole plan is monstrous," Claire said.

Myk nodded. "Probably because a couple of monsters came up with it."

"What's the plan?" Brett asked.

"Ideally, we would catch the bastards in the act of trying to steal the technology and send them both to prison. But I would settle for somehow convincing them that the enzymes are not viable."

Lana made a shocked sound.

Myk felt his shoulders tense under the scrutiny of the other three in the lab. Neither Brett nor Claire had said anything, but Myk could sense their questions.

"I'm not sacrificing Lana's safety to catch the bad guys." Not this time. He'd made the last compromise of innocents that he was going to make on his last case.

Brett nodded in understanding. Claire gave Lana an interested once-over and Lana just looked perplexed. Good, it didn't hurt to stump her brilliant brain once in a while.

Myk turned to Brett. "Elle was right. I do need your help. Now. We've got two primary targets that need twenty-four/seven protective surveillance."

"And there is only one of you."

"Right."

"TGP doesn't want to bring another agency in for manpower?" Brett asked.

"They would, but Elle and I convinced them to let you all handle the slack." He trusted Elle's newly merged company mates more than unknown federal agents.

Claire laughed and shook her head. "I knew the merger was a good idea. Elle is bringing in business already."

"She's a natural," Myk replied. "She didn't get the money to buy that car of hers working for the government."

Brett nodded, looking pleased. "You're right about that. Her security services were ranked at the top worldwide even when the company was primarily her cover."

"Now that she's focused on it full-time . . ." Myk let his words trail off.

Claire grinned. "Watch out."

"Exactly," Myk and Brett said at the same time.

Myk left Lana working in her lab. Feeling uncomfortable leaving her alone, even inside ETRD, he assigned a security guard outside the lab with instructions to alert Myk if Lana had visitors or if she or Casey left the lab.

He was in the middle of bringing Brett, Claire, and their team up to speed in Elle's former office when he got a text from Alan Hyatt.

> Followed a feeling. Found another interesting family connection. Former security officer Ramirez is related to Anibal Vega.

That was bad news on so many levels Myk didn't even want to start counting them.

Casey measured growth levels on the *Lathyrus odoratus*. He had to double-check his measurements after writing down Nisha's extension number in one of the boxes instead of the measurement he'd taken. Okay, so his full attention wasn't on his job this morning.

Who could blame him?

He had a date with the most scintillating, intelligent, and exquisitely beautiful woman in the world. None of the women he'd dated since coming to ETRD had measured up to Nisha, but he'd been so sure he didn't have a chance with her he'd never even bothered to ask her out.

Not until Myk gave him that pep talk. For a spook, the guy was pretty cool.

Casey usually preferred braniacs for company. They understood him, but Myk was smart in lots of ways. And he treated Casey like a person, like another man to shoot the breeze with. Not a big science geek.

Nisha didn't think Casey was a geek, either.

The way she'd responded to his kiss. Oh, man. Even if he hadn't been able to convince her to go out with him, Casey would have been wanking off to that memory for months. The prospect of making more memories like it, of actually spending time with the exotic materials expert, blew his mind.

His extremely pleasurable musings were interrupted when the growth lab's door opened. The evening security team lead, he thought her name was Ramirez, walked in with two other guards that Casey didn't recognize.

"Dr. Billings, what are you doing in here?"

"My job. What are you doing here, Ms. Ramirez?"

The three security guards gave each other a look and then Ramirez turned cold eyes on Casey. "I'm looking for Dr. Ericson."

"Oh?"

"Yes."

Casey wasn't like Lana. He didn't overhear stuff and then later put together whole pictures that no one would expect him to have. He was more a here-and-now person. But he was observant and he had done extremely well in scientific scenario building. Human scenarios were very similar, even if other people might not see it that way.

What he observed now was a team lead security guard who had not been on duty when Casey had arrived that morning. He knew for sure she hadn't been on duty because he'd stopped at the security desk to ask if they knew where in the building Nisha was. As the expert on exotic materials, she was in other scientists' labs more often than her own office.

The team lead, denoted by a different uniform shirt, had been a man. Casey had thought it odd because Ramirez was always on duty as the team lead on the day shift. He'd made a mental note to ask Lana if she knew what was going on, but then his curiosity had flown the way of cuckoos when Nisha had agreed to go out with him.

Ramirez was currently accompanied by two guards Casey had never met. He knew all the staff at ETRD by name, or tried to. It kept his observation skills sharp and, he hoped, improved his interpersonal relationship skills. He'd never seen these two.

Add the previous anomalies to the newly discovered fact that someone wanted Lana's enzymes for spurious purposes and he had a situation that didn't imply efficacious results.

Ramirez glared at him. "Is she around?"

"No." Technically that wasn't a lie. Lana wasn't around that growing room. "Is it something I can help you with?"

"No. Where is she?"

Now, that was another interesting anomaly. Everyone at ETRD knew that talking to Casey was as good as talking to Lana and vice versa. Unless it was a management decision that was needed and even then, most of the scientists would run stuff by Casey if Lana was busy.

"She's having coffee somewhere with the new security chief. He's jonesing for her." So, that was a half blatant lie, but he could always apologize later if it had been an unnecessary one.

Ramirez's eyes narrowed and she looked around the room as if expecting Lana to suddenly appear. Casey could feel the sweat break out on his palms. If the guards checked the other growing rooms, they'd find his boss and he'd be busted. But not before he had a chance to alert security.

If he pressed the panic button again and it turned out to be another false alarm, he'd feel like an idiot. But he wouldn't let that deter him. Somebody wanted Lana's enzymes and Casey had a bad feeling about the usually surly security guard and her companions.

"How long will she be?" Ramirez asked.

"I don't know. An hour, more maybe. I think she likes Myk."

"No doubt. You pushed the panic button when you found them kissing yesterday, didn't you?"

He felt his face heat. "Yes."

"We don't have an hour," one of the guards said. Casey was rapidly drawing the conclusion the security guards were fake.

Ramirez glared the man into silence and then locked gazes with Casey. "Where are the enzymes kept?"

"You mean the ones for the *Oryza sativa* and *Phaseolus vulgaris*?"

"Yeah, whatever."

"The enzymes Dr. Ericson is working on right now," one of the bogus guards added helpfully.

This was definitely not looking good. "Why do you want to know, Ms. Ramirez?"

She pulled a gun from behind her and pointed it at him. "Because I want them."

He saw guns on TV all the time, but looking down the barrel of one was nothing like that. It scared the hell out of him. The weapon in Ramirez's hand looked black, cold, and deadly. The expression in her eyes wasn't much better.

"We have some in the refrigerated storage in the lab." If he cooperated, maybe they would leave. Without Lana.

"Lead the way."

He left the growth room, praying all the time that Lana wouldn't choose right then to come out of the other one. His boss was a really great woman. She'd given him a chance when a lot of lead scientists had ignored his credentials because of his youth.

And she'd become a good friend since then. She didn't think he knew, but she'd been hurt before for her science. He wasn't exactly sure what had happened, but she'd said a few things that could only be interpreted in one direction.

He wasn't going to let her be hurt again. Not if he could help it.

He tried to sidle close to the panic button on his way to the cold storage, but Ramirez told one of the other guys to keep him away from it. The guy did it with a shove to Casey's back that sent him stumbling forward right into a lab bench.

He righted himself and glared at the guard, but didn't antagonize them with words.

He scanned his thumbprint to open the refrigeration unit. The lock clicked and the door's seal released with a long hiss. He pulled it open. He grabbed the samples they wanted, knowing the enzymes wouldn't do them any good. Not unless they wanted more rice or beans for dinner.

"Okay, here you go."

"Take it," Ramirez told one of the fake guards.

"What about him?" the guy asked with his chin pointed toward Casey.

Ramirez didn't answer, but gave the guard closest to Casey a look.

Casey felt a sharp blow on the back of his head and then the world around him went dark.

Chapter 15

Lana came out of the growing room and took off her gas mask. Casey wasn't in the lab and that surprised her. Measuring growth on the *Lathyrus odoratus* usually went faster.

She was cataloguing her own data when Mykola came into the lab closely followed by a man she'd never seen. He had dark hair and looked like he should be wearing army fatigues, not a suit.

Mykola's expression was as grim as she'd yet seen it.

"What's wrong?" she asked.

"The security guard that was fired, Ramirez, she has a distant family tie to Anibal Vega."

"So? We're all related to each other if you go back far enough."

"So, if she was feeding Vega information, he knows about most of Elle's security measures."

"Because the security staff was kept in the loop."

"Exactly."

"But you can't be sure she has anything to do with Vega. Having family ties wouldn't necessarily mean she'd ever met any of her Vega relatives. I've got distant cousins I wouldn't know from a rock star if they crossed the street in front of me."

"Cartels rely heavily on family connections, and Ramirez didn't strike me as supremely loyal to ETRD."

"Being surly does not equate to approving a conscienceless megalomaniac's business practices." They should get Casey in here. He was better at human scenario prediction than she was. "Wouldn't she have made a bigger effort to ingratiate herself into her job if she was spying on ETRD for the cartel?"

"Maybe. Maybe not. I'm not taking any chances that she leaked information to the cartel. We're upping security until we know how much of it has been compromised. You and Casey are going to have bodyguards twenty-four/seven. And not members of ETRD's current staff. Speaking of, where's Casey?"

"In the *Lathyrus odoratus* growing room."

"The one that doesn't stink?"

"Yes."

"You want to bring him out here so we can debrief him on protocol from here on out?" Mykola asked the stranger he'd brought with him into the lab.

"Sure thing."

"So, is he Casey's bodyguard, or mine?" Lana asked.

"Casey's," Mykola bit out. "I'm your bodyguard."

Man, was he snarly. "But you're lead on the case."

"And you are the primary target. Don't worry, I've got a backup for the times I need to be somewhere you aren't."

"I wasn't worried. I just . . . this isn't how you usually run a case, is it?"

"You'd know so much about that?"

"Practically nothing." She gave him a wry frown. "But I can guess."

"Your guesses are smart ones, doc. I'm taking lead on your

personal detail because no way in hell am I letting another man spend the night in your apartment."

"Oh." That was good. She really didn't want a stranger living with her. She wanted Mykola.

But that was a whole other issue entirely.

The bodyguard came out. He had a clipboard, an employee ID badge, and a cell phone in his hand, but no Casey. "The only things I found in that room besides plants are these."

Lana shook her head. "No. That can't be. Casey wouldn't leave his badge behind. He can't get into secured areas of the building without it, including our lab."

"Could he be in one of the other growing rooms?" Mykola asked.

Lana was shaking her head even as she headed for the growing room not being used at the moment. They were prepping it for a new cycle with the enzymes, but there was no reason for Casey to be in the room right now. Still, where else could he be?

But when she went inside it was empty, as she had expected it to be.

When she came out, Mykola was on the phone and he didn't look pleased. "Get your happy ass in here right now," he growled into the phone.

"Mykola, what's going on? Where's Casey?" Lana asked.

Maybe he was with Nisha. She should have thought of that possibility first off, though Casey leaving his phone and ID badge behind in the growing room made no sense to her. But he was a young man in love. They did crazy things, according to songwriters and poets.

"I don't know."

"Try Nisha."

Mykola nodded, immediately picking up the phone and asking security to patch him through to the other scientist.

When she could tell from Mykola's side of the conversation that Nisha had not seen Casey since first thing that morning, something inside Lana went icy. She was jumping to ridiculous conclusions. She had to be. There was no reason to believe Casey hadn't just decided to go get coffee, or something.

He'd left his badge and cell phone behind because he was still floating on the cloud of Nisha's acceptance of their date. And he was just being spacey. It happened sometimes. He'd left his cell phone behind more than once.

It used to really upset Lana. The ETRD-furnished phones had GPS locators in them. She felt safer for him when Casey had his on his person.

"Mykola?" she asked in a voice she knew pleaded with him to tell her that her assistant was okay.

She hated that. She didn't want to think the worst. She didn't want to live afraid. Not for herself and not for Casey.

"The guard we had posted outside your lab said no one entered or left while he was on duty." Mykola's grim expression had darkened by several degrees. "He just amended that to three security guards coming inside and leaving about ten minutes later."

"I didn't see any security guards," Lana said, her brain screaming at her to do something while her heart froze in her chest. "I was in the enzyme growing room."

"The security officer said Casey didn't leave with the other guards, but he isn't here," Mykola growled.

"He's left his cell phone lots of times, but he wears his ID badge on a neck lanyard. There is no reason for him to have taken it off," she said through numb lips, fear leaving its foul taste in her mouth.

The ETRD security guard arrived, out of breath and looking very, very nervous.

She didn't recognize him, but unlike Casey, who seemed to

know everyone, she rarely registered the faces of the people around her.

Mykola towered over the hapless guard. "You said no one came into this lab."

"I thought you meant people besides security personnel."

"Did I make that distinction?"

The guard looked around with a desperate expression, but no help was forthcoming. "No."

"So, three guards came in?" Mykola asked in a deadly quiet voice.

"Yes." The guard nodded, as if his affirmative would not be enough to convince Mykola.

"Who?"

"Uh . . ." The trapped expression that came over the guard's features did not bode well.

Lana's nails dug painfully into her palms.

"I don't think you're going to like the answer."

Lana wanted to scream at the man to just tell them.

Mykola simply glared. All silent, scary intimidation.

"It was, uh, Ramirez and two guards I didn't recognize."

"Ramirez, who no longer works here?" Mykola asked through gritted teeth.

"Uh, yeah."

"You let a guard who no longer works for ETRD and two strangers into Dr. Ericson's lab. *And you didn't call me?*"

"I didn't know that, at the time. I mean about Ramirez. I just started working here a couple of weeks ago. I don't know all the officers on the other shifts."

"But you recognized Ramirez?"

"Yes."

"You are now aware she was fired yesterday."

"I wasn't. Not until I got up to the station and read today's updates."

"You hadn't read the updates when you came down to

stand guard outside Dr. Ericson's lab?" Mykola asked dangerously.

"I was uh, I'm uh, well, see, I'm buying a house and I had to talk to the loan officer this morning first thing. I could have lost the lock on my loan, sir."

"When you discovered your error, why didn't you call me?" Mykola asked.

The guard looked away. "I didn't want to admit I'd messed up like that. I'm new on the job and Ms. Gray raised the bar on standards for our behavior. I love this job and I was really looking forward to the training we're all going to take."

"You're going to have a hard time paying that mortgage you are so eager to get without a job, aren't you?"

The security guard looked sick.

Mykola glared. "When the three guards left, you are absolutely sure it was the same three people?"

"Yes, sir. Definitely. The only difference was they were pushing a transport cart."

"And you didn't find this odd?"

"Uh, well, all the guards know that we're more grunt labor than anything. I mean we get asked to move stuff around the facility all the time. We're expected to be like James Bond or something, but we're treated like janitorial staff. Ramirez was saying so all the time."

"It never occurred to you that you were being asked to move highly sensitive research from one place to the next because far from being grunts, your company sees you as highly trained assets capable of ensuring the security of their projects?" the bodyguard asked.

Mykola snorted. "Highly trained, my ass." He took hold of the security guard's shirtfront. "Or are you? Are you as idiotic as you appear, or part of the conspiracy to take Dr. Ericson's assistant from the building?"

The guard blanched, but cold certainty settled inside Lana and she ignored the rest of what he had to say. She turned to her computer and pulled up a program she had hoped she would never have to use.

Mykola was saying something about getting footage from the security cameras when the GPS map filled Lana's screen, soon followed by a blinking dot. A moving blinking dot. Her relief was so great, she had to grab the bench so her knees didn't buckle.

She turned to Mykola. "Get him out of here." If the man was in on Casey's kidnapping, for she was now sure that was what had happened, she didn't want him learning of her backup plan to cover Casey's absentmindedness about his cell phone. "You won't let him go, though. Right? In case he is involved?"

"No, I won't let him go." Mykola turned to the bodyguard. "Collins, secure this man in the storage annex next to Conference Room B. Don't let anyone see you."

"You can't do that. It's against my constitutional rights."

Mykola grabbed the hapless ETRD security officer again, this time by his upper arms. "Listen closely, if Dr. Billings is hurt because of you, a violation of your rights is the last thing you're going to have to worry about."

The bodyguard left with his charge.

Lana swallowed tears that threatened to steal her ability to speak. "Don't bother with the cameras," she told Mykola.

He turned to her, ignoring her computer screen, his whole attention on her face. "Listen, sweetheart, we are going to get him back. Don't give up."

"I'm not, but I know where he is."

"How can you?"

She indicated the computer screen behind her.

"But he left both his badge and cell phone. How is he sending a signal?" He looked at her with respect tinged with concern. "You Lojacked your assistant just like you let Mr. Smith do to you?"

"Yes. It's in his watch. I gave it to him for Christmas last year. It's got lots of gadgets. He loves it."

"Does he know?"

"About the GPS locator?"

"Yes."

"No." She defied him to criticize her. "I never invaded his privacy, but he was at risk just like I was. And he kept leaving his cell phone behind. Not that it wouldn't be the first thing a kidnapper would throw away if he was taken. His badge only works in the building for location, but they left that anyway."

"They probably didn't want anyone knowing when they took him."

She nodded, barely holding it together.

Mykola rubbed her back. "We are going to find him."

"Yes. Before he gets hurt."

"Before he gets hurt," Mykola promised, that mixture of pity and respect on his face.

Then he grabbed his cell phone and dialed. "Brett, mobilize your people. We've got a GPS lock on Casey. He's moving South on I-5. I want to be in a position to retrieve him when the kidnappers stop."

"Are you going to call the police?" Lana asked.

"Kidnapping is a federal crime. If we call it in, the FBI gets involved."

"And that's bad?" she asked.

"It's unknown. I trust Brett's men. I know what kind of training they've had and what their priorities are."

He didn't know those things about FBI agents. He was putting Casey's retrieval and safety above everything, even his own case.

"Okay. Go get him, Mykola. Before they hurt him because he can't give them what they want."

"We will."

"You won't leave him in custody so you can assess the situation?" That seemed to be what federal agents did, but she knew Mykola wasn't acting like your typical agent.

"We're not going to risk the Vega Cartel getting him out of the country. We'll move in as soon as we get a window of opportunity. And if we don't get one, I'll make it."

"I believe you."

Lana watched the blinking dot that represented Casey move slowly on the GPS map. He and his kidnappers were still headed south of L.A. but had taken a turn eastward, toward the desert. That scared her. The population thinned out that way.

No one would see Casey dragged from the car. Or worse.

Claire Adams was working on Lana's computer while simultaneously talking into her Bluetooth headset and updating someone, probably both Mykola and Brett Adams, as to Casey's location. "I'm patching the GPS locator through to you now, Brett. Tell me when you have it on-screen."

Claire did some more typing and clicking, and then said, "Good," into the phone.

She met Lana's gaze over her shoulder. "They're directly linked now."

"That's good, right?"

Claire nodded. "They're going to get him back."

"They have to. He shouldn't be hurt. Casey didn't do anything wrong." Just saying it wouldn't change anything. Lana knew that. But the words tumbled out anyway.

"Myk's a good agent and my gorgeous hubby is no slouch. Remind me later to tell you about the time he saved my life."

Lana wanted to share the other woman's certainty. Only

no one had ever saved her. She'd had to do it herself and the cost had been enormous. She had to believe it would be different for her assistant.

"He can't help them. But they won't believe him. They'll hurt him to make him try."

"We won't give those lowlifes the chance." This time it was Collins who spoke. He'd stayed behind with Lana and Claire when Myk left.

He was under strict instructions not to let *anyone* into the lab. Not even Frank.

"Maybe you should have gone with them. They already took Casey." Lana's gaze skittered around the lab as if he would suddenly appear. She could only wish. "They won't be coming back for me."

"We aren't taking that chance." Collins could look almost as scary as Mykola.

She found that strangely comforting. "Are the other members of Brett's security team like you?"

"No way." He smiled. "I'm the charming one. The rest are a bunch of degenerates with hides tougher than titanium."

"I'll be sure and tell Sammi you said so," Claire threatened.

Collins actually looked a little worried. "That she is the exception should go without saying."

"I hope, for your sake, she agrees with you," Claire teased and then tensed. "They've stopped." She listed off an address.

"Does that sound familiar to you?" Collins asked Lana.

She shook her head. She didn't know of any research facilities in that area, but then the cartel wasn't likely to advertise one if they had it.

"I'm looking it up right now," Claire said. Whether to them or into the phone, Lana couldn't tell. "Good news."

"What?"

"It's not an airfield."

"What is it, though?" Lana asked, not feeling appreciably heartened.

"A warehouse."

Collins frowned.

"How far are Mykola and Brett from Casey?" Lana asked, not liking the frown on Collins's face.

"They're about fifteen minutes behind at this point."

So much could happen in fifteen minutes. Images flashed through Lana's mind. Mental pictures she so didn't want to experience right now. Memories of pain she could not bear to think of Casey going through.

She heard an odd sound, like the whimpering of a trapped animal. She couldn't think where it might be coming from.

A hand landed on her shoulder. "Maybe you should sit down for a little while, Dr. Ericson."

Her gaze flicked up to Collins. "I . . . Sit down?"

"Yeah. I think that would be a good idea."

"There are chairs. In my office. I don't go there much. But I can't see the monitor from in there."

"Don't you have the program on your office system?" Claire asked without looking away from the screen which she had split into two windows. One showed the GPS map and the other kept changing, like Claire was clicking through web pages.

"Yes. Maybe. I think so." Lana fought the thoughts trying to take over her mind, trying to remember if she'd put the GPS locator program on both systems.

Collins looked worried. "Let's go find out."

"I can't. What if he moves? I won't see. Why are you worried? You think something bad is going to happen, don't you?"

"I think that if I let you faint and fall down and bruise something your lover is going to shoot me."

"My lover?"

"Myk."

"Oh, yes. He, is." She hugged herself. "He promised to get Casey back."

"He seems like a man who puts a lot of store in keeping his word," Collins said, instead of reminding her that he'd been there when Mykola had made that vow.

She knew that, it was just . . . her thoughts were disjointed.

"I'll tell you if he moves," Claire said. "I really think you should go sit down for a minute."

What if sitting down put Casey at further risk? It wasn't a rational thought, but Lana wasn't feeling particularly rational right then.

Collins took Lana's arm in a gentle grip. "There. Problem solved."

He led her to her office.

She sat down, only to pop back up again. "I should be doing something."

But there was nothing she could do.

Only wait and pray that Mykola kept his promises better than anyone else in her life ever had.

Myk spun the car into the warehouse parking lot. He scanned the lot for the sedan ETRD's records had listed as Ramirez's automobile. There was no guarantee she'd taken it to ETRD to kidnap Casey, but there was a chance. And that was worth a look around the parking lot.

"There it is," Brett said from beside him, pointing near one of the secondary entrances to the warehouse.

Myk spoke into his headset. "We've located the kidnapper's car."

Brett gave the location.

"Roger that," was repeated three times by the team points.

Myk brought his restored Land Rover to a halt behind the sedan, blocking an easy escape. He and Brett were out of the car and headed toward the door as two steel-gray Escalades pulled into the lot, each SUV heading for a different entrance.

Myk pulled on the door, but it didn't budge. "It's locked."

"Do we incapacitate the lock?" Brett asked.

Myk asked into the headset, "Any other entrance viable?"

He was waiting for a response when he became aware of the thwap-thwap-thwap of helicopter blades coming from the roof.

Chapter 16

"They're warming up a copter. Get to the roof, whatever it takes," Myk instructed the team through his headset as he pulled his gun and shot an arch of bullet holes into the door around the handle, separating the door from its locking mechanism.

He turned to Brett. "With me?"

"On three."

One. Two. Three. They kicked the door in together, severing the door from its handle and lock.

Claire's voice came over the intercom. "Building schematics show access to the roof in the south stairwell. The warehouse is three stories high. There's a freight elevator on the east wall."

Brett drummed out directions to his operatives as he and Myk ran up the stairs toward the roof. "Team A, cover the elevator and the exit for the other stairwell. Team B, search the warehouse floors, starting with the ground level. Team C, you're up on the roof with us."

Myk tried to remember how long a helicopter took to warm up. They had three, maybe four minutes before the copter could go airborne.

He and Brett tore up the steps. The door at the top wasn't locked. They burst through it, dropping and rolling to opposite sides of the entrance as they came onto the roof. Myk landed in the one-knee, one-foot pose that gave him maximum maneuverability, his gun trained on the group headed toward the helicopter.

Ramirez and another man were dragging a struggling Casey toward the helicopter.

The redheaded scientist was doing his best to get away and swearing loud enough to be heard over the noise of the moving blades.

Myk shouted, "Let him go." He didn't wait for them to comply but shot the ground at Ramirez's feet.

Cement chips flew up, gouging her through the polyester blend pants of her ETRD uniform.

She yelled in pain and Casey yanked himself from her temporarily slackened grasp. Brett shot the other man holding the scientist, in the leg. He went down and Casey ran toward Myk and Brett, going straight for the stairwell and safety.

Smart man.

Myk was going to tell him he approved. Later. Right now, he was going to keep his own ass from getting shot off. Ramirez had a gun and the bitch knew how to use it. Myk rolled toward the entrance to the stairway, shooting toward Ramirez and the helicopter the whole time. Brett was doing a damn fine job of keeping the injured man pinned in place with directed fire.

Ramirez jumped into the helicopter and it started rising. The injured man tried to get to the lifting helicopter, but no way was he going to make it. Just to make sure, Myk shot at the helicopter, encouraging a faster liftoff. He wasn't about to shoot it down and deal with that red tape, but he'd settle for a perp to interrogate.

No surprise, his bullets bounced right off the obviously armored chopper designed to look like a civilian copter.

A gunman from inside the chopper targeted his downed comrade through a small hole in the window. A bullet went through the window, shattering the bullet-resistant glass, and slammed into the thug's shoulder, followed closely by the report of an armor-piercing sniper rifle.

The chopper went up and away in a rapid defensive retreat.

Trusting Brett's team to cover him, Myk rushed to the downed perp.

He was moaning and whining about his pain in Spanish. Myk ripped the perp's pant leg at the tear and gave the wound a cursory examination.

He shook his head and bit out in Spanish, "Stop your whining. It's a flesh wound. You'll live. For now."

The man spat at him. "Pig cop. Get me a doctor."

"You wish I was a cop, asshole." Myk grabbed the wounded man's shoulder and yanked him to his feet. "Let's go."

He met Brett and the rest of his team at the door to the roof. "Nice aim."

Brett nodded and then turned to Team C. "Police the casings. I want this roof pristine before the local law enforcement shows up."

"Will do, boss." Then the team got to work.

Brett grabbed the perp's other arm. "Let's go. Claire told Lana Casey's okay, but the doc is going to need to see for herself before she comes down off the ledge."

"She has a history." And had no doubt gone through emotional hell waiting to hear if they succeeded in rescuing Casey.

"Elle briefed us."

Myk nodded. Nothing else needed to be said. He was glad Brett was the kind of man who understood that.

Casey was waiting at the top of the stairs.

Brett frowned. "I told you to wait on the ground floor."

"I wanted to make sure Myk was okay. He's my friend."

Well, hell.

Myk left the perp to Brett and grabbed Casey's shoulder. "I'm golden."

"Okay. Good. I'm golden, too. Because of you guys. They were going to take me to Mexico. And probably South America after that. I would have . . . It would have been . . . I . . ."

"I know. Let's go."

Casey nodded and then winced, his hand going up to gingerly touch the back of his head.

"You okay, kid?"

"He," Casey said with a jerk of his shoulder in the wounded perp's direction, "hit me on the back of the head. Knocked me out. I woke up in the trunk of a car."

Casey was vibrating and Myk wanted to get him out of there.

"You good to walk?"

"Yeah. I think so."

"Try for me."

"I will, Myk." The younger man looked so sincere Myk figured he'd make it.

They took the elevator for Casey's sake and by the time they reached the parking lot, the SUVs from the rest of Brett's team were gone.

"One of the units will come back to pick up the cleanup team. Claire will monitor the LLEO's radio transmissions and direct our guys to a clean meet," Brett said, referring to local law enforcement.

"You work outside the law a lot?" Myk asked, impressed and a little envious.

"When we have to."

He got that. Had wished more than once on his last assignment he'd had that kind of leeway.

"You've got a base of operations here?" Myk didn't want to take the perp back to ETRD.

He didn't want the perp on the company's surveillance videos because he wasn't filing a full report to Whitmore just yet. He'd played it by the book on his last job and two children and their mother had lost their lives because of it.

He was never losing another innocent to protocol.

"We've got a house on the beach."

The house turned out to be an isolated fortress on a steep cliff overlooking the ocean.

"How the hell did you get access to this place?" Myk demanded of Brett as they drove through the security gate.

"Wolf designed it as a vacation home for a friend."

The private, winding road led to a huge house of what looked like white stucco, but Myk would bet his last paycheck was damn near impenetrable cement. It soared toward the sky in impressive beauty.

"Rich friend."

"Yes."

"Mercenaries make a lot, do they?"

"*We* did. And we survived to enjoy what we earned. We had a lot of compatriots that weren't so lucky."

"Obviously, this guy was one of the lucky ones."

"I never said he was a former merc."

"You didn't say he wasn't, either."

"True."

They pulled up to the house and got out. They were pulling the wounded cartel henchman from the back of Myk's Land Rover when Lana's car came screeching up the drive.

Collins was driving and he'd barely stopped when Lana

hurtled from the car and started running for them. Myk couldn't tell if she was headed for him or for Casey.

It didn't matter, because Casey threw himself at her. "Thank you. I can't believe you Lojacked me, but thank you!"

"You kept forgetting your cell phone."

"A lot of good it would have done me. Ramirez knew about the GPS locator in it."

"She didn't know about your watch, though." Lana's pale face had a smug cast to it. "No one is kidnapping my assistant and getting away with it."

Cursing in Spanish had Lana's head snapping up and around. She glared at the wounded perp. "What is he doing here?"

"Answering a few questions." Myk ushered her and Casey toward the front door. "Let's get inside. I want Brett's field medic to take a look at Casey's head."

"Casey's head? What's the matter with your head?" she demanded of Casey as they crossed the threshold into a spacious marble foyer.

It had a fountain that fed an indoor pond with tropical plants surrounding it. Very aesthetically pleasing, but it would also make good cover for someone who knew their way around the house.

Myk answered Lana's question when it looked like Casey wasn't going to. "Whiney-boy back there knocked Casey out with a blow to the back of his head."

"How did you know he knocked me out?" Casey demanded. "I didn't tell you."

"An educated guess. I was right, wasn't I?"

"Yes." Casey glared at Myk. "I didn't want her to worry." Myk sighed. "Too late."

"He hit you? Knocked you out?" Lana's voice rose with each word.

Surprising him and Casey, who gasped, she jerked away

from both of them, then spun around and marched back to the fake security guard.

"You spineless bottom-feeder!" She punched him right in the stomach.

The perp oofed and then screeched when she followed the punch up with a kick to his shin.

No one else moved. Or spoke.

Myk was in shock, but pleasantly so.

"What are you all staring at?" she demanded.

"I thought you were a pacifist," Myk said, doing his best not let his budding humor show.

"I kicked the uninjured leg."

That did it. He laughed.

She glared.

Brett whistled. "Damn, Myk, I think the doc might be a keeper."

Myk just shook his head. "Where's your medic?"

"Here." A man who looked like a soldier and too young to be a medic stepped forward. "I've got an examining room set up here on the first floor." He turned, clearly expecting Casey to follow.

Showing his good sense, the recently kidnapped scientist did just that. Lana started to trail after them, but Myk snagged an arm around her waist and pulled her back. "Where do you think you're going?"

"To make sure he's okay."

"He's fine. He's in good hands, and doc?"

She turned to look at him.

"Give him some space."

"I just want to make sure he's not seriously injured."

"Give it a minute, then we'll go check on him. Okay?"

"But . . ."

"He needs a chance to assimilate stuff a little." Myk

wouldn't be surprised if Casey needed a chance to let off steam through some tears. It was a natural reaction after what the younger man had been through, but Myk figured Casey wouldn't want to cry in front of his boss.

The perp yelled. "Hey, what about me? I just gave him a little tap. I got shot. I know my rights. You got to let me see a doctor."

Myk had the guy pinned to the wall, his hand fisted in the scumbag's shirt before Myk realized what he was doing. "Thirty-three people."

The guy gave him a belligerent glare. "What? That supposed to mean something to me?"

"It's the number of people your employer has had killed in the last six months pursuing his deranged plan to increase his power. *That we know of.*"

"So?"

"So, you piece of shit, those people had rights, too. They had the right to pursue their livelihoods without the threat of some sociopath cartel *jefe* ordering their deaths with less thought than he orders dinner. You get me? In this house? You are the only link we've got to that son of a bitch and your life is only worth what you can tell us." He snapped his fingers in the cartel thug's face. "That's your rights."

The bastard finally had the intelligence to start looking a little worried.

"Mykola."

"What?" he ground out without looking at Lana.

He didn't want to see the disappointment that was bound to be on her face right now. He had to do what needed doing, but that didn't mean it wasn't going to rip him up to lose her over it.

She was the idealist, after everything. He was a pragmatist.

And he was going to protect her. Whatever the cost.

"I went a little crazy after my stay in Turkey."

"Yeah?" Did she think this was a blip in his sanity? That he was going to calm down and realize he needed to turn this scumbag over to the authorities?

"Yes. I wanted to know if my parents loved me, if they ever had."

Oh, damn. "I'm sorry about that, sweetheart. I really am."

"Don't be."

"So?" He knew she had a point. His brilliant head geek might have a convoluted way of thinking, but she always had a final destination in mind.

He just hoped it didn't lead to her telling him she couldn't tolerate him or his methods.

"I developed a truth serum that is to sodium pentathol what morphine is to aspirin as a pain reliever. It doesn't have any long-term side effects, but it's extremely effective."

Despite the cool air in the marble foyer, sweat broke out on the thug's brow. Apparently, his grasp of English was better than good. He had something to hide, something his employers didn't want him sharing. Or he wouldn't be so nervous.

Even so, Myk wasn't nearly as interested in the perp's reaction as he was to Lana's. He spun to face her, dropping the cartel henchman, who swore as his weight settled back onto his wounded leg.

She was smiling softly at Myk, no condemnation anywhere on her face. "I changed in that prison lab, Mykola. I still don't believe in violence as a solution, but sometimes it is necessary."

He nodded, the level of his relief at her acceptance acute.

"We have to stop the sociopaths who think they can use my research to instigate a new power structure."

"Yeah, doc, we do."

She smiled. "Together."

"Together." So long as her involvement kept her completely, totally, indisputably out of the line of fire. "How long will it take you to whip up a batch of your truth serum, doc?"

"A few hours, but I need my lab."

"I'll take you back to ETRD." He turned to Brett. "Get his scratch disinfected and bandaged, then lock him up until we get back."

"No problem."

"Keep an eye on Casey. Find out if he overheard anything else. Make sure he rests."

"Will do."

"TGP's research agent identified a Vega office in Mexico. Maybe Claire and Alan can collaborate and pinpoint the location of Vega right now."

"I'm on it," Claire said. "You got his deets?"

Myk beamed the info from his phone to hers. "As far as TGP is going to know right now, there was an abortive kidnapping attempt on Casey."

"Got it."

"I want to see Casey before we go."

Myk thought about the best diplomatic answer to Lana's demand. "No."

"What do you mean, no?"

"He needs a chance to get himself together, without worrying about whether or not he's letting you down or not acting like a man in front of his mentor and friend."

Lana stared at Myk, a myriad of emotions swirling in her beautiful hazel eyes. "Oh."

"You can see him when we get back."

"What if he wants to see me now?"

"How about if I ask him?"

"Why is it okay for you to see him and not me? Aren't guys more worried about looking weak in front of other guys?"

"Sometimes, but not this time."

She frowned, but nodded. "Go ask him."

Casey was exhausted and in pain. "It's just a bump, though."

"You've got a tough head," Myk said.

"Yeah. I guess. I knew something was wrong. When Ramirez showed up. I'd seen the morning's team lead and it wasn't her."

"She was fired yesterday."

"Oh, wow. Wish I'd known."

"Lana's going to feel guilty for not telling you."

"It wouldn't have made any difference. I lied to Ramirez, so she wouldn't go looking for Lana. Something felt off and I wasn't taking any chances. I was hoping they'd leave if I gave them the enzymes, but they decided they would use me, too."

"You've got good instincts."

"Thanks. I feel like such a wuss right now, though."

"Why?"

Tears flooded the other man's eyes. "Because I'm still scared."

"That's understandable. You're not weak, though. You're strong and I'm impressed."

"Yeah?"

"Definitely."

"Thanks."

"Lana wants to see you."

"Could I . . ."

"See her later?"

"Yes. I don't want to hurt her feelings."

"But you don't want her to see you like this."

"Right." Casey looked awed. "How did you know?"

"It's natural."

"You don't think it will hurt her feelings? I don't want to upset her. I don't blame her or anything dumb like that. I wanted to protect her, and I'm glad I did."

"But now you have to deal with the aftermath of what that cost."

"Exactly."

"You're going to be fine, Casey, you really are."

"I believe you."

"Lana needs to whip me up some truth serum."

"Serious?"

"Yep."

"She's a woman of varied and inexplicable talents."

They both laughed, and Myk was still smiling when he explained to Lana that Casey said he'd see her when they got back from ETRD.

Thankfully, she let it go at that.

He didn't tell her how Casey had sacrificed himself for Lana's well-being. That would come later, when Myk could hold her when *she* cried.

Lana showed an incredible ability to focus when they got back to her lab. She didn't ask questions about Casey's rescue, what the plan going forward was, or anything else. She did one thing and one thing only. She worked.

Myk had no desire to interrupt her. And there were a couple of things he had to take care of himself. He'd brought Collins with them. He left the bodyguard and Lana in a locked lab while he interrogated the ETRD security guard who had made the mistake of letting the kidnappers in. Twenty minutes and several questions later, he was satisfied the man was poorly trained and truly enamored of his job.

His anger pushed him to fire the idiot, but instead, he assigned the security guard to the first group of trainees leaving for Oregon the following Monday. He ignored the man's effusive thanks and made a necessary trip to ETRD's main security office.

Forty minutes later, he was back in Lana's lab.

She hadn't moved from her position at the chemical lab bench.

"How's it going, doc?"

"Without incident."

He looked at Collins.

The guard shrugged. "I think that's good. She hasn't cursed once or dumped anything out and started over."

"Of course not. I don't make mindless mistakes." She sounded mortally offended.

"Glad to hear it."

She carefully picked up a tray of test tubes and carried them to something that looked like a microwave in the wall. She put the tray inside the unit, pressed a series of buttons, and it started with a quiet whir.

She turned to face him and Collins. "Right. The chemicals need to agitate for twenty-seven minutes exactly and then be left to rest for another hour before being brought to temperature and kept there for six minutes. Once it cools to ninety-eight degrees, it is usable. It will remain viable as long as it is kept at a temperature between sixty and one-hundred-two degrees Fahrenheit. Note, it is best to use it at moderate temperature."

"So, you're saying we've got a couple of hours of waiting?"

"Pretty much."

She'd told him it would take a few hours to make the serum, but that didn't stop him from wishing there was a way to speed the process up.

"We can use refrigeration to bring it down to usable temperature as long as we watch the drop in heat closely."

"You reading my mind, doc?"

"More like your expression."

"I have a great poker face."

"But you don't hide your impatience to interrogate the Vega lackey well at all. Two different things."

He wasn't so sure about that. Too many of his defenses disappeared around this woman.

"You want to know how Ramirez got into ETRD after being fired?" he asked in what he thought was a pretty brilliant change of topic.

Chapter 17

"**H**ow?" Lana asked, really curious.

Ramirez had been fired the day before. She shouldn't have been able to get into ETRD on a visitor pass, much less with access to the labs.

"She used an I.D. badge."

"Didn't they take hers?"

"Yes."

"She had a duplicate."

"Must have. A well-run cartel like Vega's would plan for contingencies like her getting fired."

"That's scary."

"It shouldn't be. Criminal mastermind or not, the guy and his minions couldn't plan for the contingency of you." Myk grinned at her.

Warmth suffused Lana at his approval. "You don't think I'm a nut job, Lojacking my assistant?"

"I think you saved him a lot of pain and probably his life."

"What about Ramirez?"

"She was logged entering the building at eight-forty-five this morning and leaving again less than thirty minutes later through one of the side entrances. She logged her cohorts in

as visitors and since her security clearance had not been removed on the computer yet, no alarms showed in the system
when she did so."

"But why hadn't her clearance been removed?"

"She'd given up her I.D. badge. As you know, security is a
dual program. The badge and a biometric scan."

"One is useless without the other." She'd run into that when
she'd forgotten her ID badge at home.

"Right. Duplicating the badge with its computer chip inset
is an expensive and tricky process."

"So, it never occurred to security that she might have done
so."

"No."

"And they put taking her clearance away on the bottom of
their 'to do' list."

"Near the bottom, anyway." Myk looked and sounded disgusted by that fact.

"I can't believe it."

"I could. Mr. Smith accepted the Head of Security's resignation on my recommendation ten minutes ago."

"But he was going to retrain at that place in Oregon."

"You can't train instincts and his sucked." Myk glowered,
clearly upset by what he saw as the other man's incompe-
tence. "He gave an important job to a family member whose
biggest recommendation for hiring was her distant familial
tie. When she began undermining the security staff with talk
about how the scientists here are treated like elitists while the
security force is treated like glorified custodial staff, he did
nothing more than give her a verbal warning. Even officers
with good instincts were having them subtly undermined by
her rhetoric."

"She primed the other guards to ignore things out of the
ordinary." It was a clever, if diabolical plan.

"Exactly."

"I hope I see her again one day. And I hope I have my stun gun out, primed to use." Which wasn't the kindest of sentiments, but that evil bitch had tried to kidnap Lana's friend. She deserved a painful jolt of reality.

"*You have a stun gun?*" Collins asked, sounding shocked.

She nodded, trying for nonchalant, rather than a kook who was way too worried about personal safety. "It looks like a cell phone. An attacker goes to grab it from me and gets a heck of a shock. Literally."

"You've got hidden depths, Lana-love." Myk didn't appear in the least like he thought she was an egg shy of a soufflé.

In fact, he looked impressed. And that helped something inside her that had been squirrelly since admitting earlier that she'd given Casey a watch with a GPS locator in it.

"You should see my can of mace. It looks like a pen," she said proudly. "It only holds one dose, but hopefully that's all I'd ever need."

"Not a tube of lipstick?" Collins asked with raised eyebrows.

Lana laughed. She couldn't help it. "Do I look like a woman who would carry around a tube of lipstick?"

"If I say no, does that get me brownie points or the rubber boot?" Collins asked with a grin and a wink.

Myk drew himself up to his full intimidating height and glowered down at the bodyguard with an exaggerated air. "Flirting with the doc is going to get you the wrong end of my boot, and it has a steel toe, not rubber."

Even Lana could tell he was joking. Mostly.

Collins laughed, but gave Myk a look that said he got the message.

That had Lana rolling her eyes. "If you get tired of playing Neanderthal, I've got something in my *Lathyrus odoratus* growing room I want to show you."

"I thought it was Cro-Magnon man."

"Let's just say you're primitive. Very."

"Works for me." He inclined his head to Collins. "Alert me immediately if anyone attempts entry into this lab."

Collins nodded and took a sentry position beside the door—all official and military-like. It reminded Lana of memories long buried, but she admonished herself that this time the soldier was on her side. Not her captor's.

That made all the difference.

Lana had never felt protected. Not even when Mr. Smith gave her the belly button ring with a locator in it. That was a passive stratagem intended to get her back. It was not the same as Mykola taking proactive measures to make sure *nothing* could happen to her.

"Thank you," she said to Collins.

"Just doing my job, Dr. Ericson. And if you don't mind my saying so, I'm glad to be called in on this assignment. We all are. You're doing something good here and nobody should be able to get in the way of that."

"I . . ." She didn't know what to say.

"It's okay, sweetheart." Mykola brushed hair that had come loose from her ponytail behind her ear. "Not everyone is as blind as your family to the true value of what your brain can do."

She felt tears well up and she spun away, not wanting Collins to see. "Thank you. Again." She crossed the lab to the growing room.

Mykola followed her with that silent tread of his. How he managed to do it with steel-toed boots, she had no idea. But even if she couldn't hear him close behind her, she could feel his presence. It made her feel so many things, safety only one of them.

He stepped into the room right behind her. "I'm glad whatever it is you want me to see is in the place that smells like flowers, not rotting corpses."

She grinned, but didn't answer.

The door shut, sealing them into the fragrant, silent room. Perfect.

She didn't need an audience for what she wanted to show him. Her gratitude.

Myk leaned back against the door. "What did you want me to see, doc?"

She stopped right in front of him and reached up on tiptoes. "This."

Lana kissed Myk. Long and sweet.

Damn.

If this was what she wanted to share with him, he was all for it.

When she ended the kiss and stepped back, he grabbed her shoulders to stop her from getting too far away. "What was that for?"

Under the growing lights, her eyes were shiny with suspicious moisture. "You saved Casey. You didn't try to use him to further your case. You cared and you kept your promise."

"I always keep my promises, sweetheart."

"I believe you."

Those two words went straight to his heart and his dick. While a big neon sign flashed *DANGER—Emotional Waters Ahead* in his mind, his body vibrated with the need to get closer to her.

But some things needed to be said first. "You are as responsible for keeping Casey from being taken out of country as those of us who went chasing after him."

She hadn't just been paranoid for her own safety, but as soon as she'd recognized the potential danger to Casey, she'd done something to mitigate it. Lana was a doer and the world needed more people like her.

"I never wanted him to go through what I did in the prison lab," she said in an almost whisper.

"He won't. We'll make sure."

"Yes." The trust shining from her eyes was a damn potent aphrodisiac.

His cock was filling fast and his fingers itched to take that ponytail holder from her strawberry-blond, silky waves. "If Collins wasn't out there, I'd make love to you right now."

"We can lock the door from the inside."

"He'll know what we're up to."

"Does that worry you?"

"Nope. I assumed it would bother you."

She leaned past him and locked it, then looked up at him with a naughty twinkle in her hazel eyes. "Does that answer your assumption?"

"Come here."

But instead of waiting for her to comply, he pulled her into his arms. "You feel so good against me."

"I concur." She tilted her head back.

He accepted the clear invitation and kissed her. There was nothing slow or gentle about this meeting of their mouths. They devoured each other, rubbing their bodies together, staking claims he had no desire to analyze the meaning of.

All he knew was that it felt damn fine. Too good to worry about a bunch of emotional stuff like a teenage girl.

Intense pleasure gripped him low in his gut and he was once again in risk of creaming his pants. He pulled back. "How do you want this?"

"There's an empty growing table in the back of the lab. Casey and I use it for paperwork sometimes. We like this room."

He made what he hoped was an intelligent sound and grabbed her wrist, dragging her toward the area she had indicated.

The empty table was just the right height. Sexy images of what they could do here flashed before his eyes. He had to get them naked. Right now. He could ask her to take her clothes off, but he'd rather be the one to do it.

He stripped her, starting with the lab coat that had been featuring in his fantasies since he first walked into this lab. Today's T-shirt was hot pink and had Tinker Bell on the front. He thought the fairy with Mae West curves particularly appropriate for his own sweet little vamp. Her bra was all lace and the same color as her T-shirt. Would her panties match?

He'd know soon enough.

He had no patience for a slow striptease today. It hadn't taken Casey's words for Myk to realize he could have lost Lana today, but they'd confirmed the fact.

As sexy as the bra was, her naked skin was even more sensual. He undid her pants and pushed them over the gorgeous curve of her ass. How right he had been. Her G-string panties were nothing but a triangle of hot-pink lace.

Delicious. But they had to go, too.

When he had her completely naked, he stepped back and just looked. She didn't rush him, or ask why he was staring, or any of the things that women often did when they were feeling self-conscious.

Her mouth tilted in a half smile and she put her hands on her hips, pushing her generous breasts into prominence. "Like what you see?"

"Like is an anemic word for my reaction to your nude body." He indicated the now rock-hard dick behind his zipper. "I could drill nails with my cock right now."

She laughed softly. "I'd rather you drilled me."

Oh, damn. Just damn.

He picked the lab coat up off the floor. "Wear this?"

"Fantasy?" she asked in a low, teasing voice.

"Oh, yeah."

She crossed her arms and tapped her chin and made him wait several seconds for her answer. "Okay, on one condition."

"Name it."

"You keep your clothes on. Just take your leather pants down far enough to get your penis out."

His knees about buckled at her words. "Fantasy?" he asked in a choked voice.

"Oh, yeah," she said, copying both his words and his tone.

He put the coat on her and then lifted her to sit on the edge of the growing table. "You turn me on so much, doc."

"Uh huh . . ." She was too busy sliding her hands under his T-shirt to talk.

He liked that, so he didn't even think about complaining.

He pushed the edges of her coat apart so that her rosy-tipped breasts were framed by the white fabric. Talk about decadent. "Beautiful."

"You get turned on by odd things."

"This from the woman who wants me dressed while I'm inside her."

"Don't pretend it won't turn you on, too."

"Baby, everything I do with you turns me on."

"Good."

"Fantastic." But he was done talking. He wanted to taste. And he wasn't going to make love again without finding out if her nipples were as sweet as they looked.

He pushed her back until she was propped up on her elbows.

"I'll never be able to work at this table without thinking of us, like this, again." She didn't sound like that bothered her.

He just winked and then leaned forward to lave first one hardened peak and then the other.

She moaned, letting her head fall back.

Lana arched her back toward the hot lips teasing at her nipples. How had she lived so long thinking this was barely worth the effort?

The answer was that sex had never been like this before. If it had, she'd be an addict.

Her hips canted off the table of their own accord, her body desperate for the joining Mykola had promised her. The man always kept his promises.

"Always, doc, always," he said against her breast, letting her know she'd once again been babbling out loud.

She had to control that trait, or she was going to blurt something out loud neither of them was ready to hear her say. Something she had yet to even allow her mind to fully grasp.

That thought disintegrated along with every other one as he took one turgid tip into his mouth. Hot suction sent pleasure pulses straight to her already contracting vaginal walls. She'd never realized there was such a direct correlation between stimulation to her nipples and near orgasmic muscular shudders in her pelvic cavity.

She'd always liked having her breasts touched, but too many men thought that large meant insensitive. They groped, squeezed, and pinched without building up to the pleasure that Mykola just seemed instinctively to know how to create.

She jerked up and down with her hips, but the only titillation he gave her was his mouth to her breasts. He was so very good at that. He tugged on her tender flesh with teeth pressing just hard enough to give pleasure and no pain. He tickled the tops of her nipples with the tip of his tongue, making her cry out from the jolts of bliss zinging through her.

He suckled, pulling the carnal delight out of her one tug at a time. It was too much and not enough and everything in between.

"Please, Mykola. Inside me. Now." She had never wanted so much. She had never begged, or moaned like this, either. Not before him.

The sound of his zipper going down was a symphony of pleasure to her ears. Then other sounds, a tear, a growl from him as his hands were busy where she could not see. And then his penis was there, the big head pressing against her entrance made dewy in welcome.

"Please," she begged some more. "Make it hard and fast."

He did, pulling her hips until her bottom rested right on the edge of the table. He slammed into her and she would have slid backward but for the lab coat whose sleeves held her in place while he pinned the bottom of the garment to the table with his thighs.

He was so big and he went so deep, hitting her cervix with thrust after thrust.

The pleasure didn't build so much as explode through her, bringing a massive orgasm that stopped her breath so she couldn't even scream.

He didn't have the same problem and his shout was deafening.

Afterward, he wrapped her up in his arms as he kissed her back to earth, talking sweet nonsense in her ear about her beauty and how much he wanted her.

"You're amazing, Mykola," she panted.

"You're the incredible one. I've never been with a more responsive woman."

"Sex just isn't like that for me," she admitted, the realization of why that might be settling in her heart and head at the same time.

She wanted to believe it was just Mykola's immense sexual talent and experience, but unfamiliar emotions from deep within her soul said it was more than that.

"It's not usually like that for me, either."

She forced herself to meet his gaze, to accept whatever she found in the dark brown depths of his eyes. "But it is sometimes?"

His jaw went granitelike and he stood up, pulling away with care, but inexorably. "I don't talk about my past exploits with my current partner."

"Is that all sex is to you, an exploit?"

"That's not what I said."

"That's exactly what you said."

"Look, we need to get back to the case. Is there somewhere in here we can clean up?" He looked around. "You water the plants with something, right?"

"The growing trays are equipped with soaker hoses."

"Oh." He wrinkled his nose. "Maybe you've got paper towels, at least?"

"There's a sink." She and Casey used it to wash their hands after mucking about in the dirt. "It's behind the small divider over there."

She wasn't sure why the building designers had put the wall up between the sink and plumbing area for the hoses and the rest of the growing room. It would have made more sense to her to have the sink by the door, but she was the scientist, not the architect. Though she'd come to work very soon after ETRD opened its doors, she'd had nothing to say about how the labs or their connected rooms were set up.

They cleaned up in silence, but afterward, they still smelled like sex to her sensitive nose. She kind of liked it, even if she didn't particularly enjoy feeling like a soon-to-be *past exploit.*

No matter how he defined what had just happened, for her it had been earth-shattering. And life changing. It might come with a cost and pain would very likely be her final emotion from this relationship, but she knew now she would not die never having been in love.

After straightening her clothes, she turned to him with a smile tinged with inner sadness. "I'll never look at my lab the same way again."

"That would have never happened in your lab." He didn't return her smile.

"Oh, really?" He'd seemed just as hot for it as she had been, but then her experience was admittedly dismal compared to his.

"Really. Elle installed security cameras in all the main labs. They run on a random pattern, but I would not risk having our naked asses caught on one." Now he smiled, but it was a bad-boy smirk accompanied by a wicked little wink.

No regrets or emotional baggage weighing him down.

"Your behind wasn't naked," she pointed out in her own effort to keep it light.

"Actually, it was, just not the rest of my body." He leaned down and spoke right in her ear. "You wanted it that way, remember? Did it do it for you?"

In ways she could never explain to him. "Yes."

"Good. I aim to please. Can we put your serum in the refrigerator yet?"

So, that was that? Well, what had she expected? He'd told her their *fling*, for lack of a better word, wasn't about hearts and roses. At least not for him.

No matter how out of this world the sex was, she couldn't mistake his consideration for her pleasure as anything other than sexual prowess. Certainly not emotion that matched her own.

"No, but soon. I'll get a cooler ready for transport so we can head back to the beach house while it is cooling."

"I like the way your mind works, doc."

"Thanks." He wouldn't say that if he knew the three little words flitting through her mind right now though.

And if it killed her, she wasn't going to say them out loud.

Chapter 18

When they came out of the lab, Collins was arguing at the door with a furious Nisha. "What do you mean you can't let me in here? I have clearance for all the labs in the building! Where is Lana? She was supposed to meet me for lunch."

"She's not available right now, ma'am."

"Not available?" Nisha demanded. "I don't believe it. I'm calling security." She spun on her heel, clearly intent on leaving to do just that.

Collins reached out to grab her. She spun and kicked out, missing his groin only because he did a quick turn and deflect.

"Damn, she's not exactly your traditional Sunni woman, is she?" Mykola asked.

"First of all, she's not Sunni. She's from India, but she's an American citizen and she's not Islamic at all. Second, no, she's not traditional anything." They needed to rescue Collins before one of Nisha's well-aimed blows landed where she intended it to. "I'm right here, Nisha."

The golden-skinned woman stopped struggling with the bodyguard and looked past Collins. "Lana! You missed our lunch and you didn't answer your phone and Casey isn't answering his, either. And you've got G.I. Joe guarding your door. He won't let me in the lab."

"Let her by," Mykola told the other man. "Why didn't you call me?"

Collins stepped aside. "I would have, but she required my full attention."

"He means I would have forced my way past him if he had picked up the phone. Are you the new head of security?" Nisha demanded of Mykola, giving him the evil eye.

"I am the *acting* head of security."

"So, you *are* responsible for this man not allowing me access to this lab?"

"Yes."

Nisha's eyes narrowed and Lana worried for Mykola's safety, no matter how good an agent he was. "He had a good reason for ordering extra security measures."

"Really? I notice they aren't in effect in the other labs. What's going on, Lana?"

"A very dangerous South American cartel attempted to kidnap Casey today."

Under her dusky complexion, Nisha paled. "Casey? Is he all right?" She looked around the lab, her expression agonized. "Where is he?"

The naked emotion on Nisha's face wasn't mere worry. It went much deeper than that. The woman loved Casey. *Was in love with him*. Lana wondered for how long, but didn't dwell on that.

What was important right now was reminding Casey what was good about his life and helping Nisha to see that the man she cared for was okay. Her concern for Casey was a beacon no one could miss. She hadn't once asked why he'd been kidnapped, or if anyone else at ETRD was at risk. Her entire focus was on Casey's well-being. A situation like this could bypass barriers Nisha would never have let down otherwise.

Both she and Casey deserved a chance to explore the very real emotion they felt for one another.

Love didn't always come at the right time or to reciprocating people, but for Nisha and Casey, it was all there. And Lana wasn't going to let anything stand in their way. Not Anibal Vega or Ahmet Musa. And not Agent in Charge Mykola Chernichenko.

"Casey is fine." She didn't mention the possible concussion from when that stupid thug knocked her friend on the back of his head. "If you wait a few minutes, we'll take you to see him."

"Like hell we will," Mykola said.

Lana ignored him.

Nisha did too. "Is he at home? I'll go now."

"No. He's someplace safe."

"And he's going to stay that way," Mykola firmly inserted.

Lana frowned at him. "I'm not proposing we compromise his safety. I wouldn't *do* that."

"She's an unknown. We can't take her to the beach house." What he didn't say, but she knew he was thinking, was that no one but they and Brett Adams and his team knew where the house was.

Clearly, Casey and the others would be safer if it stayed that way, but Lana wasn't a threat.

"I . . . He's safe." The usually supremely confident scientist looked uncertain. "I shouldn't bother him."

"Casey won't see it as a bother, believe me."

Nisha looked away and sighed. "He's so young."

"Does that really matter?"

Nisha was silent for several seconds, but then shook her head resolutely. "No. No, it doesn't." She took a deep breath and let it out, like she was letting go of a wearying burden. She let her gaze settle back on Lana. "I fell for him the first time I saw him. He's so sweet and attractive. So different from the men back home, both in how he looks and the way he treats me. Like he recognizes and respects my intelligence, but still sees my femininity. I haven't dated anyone else in more than a year. But I thought it was wrong to pursue something with him."

Lana smiled. "And then he pursued you."

"Yes."

"Are you glad?"

"Yes. I still wasn't sure this morning, though. I was meeting you for lunch to talk it over."

"I figured as much."

"He told you he asked me out?" Nisha asked.

"He told me he wanted to. I encouraged him. And then, yes, he told me he did it and that you said yes."

"That's a relief. I was worried you wouldn't approve and that would make it hard for him at work."

"You should know me better than that."

"Lana, I don't think anyone working for ETRD knows you well enough to guess how you would respond to anything but a chemical reaction."

"Casey does."

"He's your friend."

"Yes."

"He's mine, too."

"But he's more, isn't he?"

Nisha drew herself up. "Yes. I hope he's as ready for a relationship as he thinks he is."

"He may have boyish features, but he's twenty-four. Not a child."

"I'm thirty-two."

"Still young."

Nisha laughed softly. "You think so?"

"Definitely."

"What if he changes his mind down the road? My feelings for him are only going to grow."

"You don't think his for you will?"

"I don't know."

"He compares every woman he meets to you. They all come up lacking."

"He told me that."

"Did you believe him?"

"I wouldn't have said yes to the date if I didn't."

"Then believe *in* him. And in what you two can have together. He's not going to break your heart. I know him."

"Even if he were, I'm willing to take the risk." Her eyes said it all. "I have to."

Lana was going to hug the other woman, even if that sort of thing wasn't her usual way, but Mykola inserted himself between them.

He looked ready to grind bricks between his teeth. "Speaking of risks, taking you to see Casey might not be the best course of action."

Considering his expression, the words were surprisingly diplomatic.

Lana's weren't. "You're wrong."

"Lana—"

"No. This is too important to let Vega's actions mess it up. This thing between them is the real deal. Anyone with eyes can see that. Casey *needs* to see her. He's going to be worrying about telling her what happened and what her reaction will be. He's going to be concerned that the fact that he was kidnapped will make him a bad relationship risk. He needs to see that Nisha still wants to go out with him and see where their relationship can go."

"You don't think he's got other things on his mind right now?"

"Right. Because you wouldn't allow emotional considerations to take your mind off target, you assume Casey's the same way. But the target is his life and a really important part of that is Nisha."

"They haven't even dated yet."

"They've known each other for two years. They care about each other. You don't have to have sex to fall in love." Though it sure could make you see your emotions more clearly when you did.

She didn't tell Mykola that. It wasn't something he'd want to hear.

"Casey's going to be worried that what happened to him has messed up what he was hoping to build with Nisha. We can't let Vega and Musa win that way."

Surprising her, Mykola rested his hands on her shoulders, rubbing along her clavicle bones with his thumbs. "Being kidnapped does not mark a person as a relationship leper."

Like he would know. "It can."

"Did it for you?"

"I never told anyone exactly what happened to me, but I alluded to it with a couple of the men I tried dating when I started working here. They dropped me fast. One even admitted that dating me wasn't worth putting his own safety at risk."

"That bastard."

"But that's not how I see it," Nisha passionately interjected. "Casey's work may be more obviously targetable, but my own knowledge of exotic materials is matched by less than a dozen people in the world. I know that puts me at risk, but I'm not about to live my life letting fear dictate my actions."

Lana turned away from Mykola and the false sense of comfort from his touch. "Good for you. Now, we just have to show Casey you feel that way."

*   *   *

Myk called Brett while he waited for Lana to pack some things to take to the fortress on the ocean.

"One of my men could have packed for her," Brett said.

"She agreed to stay at the beach house until this situation is contained. She didn't even argue." He thought that had more to do with the fact that Casey would more readily co-operate with staying if she did than her own safety, but still it had been a huge concession for her. "Letting her pack her own clothes seemed like a pretty small reward to offer her."

Brett grunted an agreement. "Collins is watching your six?"

"Yes. Although considering his altercation with Nisha, he's probably due a hazard pay bonus."

"All the operatives on this mission are getting hazard pay."

"And TGP is covering it?"

"It's cheaper for them than keeping a team of their own containment agents for cases like this that require more man power."

"I guess you can hide a lot in a budget for an agency no one knows about."

"Don't you believe it. The CIA hides plenty in theirs."

"True."

"You do realize that once this other scientist comes to the base, she's going to know where it is."

"The TGP background check on her was a hell of a lot more thorough than ETRD's on their security guards. She's clean."

"I hope you're right."

His gut told him he was. Besides, it was important to Lana and, like it or not, that made it important to him. "According to Lana, seeing Nisha is exactly what Casey needs."

"She could be right about that. He's only mentioned the woman's name a total of thirty times since you all left."

Mykola fought a chuckle and lost. "Young love."

"Love at any age can turn a man into a blithering idiot."

"Speaking from experience, are you?"

"Claire ran me ragged."

A month ago, Myk would have made a sarcastic comment, but he couldn't make the words pass his lips now. Not when he was allowing Lana to pack her own things. He'd calculated the risk and determined it was minimal, but the longer the time from the aborted kidnapping, the higher the risk of Lana returning to her apartment.

Anibal Vega wasn't the type of man to give up. However, he had to make plans since his initial attempt to grab one of the scientists working on the enzymes had failed. That made this little trip low risk.

The problem was, any other civilian would have gotten a resounding no from him if there was *any* risk.

"Her serum should be ready when we get to the house." No use dwelling on that which remained inexplicable.

"She's a woman of hidden depths, isn't she?"

"Yeah." And didn't that make him feel ridiculously proud?

"Casey overheard a conversation between Ramirez and a man she called *jefe*."

"Vega."

"That's my guess."

"What was it about?"

"She told him she'd taken the assistant instead of the lead scientist. From her side of the conversation, it didn't sound like Vega was happy with the substitution. They were speaking in Spanish and she assumed Casey couldn't understand them, or she didn't care if he overheard. Regardless, he pretended to be as monolingual as she thought he was. He's a smart kid."

"And then some."

"She talked about meeting Vega at the airstrip and going parasailing."

"That doesn't make any sense."

"No, but Casey's still pretty shaken up."

Something niggled at the back of Myk's mind. He yelled out, "Hey, doc, you know anything about geography?"

"Some," Lana called back from her bedroom.

"Aren't there some islands off the coast of Vietnam called Parasail?"

"Paracel," Nisha said from her place on the sofa. "They're a pretty much unpopulated group of islands that both Taiwan and Vietnam lay claim to. Some think they've got untapped oil and gas reserves around them."

"I think we've got our storage spot for the scrap metal," Brett said after Myk repeated what Nisha had said to him.

"We've got to get that information to Whitmore. If any of the barge crew are still alive, they are probably on those islands somewhere."

"Right."

"If I tell Whitmore, I'm going to have to tell him how I got the information."

"You don't have to tell him *how* we got Casey back or that we have a Vega henchman in custody to tell him Casey overheard something Vega wishes he hadn't."

"True."

"We should confirm our guess during interrogation of Vega's man before we tell anyone what we suspect."

"Even more reason to interrogate the little bastard as soon as possible," Myk muttered.

"You got that right."

Myk walked into the dining room, away from Nisha and the door to Lana's bedroom. "I'm going to have to resign after this case."

"You want a job, we've got one for you."

"And work for my little sister?"

"There is that." Brett, the bastard, was laughing.

Mykola said, "We'll be there in thirty-five minutes," and clicked the phone shut.

He was not going to work for Elle, but he wasn't going to be able to keep working for the feds any longer, either. There was a reason for protocol, even if he couldn't make himself stick to it.

One dose of Lana's truth serum and ten minutes later Vega's henchman became loquacious as all hell. He also got teary eyed. Although he couldn't seem to help answering their questions, he was aware enough to realize that if Vega ever got hold of him after this, death would be the easiest outcome he faced.

It was good thing Mykola spoke Spanish, though, because the man slipped into it pretty much immediately.

His name was Jorge and he was merely a hired henchman, not family to Vega like Ramirez. He knew more than he realized, and not all of it useful for this particular investigation, but Mykola took note of everything Jorge said.

He would compile it, and later, he would share it with the other federal agencies who might find the information of interest.

According to Jorge, Ramirez had planned to take Casey directly to the airstrip near their office in Mexico. From there, they would go to the Paracel Islands, just as they'd surmised from Casey's garbled memory.

But what Casey hadn't known from the little he overheard was which of the islands they would be headed for, the coordinates of the airstrip in Mexico, the exact location of the office within the Vega compound that the man himself used. or Anibal Vega's personal e-mail address.

Jorge hadn't realized he knew that one, but it had been in the header of an e-mail Ramirez had sent to him with instructions for the abduction.

It took several hours, but finally, Myk was satisfied with the information he had obtained.

* * *

Myk found Lana in the bedroom Brett had assigned to them. He didn't know if Lana realized yet that they were sharing, but she didn't seem surprised to see him.

"How did it go?" she asked.

"That serum is scary stuff, doc."

She nodded. "I decided not to use it with my parents. Truth isn't all it's cracked up to be."

"They do love you, sweetheart, even if they don't understand you." The cards he'd found on her dresser had all been personalized and quoted sentiments that indicated a depth of feeling he'd be willing to bet her family had been incapable of expressing in person.

"That's the conclusion I came to. They let me turn their attic into a fortress and never once said a thing about it. Ultimately, both my brother and my parents encouraged me to go with Mr. Smith when he came recruiting."

"I'm glad."

"Yes?"

"I wouldn't have met you if you hadn't started working for ETRD."

"You're glad you did, even knowing Vega tried to kill your sister because of me?"

"He tried to kill her because he's a megalomaniac without a conscience. That's not your fault."

"That's not what you said the first time you came into my lab."

"I was wrong."

"I bet you don't admit that often."

"As often as I need to. Which happens rarely."

She rolled her eyes, but smiled. "Like I've said before, arrogant."

"Confident."

"Whatever."

He leaned down and kissed her. Couldn't help himself. "I'm

meeting with Brett and Claire to discuss the best course of action from here on out. I wondered if you wanted to sit in."

"Are you in the habit of inviting civilians into your planning meetings?"

"I think you know the answer to that."

"Then why me?"

"You are smart, sweetheart. Maybe the smartest person I've ever met. I think you could add to the discussion."

"Seriously?"

"Baby, your family may not have seen the benefit of your incredible brain, but I'm not them."

"Wow."

"Will you?"

"Yes."

"It might get sticky, with the whole mostly pacifist thing."

"I can handle it."

"I believe that."

"Let's go."

"Wait. What about Casey? He's very good at scenario building."

"He's got good instincts, too. He figured out that something was up with Ramirez even though you hadn't yet told him she'd been fired. He lied and told the kidnappers that you were out of the lab before they revealed their intentions."

"He was protecting me," Lana said, awestruck.

"Yes. He's your friend."

Her eyes filled with tears.

Myk pulled her into a hug. "It's okay, doc."

"He could have been hurt because of me."

"Nah, he's probably alive because his instinct was to protect you."

"What do you mean?"

"If they had known you were in the lab and that they

could take you instead of him, do you think they would have left him alive and capable of telling us what had transpired?"

"Oh."

"Yes, oh."

"I want to kick Vega, and not in the shin."

"Hell, sweetheart, I'd let you use your stun gun there. The man deserves it."

He was rewarded with a laugh.

Chapter 19

Lana would have asked Casey how he was doing, but there was no need. Sitting across from her at the large glass dining table, he was positively glowing with happiness. Nisha sat beside him and looked equally enamored with life.

"You look awfully pleased with life for a man who survived a kidnapping attempt," she teased him.

"How's the headache?" Mykola asked Casey as he took his own seat at one end of the table, to Lana's left.

"What headache?" Casey asked with a grin.

Nisha shook her head, but she was smiling, too. "He has taken a pain reliever and the medic confirmed he has no signs of concussion. Nevertheless, after this discussion, I will be making certain he rests."

"I guess scientists are harder headed than I thought," Brett drawled from the other end of the table. "Here I thought that was just computer experts." He gave a sidelong teasing glance to his wife on the right.

"Maybe almost as thick-skulled as former mercenaries?" Claire mused.

"I'll show you thickheaded." Brett turned his bright blue gaze full on his wife and winked. "Later."

Lana could feel the heat of that look from where she sat farther down the table. The intensity of the two security experts' relationship was as obvious as the reaction in a vinegar-baking soda chemistry experiment.

"I said thick-*skulled*." But Claire was smiling like a woman does when she's contemplating something very pleasant.

Brett shrugged and winked again. "Whatever."

"You can save show-and-tell for another time," Mykola said. "Let's focus on the plan for right now."

"Did you get enough from that guy to make a plan?" Casey asked.

Mykola and Brett had interrogated the man together and they took turns telling the rest of them what they'd discovered.

"You got Vega's e-mail address?" Claire asked, practically salivating.

Brett smiled at his carrot-topped wife. "I thought that would make you happy."

"It will make it a whole lot easier to locate his ISP and the computer he's currently using to retrieve his e-mail."

"And if it's a laptop?" Nisha asked.

"Vega still has to sign on to a server to send and retrieve e-mail. Servers are location static."

Mykola looked up from his notes. "We're pretty sure that right now, he's working from his Mexican office."

"Right. That will make it easier to locate the system, won't it, sugar?" Brett asked.

Claire nodded, looking keen to get started on her computer hacking. "Definitely."

"But he could keep his plans to fly to the Paracel Islands. He's got the enzymes and he's unaware they don't work on metal. It would make sense for him to want to try them out," Casey said.

"I've been thinking about that. What about informing the Taiwanese government that the islands are being used for criminal activity?" Brett asked.

"I've already briefed Whitmore to that effect without revealing the source of my intel. I may have overstated what you heard in the course of your aborted kidnapping," Mykola said to Casey.

Casey shrugged. "Why not tell him about Jorge?"

"Because we would have to release him to the FBI and we weren't ready to do that before interrogating him."

"Are you going to now that you have?"

Brett and Mykola gave each other significant looks, like they were trying to decide how to answer that question.

"The only two significant side effects of the truth serum I created are the need to sleep once it wears off and memory loss. Jorge won't remember being interrogated, or anything else that happened one to three hours prior and post to taking the drug." Lana didn't want to be responsible for Mykola stepping so far outside the box of his job as an agent that he couldn't get back in.

"So, we could turn him over to the FBI and he wouldn't remember being here?" Brett asked skeptically.

Lana wished she could give a definitive yes, but she couldn't. "That's a strong possibility if you move him while he is still sleeping off the effects of the drug."

"We can't risk him knowing the location of this house," Mykola said.

"We blindfolded him on the way," Brett replied. "Even if he does have memories of the house itself, all he would remember was that it was by the ocean. There's a hell of a lot of ocean in California."

Casey looked thoughtful. "He could be a bargaining chip."

"True," Mykola said with an approving look at Casey.

"You don't sound like a man who is following procedure," Lana said to Mykola with concern.

"I'm not. I'm doing my job."

"They're not the same thing?"

"Not in this instance."

"But I think what Lana is saying is that they can be, at least to an extent," Claire remarked.

"Exactly. If you did a thorough job interrogating him, there's little if anything you and Brett will be able to get from him in a subsequent session. As bargaining chips go, he's not great. He's not related by family to the Vega Cartel and he's not high on their organizational pyramid." Lana had to get Mykola to see reason. "There's no compelling reason to wait to turn him over to the FBI."

"I'll inform Whitmore we have a perpetrator in custody and ask him how he wants me to proceed." Mykola gave her a questioning glance. "Will that make you happy?"

"I just don't want you to lose your job trying to keep me and Casey safe."

"That should be my job, but politics and directives get in the way. I won't let them in this case."

"I appreciate that more than I can say, but please, don't do anything stupid."

Mykola reached out and tugged her ponytail. "No plans on being stupid, doc."

She found herself smiling and wishing she could lean across the table and kiss him. She forced herself to stay where she was.

"Do you think the Taiwanese government will succeed in catching Vega?" Casey asked.

"With the CIA's help, they've got a chance." Brett didn't sound too hopeful despite his words. "With the scrap metal, and lost barges, they should be able to connect Vega to the hijackings."

"Which would ensure he got a prison sentence. Right?" Nisha asked.

It was Claire's turn to look doubtful. "In a perfect world, yes."

"But we don't live in a perfect world," Lana said with a sigh. She should know.

"No, we don't." Mykola's tone was bleak. "I don't want to rely on catching Vega with his pants down. He's a cautious man. If I was him and I lost out on getting my scientist, I'd try the enzymes in my own labs, rather than taking them to the Paracel Islands. And I'd make another try for the scientist."

"But don't you think he'll wait to make the try until he's sure he can't make the enzymes work on his own?" Brett asked. "Like you said, he's a cautious man. He shouldn't attempt a second kidnapping until he's sure it's necessary."

"I concur with that scenario," Casey said. He frowned. "But I wish there was a way we could be sure."

Claire sat up straighter, excitement emanating from her. "Maybe we can. I've been working on a program that turns the microphone on a person's computer into a listening device. I can try to get it onto whatever system or systems Vega is using to retrieve his e-mail."

"Do you think you can do it without detection?" Mykola asked.

"Yes. But if his security is good, it will take longer." She took a few notes on her handheld. "I can also monitor all incoming and outgoing e-mail correspondence to whatever systems I get into."

Mykola said, "Do it."

"What about contacting Vega?" Lana asked. "We could tell him the enzymes don't work for metals. That there is no way of designing any that would without requiring exorbitant amounts of energy for the change process."

"You mean via his e-mail?" Claire asked.

"Yes."

Claire looked like she thought it wasn't a bad idea. "If nothing else, it will encourage him to test the enzymes."

"Giving us time to figure out what his plans are," Brett said with satisfaction.

Mykola didn't look nearly as pleased as the others. "Or, it will make him more determined to come after Lana."

"What if we give them what they want?" Lana asked as an idea came to her.

Mykola erupted from his chair. "What the hell are you talking about?" He dropped to his knees and spun her chair to face him so they were looking directly at one another. The others in the room might as well not have been there. "You are not giving yourself up to keep Casey safe."

"No, I'm not. But what about giving up my research?"

"Do you really want them to be able to double their drug crops even if they can't make the metal transformations?" he asked.

And she loved him for doing so. He understood her and the fact that such an eventuality would be devastating to her.

"She's talking about all the research up until six months ago, aren't you, boss?" Casey asked.

"Exactly." She grinned at Mykola. "Until I had an epiphany six months ago, all my enzymes killed the test plants rather than transforming them for a second harvest. I wouldn't have to fake anything. My notes are all there and the research will match up with whatever it was that Ramirez managed to smuggle out of my lab. Which from the note you said you saw in the margins was the preliminary project proposal for Frank."

"If we tell them the enzymes don't work, their testing of the enzymes proves they don't work and their own scientists have no luck with the enzymes, they'll believe it's just a pipe dream like particle transportation technology." She hoped.

"Which they are closer to than they've ever been," Claire said with a laugh.

"Yes, but we're still far from transporting people," Lana replied without looking away from Mykola.

"True."

Lana bit her bottom lip and looked at Mykola. "So?"

"It's an idea worth considering, but I think we should wait on contacting him." He brushed her lip with his thumb, soothing the stinging flesh.

"Let him sweat out what we found out from his lackey," Brett said.

Mykola nodded, his focus still entirely on Lana. "And give him time to see for himself the enzymes don't work, so he'll believe your research."

"There's a hell of a lot more going on there than your status report implies."

Myk had never thought Whitmore was stupid. He'd just told his boss he had a person of interest for the FBI. During a phone call.

"We stopped the attempted kidnapping of Dr. Casey Billings."

"And took a hostage, which you are just now telling me about."

"He is not a hostage, sir. He is a perpetrator in custody."

"Duly noted."

"Are you going to get the information on the Paracel Islands to the CIA and Taiwanese government?"

"Yes."

"If there are any survivors from the hijackings they will be with the barges and scrap metal at the coordinates I gave you."

"I'll make sure the information is acted on immediately."

"If you take too long and Vega gets worried his thug knows too much, he's going to order their deaths and the pulling out of his people."

"You asked me to trust you to do your job, Myk. Now you need to trust me to do mine."

"Noted, sir."

"Thank you."

There was a few seconds of silence.

"Are you going to tell me the rest of your plan?"

"No, sir."

"Damn it, Myk."

"What you don't know, you don't have to act on." Like illegal bugging of a drug lord's computer system.

"True. I'll assume you are proceeding with caution then."

"That would be best."

Whitmore was laughing when Myk cut the connection.

Whitmore called back fifteen minutes later with directions on turning Jorge over to the FBI.

Later that night, Myk and Brett met in the living room and went over the schedule changes necessary to integrate Brett's people into the security teams at ETRD and compensate for the staff that would be gone on training. The shift alterations for the ETRD guards would not begin until Monday, but Brett's people would be there every shift beginning the next day and continuing through the weekend.

While the majority of ETRD's scientists and technicians did not work weekends, some experiments required daily checking and measuring. Lana and Casey would not be returning to work until Monday, and they would be under constant guard.

"What about Elle's wedding?" Lana asked from where she had settled beside Myk on a white leather sofa.

The thing was eight feet long, with lots of room for her to settle into her own space, but she chose to curl right up into his side. Damn if he didn't like it.

"What about it?" he asked her.

"We're going, aren't we?"

"We all are."

"My partners will be here to attend as well," added Brett.

"And up security. Not that I don't think Roman's got it covered with his men."

Lana laughed softly.

"What's funny?"

"It's kind of fitting, you know? For the Queen of Badass to have a wedding with more security than royal nuptials."

"Here's hoping she's enjoying the irony of it. I want her wedding day to be special," he admitted.

"It will be. She and Beau will be promising their love and commitment to one another. Nothing more special than that."

"You're a romantic aren't you, doc?"

"I never thought so. Maybe a little."

"I did it!" That happy screech was followed by a dancing redheaded dervish whirling into the living room.

Claire threw herself at her husband and kissed him soundly, then turned to face them, ensconced happily in her husband's lap. "I not only got the program working on the main system but I managed to identify the other computers in the compound using the same ISP and planted the program on those as well. It was a bitch mother in PMS to crack the first system, but once I got it, the others were easy."

"That's fantastic news." Lana grabbed Myk's thigh. "We're bound to learn something about his plans now."

"We already have." Claire looked deservedly smug. "According to what I overheard, they're planning to test the enzymes on six different metals tomorrow. At the Mexico facility."

"So, we were right that they aren't going to go to the islands just yet."

"Yep."

"Any word about Jorge?"

"They don't think he'll break. Apparently, Vega works very hard to keep his minions loyal. Intimidation and pain being his favorite tactics."

"He's assuming we wouldn't use nontraditional means to break Jorge."

"Exactly. Ramirez has also assured him that Jorge doesn't know anything important."

"He didn't know how much information he had stored in that pea brain of his either, but thanks to Lana's very effective serum, we got a lot from his latent memories."

"I'm glad it worked."

He put his arm around her, letting her settle even closer to him. "You're awfully smart there, doc."

She giggled.

It wasn't a sound he expected to hear from her, but he liked it. Claire and Brett were smiling at them, too.

"So, when do your partners arrive?" Lana asked.

"They're in town already, but they're staying at a hotel near Elle and Myk's parents' home."

"Why aren't they staying here?"

"The fewer people that come and go from here, the less likely our base will be discovered."

"This security stuff is a pain."

"Just be glad you're not the president."

"I am." Lana gave a visible shudder. "I am so not the political type." She shifted and laid her arm over Myk's stomach. "I heard you call Lise's husband Wolf, but I heard Elle refer to him as Joshua," she said to Brett.

"We still call each other by nicknames we picked up in the Rangers."

"What's yours?"

"Hotwire."

"And Daniel Black Eagle's?"

"Nitro."

"It's pretty cool that you are all still working together."

"Nitro and Josie are part-timers," Claire said. "They were going to quit completely, but she hasn't been able to get pregnant and she wanted something to keep her occupied. She found out she missed training soldiers. So, they run a few select training camps a year and help out as needed with the company."

"What do they do the rest of the time?"

"Daniel watches his wife while she consults on computers," Claire said. "He's a bit protective."

"We all are," Brett admitted sheepishly.

"Just wait until they adopt."

"Is that what they are going to do?"

"They've been talking about it." Claire snuggled into her husband. "Josie wants to start a family before she's thirty-five."

"That gives her some time," Brett said.

Claire rolled her eyes. "Not to hear her tell it."

"What about you two?" Lana asked.

"I want kids, but I want to wait a while. We thought I was pregnant early in our relationship, but discovered it was a hormonal imbalance from stress. We decided to wait a bit after that. I like what I do . . . being an active part of the dangerous assignments, but that has to end when I have kids. It's only fair to them."

"Right."

"So, ask me again in a couple of years."

Brett looked supremely happy about those words and Myk knew there had to be some sort of story there.

Chapter 20

Lana uncurled from her position beside Mykola when he and Brett began going over security for Elle's wedding again.

Mykola grabbed her around the waist. "Where you going, doc?"

"Upstairs." She didn't say she was going to bed because that was not what she had planned.

"I'll be up in a bit."

"All right."

He gave her an appraising look, but let her go.

Had he expected her to balk at sharing a room? Perhaps he could have asked, but she'd made no secret of the fact that in bed with with him was exactly where she wanted to be. That look had been a lot like the ones he'd been giving her off and on for the past couple of hours—while she cuddled against him as they chatted with Brett and Claire. Okay, so she wasn't usually a cuddly person. Or at least hadn't been for a very long time.

She could remember evenings watching television curled up against her mother, nights when she'd had a bad dream and her father had rocked her back to sleep on his lap. Long car rides when her big brother had let her fall asleep against him in the backseat.

She could still remember the feeling of warmth and security her family's physical closeness had given her.

Those times had come before her parents had realized what a freak she was, before they admonished her to "be normal" when they went places. Her precocious mind had embarrassed and sometimes angered them when she had questioned things other children her age took for granted. Like how the television worked, or why other children believed in Santa Claus.

She'd been four years old when she'd realized it was a physical impossibility for the jolly man in the red suit to be real. She'd taxed her mother with the truth and Mom had said it was magic.

Lana had looked sadly at her mother and wondered how she, a grownup, could not know magic wasn't real. Her mother must have read the look correctly because she'd gotten offended and sent Lana to her room. A place she had spent increasingly more time—by her own choice. There was no one to disappoint when she was alone.

However, that summer, her parents took Lana and her brother to Disney World. And she'd realized magic *did exist*—in that very special world. The world where fairy dust made boys fly and scullery maids ended up married to Prince Charming.

It would be another couple of years before she found out that another world of magic existed. That of science. But her love of all things Disney had been cemented.

Her desire to have her bedroom decorated with Mickey and Minnie Mouse was one of the few things her parents had thought was normal about her as a child. They'd changed their opinion when her tastes in décor had not changed by the time she was a teenager. Though by then, they'd given up on their daughter being anything like *normal*.

After all, she'd graduated high school before she was an official teen and was doing college course work when her physical adolescence had hit. She'd studied the changing reactions in her body like she did everything else. She was probably the only fourteen-year-old who understood what was going on in her body better than what was going on around her.

She'd often wondered as an adult why her parents had supported her accelerated learning if they'd wanted so badly for her to be like other children her age. Because support it they had, in so many ways. She would never have been able to get the education she had without their help.

So, why had they been so disgusted with the other trappings of her overactive brain?

She'd never come up with an answer. It no longer mattered. She'd finally accepted herself for who she was, even if others did not. If along with that acceptance came the realization that she was not a person who inspired deep, abiding love in others, that was her problem and no one else's.

So, maybe, she wasn't supercuddly. She didn't pass out hugs like they were potato chips and she'd never snuggled with previous boyfriends. Not that Mykola was her boyfriend.

He was her temporary protector and lover. *Temporary* being the operative word.

But inside her heart, he was so much more. He was the man she loved. Lana was in love for the first and, she was absolutely certain, the last time in her life. Love required implicit trust and she was never going to meet a man like Mykola who both inspired that trust and had opportunities to prove himself worthy of it.

He might see her as a convenient bed partner, someone to practice his amazing sexual skill on, but to her, he was *the one*—the man that if she could not spend the rest of her life with, she would spend the rest of her life loving. Even if that love was never spoken aloud.

Other women were probably not like her, but she didn't suddenly think sex was all that. She thought intimacy with Mykola was all that *and a hot fudge sundae*. She'd been attracted to him on their first meeting and had somehow fallen in love almost as quickly. She didn't understand it.

She couldn't build parameters to make her emotions logical; she just knew they were there, forever in her heart. It was those feelings that made making love with Mykola so incredibly special.

He was the only man she *wanted* to cuddle with. The single person on the face of this earth she wanted to hug and kiss the moment she saw him and before leaving him, even if it was simply to step out of the room for a moment. Not that she gave in to every urge, but she gave in to the ones that were safe to.

She was storing up experiences, memories to warm a future that would be void of what she had come to realize was the one true source of magic. Love.

Myk opened the door of the room he and Lana shared. Soft Middle Eastern music played in the background, the bedding was pulled back invitingly, but the bed was empty. There was no sign of Lana anywhere in the room, but the door to the bathroom was ajar, light spilling from within.

"Lana?"

"Go out to the balcony. I'll be right there." Her voice was different. Lower. Sultry.

Did she plan to seduce him on the terrace? He sure wouldn't fight it if she did. He hadn't made going out there off limits because the house had been built with security heightened in every feature, including the balconies off the bedrooms.

They were blocked from above by an impenetrable overhang and looked out onto the ocean with no angle available to a sniper's bullet unless he was in a boat off the shore. A sonar in the security room sensitive enough to pick up an oversized shark monitored the waters off the beach for just such activity.

He'd been craving her all day, their interlude in her lab only increasing his desire for her, not slaking it.

"Don't make me wait."

Soft laughter came from the bathroom. "I don't plan on it."

The balcony had been cleared of the two lounge chairs that had been out there earlier. There was a pile of pillows against the wall to the right. He sat down, guessing that was what he was supposed to do. The exterior light was on, bathing the outdoor area in a soft yellow glow. The sound of the ocean mixed perfectly with the music coming from the bedroom and the fresh, salt-laden air made him long to share this bit of tranquility with her.

The volume of the music increased and the lights inside the bedroom went off.

Then she was there, framed in the doorway.

It was Lana, but not. *This woman* was some exotic beauty from a foreign land. She wore a belly dancing costume of shimmering gold decorated with clear crystal stones and shiny beadwork. Her hair was brushed out in a curtain of strawberry-blond silk framing a face with kohl-rimmed eyes and glossy raspberry-painted lips.

He would never have imagined his Disney-fixated scientist could look like this.

It did things to both his heart and libido. She'd made herself up for him. Not a room full of strangers, or a classroom of women who wanted to learn from her, but for him and him alone.

She stepped forward with one foot, her body shimmying in perfect time to the music. She began to dance and Myk thought he would lose his mind. Her every move was mesmerizing, tantalizing, and looked so damn natural. As if her body had been created to shift, shimmy, and sway just that way. No male fantasy could begin to compare with the reality of his beautiful scientist dancing for him.

She glided across the balcony as if she were floating, rather than using the bare feet he saw peeking out from under the swirling skirt. Unbelievably, she enhanced the fluidity of her movements with a sheer veil that washed through the air like a floating wave around her.

She danced close and then shimmied away, keeping him tense and on edge, waiting to see what this sexy stranger was going to do next.

The music built in crescendo and her movements built with it, her body contorting in dips and whirls that made him dizzy with desire. At one point, her veil landed in his lap, covering a painfully stiff erection. She gave him a sultry little smile, showing she'd seen the evidence of his need before she covered it up.

She continued to gyrate her hips and curve her body in positions that both astounded and delighted until she did a final shimmy and dropped to her knees in front of him, her body arched backward, her arms fluttering to the ground with the final bars of the song.

She held the pose, her arms stretched away from her head, her breasts in prominent relief and the thin silk of the skirt falling between her legs to outline the curves of her thighs perfectly. He held his breath, unable to move, unable to speak.

Finally, he gained control of his vocal cords. "I'm afraid to touch you. Afraid you will turn into a mirage and shimmer away."

"I'm real." She did a small shimmy in that position. "Touch me and find out."

Needing no second invitation, he did just that, his palm reverently cupping the warm skin right below her belly button ring. "You were incredible. You *are* incredible."

"Thank you. I wanted to be. For you." She lifted herself with nothing but her tummy muscles until she was kneeling before him.

He found himself smiling. "Impressive, sweetheart."

"I told you belly dancing was good training for my body."

He wasn't about to argue. He'd never seen such control of each individual muscle in the human body in his entire life.

He reached out and buried his hand in her hair, wanting to kiss her but strangely hesitant. "That was the most amazing gift anyone has ever given me."

"I want to give you more."

"Yes."

She leaned forward and he pulled her into him at the same time so that she ended up on his lap. They kissed.

It was unlike any kiss they had shared so far. It was not merely passionate, though it was that. It was not merely a connection, a way for their bodies to acknowledge one another's nearness, though it was that as well. It was something deep.

Something beautiful.

"Let me touch you," he whispered against her lips.

"Always."

There was something permanent and oh, so beautiful about the way she said that single word.

He started by exploring the parts of her body not covered by the dancing outfit. The perfect slope of her shoulder, the swell of her breasts, her gently curved stomach, the porcelain column of her neck, and her infinitely kissable lips. He did not hurry, wanting to relearn each dip and crevice of this stranger, yet not, in his arms.

When he had caressed every centimeter of her exposed skin easily accessed in the revealing outfit, he kissed her again.

This time he put all the passion and emotion watching her dance had engendered in him in it. She responded as if she was the one who had been teased and enticed to *her* limit.

He did not know how long the kiss lasted, but his desire to be inside her became a burning need, a scorching inevitability.

Somehow he got her top and skirt off, enchanted to find that she had not worn even a thong under the swirling silk. He stripped off his own clothes as well, wanting skin on skin.

She'd hidden condoms in the cushions and covered his cock with trembling fingers while he explored her honeyed depths as she straddled his lap. She was more than ready for him. Her vaginal walls convulsed around his fingers as if trying to draw them in deeper. She was the only woman who did that to him and he'd discovered he loved it.

Then she was lowering herself onto his throbbing dick and taking him into paradise.

He made an animalistic sound that would have embarrassed him in any other situation or with any other lover.

She merely returned it.

She rode him with the same grace as she danced, twisting her hips in a way no other woman had ever been able to do while topping him. He played with her beautiful bare breasts, teasing her nipples and touching her with complete freedom.

It was incredibly erotic. Electrically so. He felt the build of his climax flash through him. He wanted her to come with him. He reached between their bodies, but she shook her head.

"Touch my breasts. Pull on my nipples," she demanded as she increased the swivel of her hips and ground their pelvises together.

Her body clenched around him as she released a glorious cry of completion, pulling him into his own orgasm, one so intense, his head swam. It was all he could do not to slip into oblivion.

She buried her head in his neck, her lips moving in a silent litany against his skin.

He couldn't begin to form coherent words, so he remained silent, wallowing in the best sex and aftermath of his life.

Long minutes later, he cleaned them both up with a small towel he found under the same cushion as the condoms.

Then, he carried her to bed.

The double wedding between Matej Chernichenko and Chantal Renaud and Beau Ruston and Elle Gray went off without a hitch.

Myk was more than a little pleased. Between him, Elle's partners, and their brother Roman, security was so tight, an unsanctioned Q-tip couldn't have gotten through.

Still reeling from Lana's gift the night before, he nevertheless watched for any suspicious activity. There was none.

Whitmore came along with other agents from The Goddard Project. They all manfully refrained from talking shop. Elle's new business partners had come as guests as well as providing additional security details. Family had come from as far away as the Ukraine. Myk's parents and *baba* were in their element.

Baba had dropped several hints about great-grandchildren and the fact she wasn't so young any longer. Her sister in the Ukraine, she informed both couples, already had three great-grandchildren. Myk thought both couples ought to have a good chance at getting a start on that endeavor with month-long honeymoons ahead of them.

He and Lana got several speculative looks themselves. Though they had both attended the wedding on their own invite, they were clearly together.

His mother and *baba* were thrilled.

Instead of being annoyed, he found himself amused by their antics as they dropped thinly veiled hints to him and speculated between themselves on what his relationship with Lana was.

When they started in on Lana, though, he got worried.

She hadn't had the best familial relationships in the past and his mother and *baba* could be terrifying. He didn't want Lana feeling overwhelmed, or to get scared off by them, so he stepped in to finally set the record straight.

He put his arm around his diminutive grandmother and kissed her cheek. He was no fool. "*Baba*, I think you should know that protecting Lana is my job right now. We're not a couple."

Baba looked up at him and got that look she used to get just before her wooden spoon connected in a single swat with his backside. "You listen to me, baby-boy, this girl, she and you are so much a couple even that blind Mrs. Cooper at the senior center could see it."

"Mrs. Cooper is the coordinator for the center, she's not blind," Myk's mother argued. "But even if it was Bernie the mailman who always delivers packages to the wrong address, he could see it yet, my son."

Myk frowned at them both. "It's *my job* to keep her safe. Aren't you listening?"

"What she is an illegal immigrant wanted by the mob, or something?" *Baba* shook her head. "Since when does an INS agent protect somebody?"

"I'm not working for the INS on this case." He couldn't tell them who he was working for, but the implication he was working for another agency should be enough.

"What, you got fired?" His mother looked horrified. "No wonder this perfectly lovely doctor does not wish for us to know you are a couple. She should not be seen dating a deadbeat."

"I am not jobless," he gritted out. "I am working for a different agency at the moment."

"Your agency loaned you out?" *Baba* asked. "This is never a good sign. Are you having, what is that thing they say? Oh, yes, a *personality conflict* at the office, baby-boy? You send them to your *baba* and I will set them straight."

"Things are fine at work." Though as he said the words, he knew them for a lie. Things had changed for him and he didn't know if he could continue to work for the government any longer.

"You do not lie to your *baba*. I know what I know and my baby-boy is not so *fine* at work. But unlike your mother, I do not think this lovely doctor scientist needs to worry about you keeping a job. You are a smart boy."

His mother drew herself up in indignation. "I never said I thought my son wasn't smart."

It was at that point the older women switched to Ukrainian and he tuned out their disagreement. He had a lot of practice doing that.

He smiled at Lana. "If they couldn't argue, I think they would both wither away."

Lana didn't return his smile. If he didn't know better, he would think she looked hurt. Really, deeply hurt. But there was nothing here to hurt her. His mother and grandmother wouldn't continue to grill Lana if he insisted they weren't dating.

Maybe she was worried something bad was going to happen at the wedding.

"Don't worry, sweetheart." He smoothed the lapel on her smart-looking dress the same color of green her eyes turned when she was excited. "Nothing is going to happen here. We've got better security than a UN meeting."

He'd started lusting the moment he'd seen her in the dress that morning. It reminded him of sex with Lana; that was enough to keep him in a perpetual state of semi-arousal.

"I'm not worried about security."

He was about to ask what she was worried about when his

baba crowed and slapped his arm. "I heard you call her *sweetheart*. That is not a term from one businessperson to another."

"I didn't say we worked together."

If possible, his mother looked even more gleeful than his *baba*. "Even bodyguards, they do not call their charges *sweetheart*. This time I must agree with your grandmother."

He opened his mouth to speak, but Lana got there first.

"I'm not his sweetheart. I'm not his *anything*. Just a scientist he's trying to protect from some very bad people." Her voice sounded choked, like she was on the verge of tears.

Only he didn't get a chance to check, because she spun on her heel and headed for the group of revelers that included Casey.

He didn't need his mother and grandmother's urging to go after her. He was already on his way. Only when he got there, Lana showed that she was as adept at avoiding a discussion she didn't want to have as he was.

He did not manage to get her alone again until they were in the car on the way back to the beach house. And then, he was focused on making sure they weren't being followed. Not that he didn't try to bring up her remarks, but she refused to talk about it.

He was surprised when she did not give him the cold shoulder in bed that night. She was as responsive as ever, even demanding. And he was more than happy to comply.

They were snuggled in for sleep when he broached the subject again. "What happened at the wedding, doc?"

"Your brother and sister got married," she said drowsily. "Not to each other."

"I know that."

"Why'd you ask?"

"I want to know why you got upset."

"Who says I was upset?"

"Don't play games. Why did you say that to my mother and grandmother?"

"I just confirmed what you had been saying."

"You sounded upset."

"It doesn't matter."

"It does if it hurts you." Except he still didn't know what *it* was.

"I'm fine."

"You *are* my sweetheart."

"You told your mother and grandmother that I'm not."

"That's not what I said."

"It's exactly what you said."

Shit. Here we go again, he thought. "No. I said we aren't a couple. I didn't want them scaring you off with talk of a third wedding."

"Sure. I get it. Go to sleep, Mykola."

He felt like he should say something else, but he didn't know what. "Good night, sweetheart." He kissed the back of her head.

She sighed, but a second later, she snuggled back into him. "Good night."

"You feel good like this." Right. Perfect. Though he wasn't about to admit *that* out loud.

She didn't answer and finally, he drifted off to sleep—still feeling like something was off, but not knowing what it was.

Chapter 21

Sunday, Myk woke up curled around Lana. It felt so damn right and natural; he realized he had some thinking to do.

He extricated himself from her and she shifted, rolling over to face him, her eyes fluttering open as she did so.

She smiled. "Good morning."

"It's one of the best."

Her pretty hazel eyes widened. "Really?"

"Yes." He didn't smile. What he was feeling was too profound. Yeah, definitely some thinking to do.

"Why? Did your boss call and say the bad guys surrendered while I was sleeping?"

"Nope."

"Then why?" That was his Lana, unashamedly inquisitive. It made her a damn fine scientist and an interesting lover.

Memories of waking in the middle of the night with her hands exploring his body warmed him from the inside out. He'd asked her what she was doing. He'd been teasing; he'd *thought* he'd known. He'd been wrong.

She'd been touching him in his sleep to learn the most sensitive places on his body without extraneous stimuli. He had shown her what happened to women who touched their men like that while lying naked in bed beside them.

It had been slow and tender and incredibly satisfying.

He answered her question with nothing less than the truth. "I woke up next to you."

She stared at him, her mouth opening and closing, but no words made it out. Her eyes glistened and he felt like he'd been kicked in the nads. Except his cock was harder than he'd ever been after taking a shot like that during a fight.

"Are you serious?" she finally asked.

"As serious as my *baba* is about keeping the family recipe for *tvorag galushki* a secret until she dies." The old woman had informed her daughter it was in her will, but *Baba* wasn't parting with it before then. It was a source of one the women's favorite arguments.

Lana took a breath as if trying to inhale courage. "Mykola, I want you to know that no matter what happens, I'm so very glad to have had a chance to know you."

Damn it. If he didn't do something soon, his eyes were going to get misty and he hadn't cried since he was six years old and his grandfather had died of an unexpected heart attack. He still missed the old man.

Myk didn't want to think about spending the rest of his life missing Lana.

He rolled on top of her and kissed her so she couldn't say anything else to provoke his emotions.

She melted under him, just like always, responding with a passion no other woman had ever shown Myk. It wasn't just physical response; Lana gave everything of herself when they made love.

He wanted to give her something.

He kissed a trail down her neck and across both breasts, sipping at each nipple for a few tantalizing seconds, before continuing down her body. He stopped to lick her fragrant navel. She'd admitted to rubbing jasmine oil into it and other key spots on her body the night before.

"That feels so good. I don't understand why it does."

He lifted his head, smiling at his sweet little scientist. "Stop trying to analyze it, doc. Maybe what happens between us is just pure magic, sweetheart."

She looked totally dumbfounded. "Say that again."

"It's magic." He dipped his head and kissed the very sensitive skin just below her navel. "You're magic to me."

She so was.

"*Mykola.*"

He didn't know what brought that tone of voice from her, but he was determined to do whatever it took to get it repeated.

He nuzzled the musky curls of her mound and she moaned. He lifted his head once again to make eye contact. He felt deep satisfaction at her dazed expression. "Spread your legs for me, doc."

She obeyed, a soft whimper sounding as his fingers found the slick folds he intended to taste. She was still swollen from their lovemaking the night before and the warm humidity between her legs called to him like the sweet nectar it was.

To him.

He didn't know if it was a chemical match, or just plain magic, but she tasted better to him than any other woman ever had. He gently explored her inner labia and then the warm, wet tunnel of her vagina. "You're so silky soft here, baby."

She hummed, whether it was agreement, or pure pleasure, he didn't know. And honestly, as long as it was a good sound, he didn't care.

He played with her, letting his fingertip just barely brush against that spot inside her that he knew drove her wild. Her body jerked and she made the humming noise again. So pleasure.

He filed that knowledge away for future reference and dipped his head to take the first sample of her warm honey.

She arched her pelvis, chasing more of his tongue, but he kept his oral caresses light and careful.

He wanted this to last and his sensual lover had a tendency to go off like a rocket.

He laved her from the bottom of her labia to the top of her clitoral hood in long, slow swipes over and over again until her pelvis was twitching like an itchy trigger finger. He gently caught her clitoris between his teeth while pressing more firmly against her G-spot, eliciting a long, low moan from her and a sudden arch of her lower body.

He flicked the right side of her clitoris with his tongue tip, repeating the jabbing and then sliding motion until she was begging for him to bring her over. He added a second finger to the first inside her and rubbed her G-spot with stiff digits.

She writhed, crying out and pressing herself into his mobile mouth. Then she was coming, whispering his name over and over, her body convulsing again and again.

He drew the pleasure out until she gasped a word other than his name. "Please."

He knew she meant he had to stop, that she was too sensitive. He loved being able to read her that way.

He wiped his mouth on the sheet and climbed up her body, his dick so hard he thought he would explode.

"Rub off on me," she said, her eyes heavy lidded with satiation.

"No. This was my gift to you."

"Not a whole gift until you come, too."

He stared at her and read in her expression a feeling he knew resided in his own heart. For his pleasure to be complete with her, it needed to be mutual.

She licked her lips. "Another fantasy for me."

"Me rubbing off on you?"

"Yes."

"You're an amazingly sensuous woman, doc."

She just looked at him.

"How do you want it?" he asked, giving in.

Because he wanted her to have her every fantasy and the thought of coming against her excited him beyond his ability to control.

She spread her legs so he rested between her thighs, his hard-on pressed against the top of her mound.

"This is dangerous, sweetheart."

"You'll be careful."

Damn right he would. He was so turned on it only took a few strokes and he was coming all over her stomach, white jets of come landing in pearlescent globs against her pale skin.

"Now, rub it in."

He didn't ask if she was kidding. He could tell by her tone she wasn't, but damn, he hadn't seen this earthy side to her. He liked it. He liked it a lot. Maybe even loved it.

He'd never before experienced the primal feeling of possession marking her with his most intimate scent gave him. "Damn, baby, this might be a fantasy I never knew about."

She smiled, still boneless from her own prolonged orgasm. "If I tell you there is a chemical in a man's sperm that works like endorphins for his partner, helping her maintain a more positive mood, does that take away the sexiness for you?"

"Nope. Just makes me hotter."

"*It's magic,*" she whispered, like it was a secret. "The science kind."

He nodded his head as the last of his come disappeared like lotion into her skin. "Magic."

They showered together later, but he thought he could still smell his scent on her afterward. He liked that more than he wanted to admit.

His phone was ringing when they stepped back into the bedroom after drying off.

He looked at the caller ID and answered. "Morning, sir."

"Good morning, Myk. I'd like to meet with you before flying back to D.C. later today."

"Did you have a location in mind?"

"I'd like to see Smith's brainchild."

"ETRD?"

"Yes."

"What time, sir?"

"We can share lunch in the employee dining room. Smith bragged about his chef."

"I'm sure the head chef isn't working on Sunday."

"If he's as good as Smith says he is, he's trained his people to prepare equally delicious dishes in his absence."

"Do I sense a small rivalry here, sir?" Something like the one between his mother and grandmother. Not an angry rivalry but there nonetheless.

"Perhaps, agent, perhaps."

Myk laughed. "I'll be there at noon on the dot, sir."

"I look forward to our meeting."

"You're a glutton for punishment, aren't you, sir?"

"I think I'm growing on you, Myk. Don't think I haven't notice you calling me sir, which is a step up from Whitmore."

Myk laughed and hung up without saying goodbye.

Maybe the Old Man *was* wearing on him. Not that he was sure he wanted to keep working for TGP, but he understood a little better how Whitmore could have pulled Elle from the field. Everyone at ETRD knew who she had worked for. Not just the select two Smith had revealed her status to.

When she heard he was going to ETRD, Lana insisted on going with him.

"Sweetheart, I already agreed to take you to work tomorrow, as long as nothing we overhear on our listening devices makes me think that will increase your risk."

"We know Vega's scientists are busy today testing the en-

zymes under various conditions, trying to make them work."
She glared at nothing in particular. "I've lost enough time in
my lab due to that man's interference. If I have a chance to
take some of it back, I'm going to."

"All right, doc. You can come."

He wasn't surprised when Casey wanted to come, too, not
when Nisha made it clear she could afford some time at ETRD
catching up on work. He took the scientists in his Land
Rover and a detail of Brett's men followed in one of their Escalades.

Lana and Casey worked on updating measurements in both
growing rooms, working together instead of separately as
was their norm. That had been Mykola's idea. He wanted one
of their guards at the lab door and the other inside the growing room with them.

"I appreciate Myk assigning a guard to Nisha today," Casey
said as he wrote down the measurements Lana had just given
him. "It makes me feel safer."

"Being kidnapped is terrifying. It leaves you paranoid for a
long time after, on your own behalf and that of the people
you care about."

"Is that why you bought me a watch with a GPS locator in
it?" Casey asked. "You care about me, huh?"

"You're my best friend, Casey."

"And here I thought you always saw me as an annoying
little brother."

Lana grinned. "Well, you can be annoying."

"I'm not mad."

"That I bought the watch and didn't tell you about the locator?"

"Yeah. I understand."

"Thank you. That means a lot."

"You think Nisha would wear one?"

Lana didn't laugh. She didn't even feel like cracking a smile. She understood what Casey felt. She shrugged. "You should probably ask her. Maybe an anklet, or something."

"Where's yours?"

"Who said I have one?"

"I'm keeping my watch on."

She nodded. "It's a belly button ring and Mr. Smith has the GPS connection for it."

"Are you going to give access to Myk, too?"

She wished she could. "He'll only be around until the current case is resolved, Casey."

"Are you serious?" Casey looked shocked. "No way. The guy has it bad for you, Lana. Maybe as bad as I've got it for Nisha."

"You're crazy." Oh, that was diplomatic. There went her nonexistent filter again.

"Not even. He couldn't keep his hands off you the first day you met. Come on, Lana. What do you think that means?"

"That he's highly sexual and knew I wanted him? I blurted it out when I first saw him. I was talking to myself again."

Casey didn't even crack a smile. "So? He had to be way into you to make out with you while his sister was still at risk from Vega."

She'd never thought of that. "You think?"

"You're the one that says I'm better at scenario creation than you."

"Don't get cocky or I'll put you on the *Oryza sativa* detail for two straight weeks." See how he liked getting what he'd started referring to as the "stink of death growing room" every day instead of every other day.

"Playing the boss card, are you?"

"It has its merits."

Casey laughed. "Right. You'd keep it up for three days

maybe before guilt got the better of you. You're too nice, Lana."

"And you take advantage of that."

"Actually I don't. That's why you trust me."

It was true. Casey had proven time and again to be a person of deep integrity. "I do."

"I know."

"I don't trust very many people."

"I figured that out. You mutter to yourself about stuff in your past sometimes."

Lana sighed. "You know about Turkey."

"Yes. I know you have almost no control over your talking when your brain is engaged in your work. So, at first I tried not to listen and then I just decided you wouldn't talk about the stuff around me if you didn't subconsciously trust me."

"Because you noticed I didn't talk about that stuff in front of other people."

"How did you know?"

"Because no one else here knew about Turkey until Elle told them."

"Cool."

She gave him a questioning look.

"It's one thing to surmise you trust me, it's another thing to *know* it."

She nodded, understanding washing over her.

Because no matter how many ways she thought to convince herself that Mykola saw her as something more than a convenient sex partner, until he confirmed it irrevocably, there was a part of her heart that was going to keep hurting. What scared her was the knowledge that that pain would be with her from now on.

When they got back to the beach house, Myk asked Lana if she wanted to sit in on the sit rep from Brett. He'd had to explain that meant situation report and then she'd both agreed and smiled, telling him she enjoyed learning his shorthand talk as much as knowing her own industry's.

Once again, he was unsurprised when Casey and Nisha asked to join them. He led them all into the living room.

Brett and Claire were sitting together on the extrawide armchair that matched the white leather sofa. They were kissing passionately.

Myk cleared his throat, but Casey wasn't so circumspect. He let out a loud wolf whistle that had the couple springing apart.

Brett just grinned at them all, but Claire turned an interesting shade of crimson.

"You got a sit rep for me, Brett?" Myk asked as he sat down on the end of the couch closest to the married couple.

Lana sat next to him and he smiled inwardly to see Nisha and Casey taking similar positions at the other end of the long sofa.

"Vega is pissed," Brett said succinctly.

Claire nodded. "None of the experiments have resulted in any change whatsoever."

"Of course not." Lana sounded happy about that fact.

Brett smiled at her. "Ramirez has tried to convince him that maybe the enzymes only work on plants."

"He's not happy about that possibility, either," Claire said, sounding worried.

"What aren't you saying?" Myk asked her.

"He hasn't come right out and said it, but I think Ramirez is in real trouble," Claire replied. "The way he was swearing and knocking things around his office, I would be surprised if he didn't hurt her, or worse."

"You think he's going to kill her?" Myk asked.

"I think it's a possibility."

"I think he's already hurt her," Brett said. "Some of the

sounds I heard during his latest temper tantrum were unmistakably flesh hitting flesh and a body hitting a wall at one point. She was talking after that, so I know he didn't kill her, but one more temper tantrum and I think he'll use his gun on her."

Myk sighed. "That would not be atypical for him."

Lana sat up. "Mykola, we have to do something. We can't let him kill her."

"She knew what she was getting into when she started working for him. It was her spying that put you and my sister at risk."

"Yes, to one and no to the other. You can't be sure she knew what she was getting into when she started working for him, or that she even had a choice. They're related. You better than anyone should know cartel *jefes* don't give their family a choice about working in the family business."

"It's true," Brett said.

"What can I do?" Myk asked, exasperated.

"I don't know. But I know you can do something. She's probably terrified for her life right now."

"She might flip for a chance at witness protection," Brett mused.

"How soon can you get an extraction team down there?" Myk asked him.

"Not as soon as the mercenary team that took over our business when we got out of extractions."

"Call them."

"I'll keep looking for some kind of map of the compound on one of the systems I hacked," Claire said and then started looking worried again. "What are we going to do to keep Rarmirez alive in the meantime? Vega's temper is on a hair trigger. He really doesn't like being disappointed."

"Were you able to hack into data on Vega's organization?" Myk asked her.

"Yep. I've got information the CIA would kill for."

"We'll figure out how to make an anonymous information drop later. Right now, I want to know if you were able to get his personal cell number and those of his employees?"

"As a matter of fact, I was."

"Okay, we call Ramirez and we offer the data."

"She is our negotiator?" Brett asked.

"Right."

"What's to stop Vega from demanding to negotiate the deal himself?"

"We tell him Lana doesn't trust men and will only negotiate with a woman. She knows Ramirez, so she's willing to talk to her."

"You're brilliant!" Lana threw her arms around Myk and gave him a tight hug. "The prospect of getting what he wants should keep her alive until we get her out."

"What if she won't flip?" Claire asked.

Myk shrugged. Not his problem. "Then we charge her with kidnapping and she goes to prison. Whatever happens from there is on her own head."

Brett nodded. "It's a plan."

Claire got both Ramirez's and Vega's numbers for Myk.

First Myk called Vega, using an untraceable disposable cell phone. He didn't bother with preliminaries. As soon as the man picked up he said, "Dr. Lana Ericson will be calling your girl Ramirez in the next few minutes with an offer you won't want to refuse."

He hung up in the middle of Vega's demand to know who he was speaking to.

Lana called Ramirez and put the call on speaker.

"Hello?" Ramirez said, sounding far from her cocky self. In fact, she sounded exhausted, the kind of tired that comes from being so terrified a person can't maintain the fear-induced adrenaline.

"This is Dr. Ericson from ETRD."

"We were informed to expect a call."

"By now, you have no doubt discovered that my enzymes do not work on anything but the plants they were developed for."

"What? They don't work on metal at all?" Now, Ramirez sounded resigned. To something terrible.

"No, they don't."

"But you said in your notes they would turn lead into gold."

"Achieving a second harvest on staple food crops *is* that to me."

"Oh."

Spanish swearing erupted from someone else in the room. Ramirez's phone must be on speaker as well. The sound of flesh hitting flesh could be heard. Ramirez made a sound of pain, then Vega said something to her in rapid-fire Spanish.

"Can the enzymes be made to work?" Ramirez asked.

"I'm not prepared to answer that question just yet."

"Once I have you in my custody, you will answer that question and much more," Vega said over Ramirez's phone.

"That is yet another reason not to trust men. I will not negotiate with *you*, Vega. Tell Ms. Ramirez I will call her tomorrow with my offer." Lana hung up.

Myk kissed her soundly. "Well, done, doc. I couldn't have handled it any better myself."

"Do you think he bought the misandrist attitude?"

"A chauvinist like him? You bet he'll buy that a successful female scientist is a man-hater. How else could he explain your decision to go into the world of academia rather than marry and have children?"

"Why do you think he's a chauvinist?" Lana asked. "Ramirez was point *man* on the kidnapping."

"I learned a lot more than I wanted to about Vega while interrogating Jorge." He'd learned that Vega was a crazy bastard who *never* gave up a pet project and who saw people as highly disposable tools for his benefit and his benefit alone.

Vega tried calling Lana's personal cell phone, but Claire had rigged it not to go to voice mail, so Lana did not pick up. Myk was sure Vega's inability to wrest control of the situation from the scientist infuriated him, which kept him just that much more off his game.

All part of Myk's overall plan. The one he had no intention of revealing until it had run its full course.

Chapter 22

Myk convinced Lana not to worry about copying her enzyme project notes just yet. He told her that he would set a date for delivery that would give her plenty of time to make sure she had a full set of files for herself. He wanted her relaxed, rather than on edge, waiting to complete the plan.

He took her swimming in the pool. They both swam laps before Brett and Claire joined them, Brett starting a water fight that finally broke the aura of tension that had been surrounding Lana.

Myk made a note to thank the other man later.

They had just finished dressing again when Myk's cell phone rang. It was Whitmore again.

"What's up, sir?"

"I just got word that Taiwanese troops with covert U.S. manpower support will be converging on the coordinates you provided for the scrap-metal stockpile."

"We can only hope they find some of the barge crews alive."

"I'll let you know how it goes down as soon as I'm briefed."

"Thank you, sir."

"Just doing my job while you do yours." Whit paused for a brief moment. "Any updates on the case?"

"We made contact with Vega. We're going to negotiate the

exchange of Lana's research for his cease and desist in attempting to kidnap her or her assistant."

"I'm assuming it is research that won't do him any good."

"You assume correctly."

"You think he'll keep his word?"

"I think we'll convince him it's in his best interests to do so."

"I see. Is this something else I can expect to be glossed over in your report."

"Yes, sir."

"Myk, TGP agents don't work this way."

"I'm aware of that, sir."

Whitmore's sigh was too damn knowing.

"I didn't intend to quit after this assignment when I took it, sir."

"You may not have intended to do so, but I would have been surprised, pleasantly I might add, but surprised all the same if you hadn't."

"How could you know?"

"I read the file on your last case. A Chernichenko does not take that kind of thing lightly."

"No, we don't."

"You're burnt out on being a federal agent."

"The red tape protects the criminals more often than the victims of their crimes."

"I know it can seem that way."

"It does."

"I understand. When Elle finds out, she'll offer you a job."

"Her partner already has."

"Before you accept it, I suggest you consider another possibility?"

"That is?"

"ETRD needs a permanent head of security who knows what he's doing."

"You think Mr. Smith would hire me?"

"I know he would."

"You've already talked about it with him?"

"He brought it up."

"It's something to think about."

"I'll leave it to you to tell him that."

"Thank you."

Well, that was a discussion he hadn't expected to have with his boss, but it had not been unwelcome.

Around two a.m. Claire found Vega's Mexico compound layout and security schematics. The extraction team was already in place, ready to take action. Two and a half hours later, a drugged, unconscious Ramirez was on a flight headed for the airstrip near the beach house.

Twenty minutes after getting that call, Myk got another from Whitmore.

He woke Lana to give her the news. "Three of Vega's people are in custody. Two are dead."

"And the barge crews?"

"Ten are alive. Three died in the firefight between Vega's men and the Taiwan troops."

"He had the other twenty killed?"

"As far as the authorities have been able to ascertain, yes. One of the victims told them his other crew members had been tossed into the ocean to drown after their barge was hijacked. Apparently, Vega kept only enough crew members alive to work as slave labor hauling and sorting the scrap metal."

"That bastard." Tears filled Lana's eyes. "That *monstrous bastard.*"

"You said it."

Lana blinked away the moisture. "And Ramirez?"

"On her way here."

"When are you going to call Vega?"

"As soon as you're ready. I figured you'd want to listen in."

"I so do." She grabbed a robe and followed him to the room where Claire had been doing her hacking. It was a state-of-the-art office located in the center of the house and harder to get to than any of the other public rooms.

Unlike Vega's in his compound. He was egotistical enough to want a corner office. More the fool him.

Brett and Claire were waiting for Myk and Lana. Claire had an earbud in one ear. "I'll be listening in on the computers I compromised, hoping to find one near where Vega is when he talks to you."

Brett looked at his wife with pride. "That way if he gives any instructions to his underlings, we'll know about it."

The phone was picked up on the second ring. "Speak." Vega did not sound like he'd been sleeping.

"Vega," Myk said.

"You. Is your scientist preparing to call Ramirez? You should tell her I do not appreciate being hung up on." The menace in his voice would have been chilling if Myk didn't know he could keep Lana safe from the other man. Absolutely.

"Should Dr. Ericson wish to speak to Ramirez she can do so face-to-face."

"What the hell are you talking about?" But as evil as Vega might be, he wasn't stupid. He ordered someone to check Ramirez's room.

Claire gave Myk a thumbs-up letting him know she'd isolated which room Vega was in. He pointed to the printout they'd made of the compound's layout. Claire nodded and circled Vega's private corner office.

Myk turned away from the others in the room and sent a text to his brother Roman.

"What have you done with my family?" Vega demanded a few seconds later, sounding on the verge of another one of his tantrums.

"What family?"

"Maria Ramirez."

"It's disconcerting, isn't it?"

"What?" Vega snarled.

"Having your security compromised. Knowing that someone can come in and take anyone they like?"

"Are you saying that's how your doctor felt? Am I supposed to feel badly for her?" the drug lord sneered.

"Not at all. After all, your team didn't succeed, did they? She, and everyone else at ETRD, knows that I will keep them safe. Your people are probably not feeling quite so secure right now."

"My people know that my retribution is terrible."

"Talk like that is not going to get you Dr. Ericson's research."

"Why would you give it to me?"

"I want your word you won't come after ETRD's scientists again."

"It sounds like you're worried, even if your people aren't."

"No. I am a man who knows how to take the shortest path to my goal."

"And your goal here is?"

"To get you out of ETRD's hair, now and forever."

"And you would trust my word?"

"Are you telling me I shouldn't?"

"Not at all, merely pointing out I would not be so trusting in the same situation."

"I see." While he talked to Vega, Myk wrote a note to Claire and asked her if anyone else was in the room with Vega.

She clicked a few clicks with her mouse and then shook her head. "I don't hear a second person breathing in the room," she mouthed.

He nodded. Good.

"You will give me the formula for turning lead into gold?" Vega asked impatiently.

"No. There is no such thing. The enzymes are DNA specific. Dr. Ericson is not convinced they can be made viable at all, but particularly not for metal transformation."

"So, why the hell should I deal?"

"Because the idea is too tempting to give up on. Dr. Ericson will give you all her research to this point. Your own scientists may be able to do what she can't. I assume they would be more motivated."

"And if I decide I want Lana Ericson to do the research for me?"

"You didn't succeed the first time you tried to take her and you would not succeed again, but *if* you come after her again, *I* will come after *you*."

"And this should worry me why?"

"Because when Ramirez was taken, that could have been you. Don't think your additional bedroom alarm complete with floor lasers will save your greedy ass."

"What the hell do you know about my security system?'

"You're just now thinking to ask that question?"

"How do I know Dr. Ericson's notes aren't forged or altered in some way?" Clearly, Vega didn't dwell on conversational topics that revealed his own shortcomings.

"We'll courier you the originals. You can have your scientists test the age on the ink she uses for her notes."

"And if I don't take your deal?"

"I'll leave the consequences to your imagination."

"I'll take it." Vega sounded angry enough to kill, but he had no one on whom to vent his wrath.

That was exactly what Myk wanted to hear. Now, they could get down to the conversation that really mattered.

"I want to know who besides yourself knows about Dr. Ericson's research."

"Why?"

"I want a guarantee no one else will come after her because you've talked up a technology that does not exist anywhere but in your mind."

"I don't share that sort of thing, even with my lieutenants."

"Are you saying no one else knows?"

"I have a partner. He is the only one besides Ramirez who knows."

"Where are the notes Ramirez originally stole on the project?"

"Where else would they be? I keep them with me. I had an unfortunate incident where copies of the notes were lost during an associate's problems with the law," he admitted.

It was obvious the other man wasn't worried about Myk's reaction to the news the notes had been shared with others, which made Myk think he wasn't bothering to hold anything back.

"So, that associate knows as well?" he asked, pushing.

"He is not a danger to your scientists."

"How do you figure that?"

"He's dead. Shot by some bastard *federales*."

Myk was that bastard, but now he knew Vega was telling the truth. He sent a final text.

"The project notes will be sent tomorrow," he lied smoothly to Vega.

"How are you sending them?"

"I got Ramirez out of your compound." He enjoyed needling the other man's monumental ego. "I think I can get a file box in."

"Fine."

They hung up.

Claire's eyebrows climbed to her hairline. "He's calling you lots of nasty names in Spanish."

"You really think he'll keep his word?" Brett asked.

"No."

Claire gasped loudly and then turned a measuring look on Myk. "You really didn't trust him, did you?"

"He wasn't a trustworthy man."

"You said wasn't," Lana said with a question in her voice.

Myk met her beautiful gaze. "He would always have been a serious threat to your safety and freedom."

"What did you do?"

"There was an explosion at the compound," Claire said when Myk didn't answer. "I can still hear from my other feeds, but the one that had been coming from Vega's office is non-functional."

"So, he's the only one who died?" Lana asked, her tone even.

"If his lieutenant was with him, he died, too. He would not have allowed anyone else to overhear that conversation. But Claire said she didn't hear another person breathing in the room."

"How did you do it?"

"Do you really want to know?"

She thought for a second and then shook her head. "Maybe not, but you'll always keep your promises, won't you?"

"Yes."

"Even if it means doing something you'd rather not have to do."

"Even then."

She turned to Claire. "He promised me Vega would never take me or get at Casey again."

Claire whistled under her breath. "I'd say that's a safe bet now."

"Yes."

"Well, as far as I'm concerned, one of Vega's many enemies got to him," Brett said.

"Definitely," Claire said with certainty.

Lana reached up and kissed Myk's cheek. "Sometimes we have to do horrible things to stop even worse things from happening." She patted his chest, right over his warrior tattoo. "No one will ever hear a negation of Claire's assumption from me." She paused to let that sink in. "I need a shower."

She left the room and Myk's body sagged with relief she had not hated him for the steps he'd known had to be taken to keep Vega out of her life.

An insane, sadistic megalomaniac like him would never have given up on his plan to turn lead into gold and flood the financial markets with precious metals. He'd had to be stopped, permanently.

He called Whitmore to update him on the arrival of Ramirez back in the country and tell him about the data on Vega's organization Claire had gathered. They both agreed it would be best to provide that information to both the CIA and the Colombian government. It would be up to both what they did with it, considering its anonymous source.

Ramirez might still be able to cop a witness protection situation if she was willing to bring down Vega's lieutenants. The choice, as Myk and Brett had already discussed, would be hers.

Myk followed Lana to their bedroom after his call to Whitmore, but she was still taking a shower when Roman called.

"It's done."

"We heard."

"Claire is a scary woman. Military intelligence should be so lucky to have someone of her caliber working on the Geek Squad."

"The explosion was contained."

"One of the benefits to having the buildings designed bomb-proof like they were. We planted the explosives in his office when the extraction team was inside getting Ramirez out. They didn't see us, and neither did Vega's people."

"Naturally."

"As we agreed, I detonated when you confirmed the information on Lana's experiments were with Vega."

"He didn't tell anyone else except Musa about the enzymes."

"That's good to know. Do I need to take care of Musa?"

"No. I've got it covered."

"Mind telling me by who?"

"Lana met some people after she broke out of her prison lab in northern Turkey. They helped her get back to the States."

"They have access to Musa?"

"Yes. He will die of what will look like natural causes within the week."

"Little brother, you have a ruthless side I never would have guessed existed."

"Only when it comes to the people I love."

"So, *Baba* was right. You are in love."

"Yes."

"Does she feel the same way?"

"She trusts me."

"From what you told me about her, that's major for her."

"Yeah, I'd say it was love. I just hope she's figured that out because I'm not going anywhere."

"Hell, Myk, I have faith in your powers of persuasion. You got Elle out of the country when she had a case of interest in her perimeter."

"Lana helped."

"Really? I already thought I liked her, now I know it."

"She was on her best behavior at the wedding."

"Yeah?"

"Yes, she has a tendency to talk to herself and not filter what comes out of her mouth."

"Sounds interesting."

"It has its moments."

Roman made a sound of amusement. It wasn't a full chuckle, but then Myk could count on one hand the number of times he'd heard his big brother laugh in the last ten years—and he would have fingers left over.

Lana came out of the bathroom and found Myk waiting for her on the end of the bed. He looked so ruggedly hand-some, such a perfect bad boy with a protective knight's heart.

"We can go home now, can't we?" she asked. This house was amazing, but she wanted her own bed.

She wanted Mykola to herself for however long she had with him.

"Can we?"

"What do you mean?"

"Can we go home?" he asked.

"What are you saying, Myk?"

"I'm quitting the TGP."

"You'd have to, wouldn't you?"

"I love that you understand that."

"I understand a lot about you, but some stuff has to be spelled out, Mykola."

"Like the fact that I'm so in love with you I'll even work for Mr. Smith so I can stay close to you?"

She stared at him, unable to take in what he'd just said. "You love me?"

"So much it hurts."

"No."

"What? Why no?"

"No one has ever loved me deep down and forever."

"I do. I will."

"Is that a promise?" she asked, tears clogging her throat.

He got up and came to stand right in front of her, then he

dropped to one knee. "It's the most important promise I've ever made."

"I drive people crazy."

"You drive me nuts in ways that excite and delight, sweetheart. I don't want you to be anything different than what you are."

"You don't mind the Disney décor?"

"I love the Disney décor. It shows you still believe in magic."

Like he'd told her earlier, she loved that he understood important things about her. "I do. I really do. Especially the magic of love."

"So, you'll marry me?" he asked.

She swallowed convulsively, desperately wanting to get the one-word answer out, but not able to get her vocal cords to cooperate.

"You can just nod."

Tears of joy spilled over as she did. And then she kept nodding until he kissed her. Somehow they ended up snuggled together on a lounger on the balcony.

She pressed baby kisses all over his face and throat. "I love you, too, Mykola. I was so sure you were going to leave and shatter my heart."

"Never." He grabbed her chin, gently forcing her gaze to meet his. The emotion there made her heart constrict in wonder. "A woman like you comes into a man's life once. Only an idiot would let you go."

A smile she couldn't have stopped if she'd wanted creased her lips. "And you aren't stupid."

"Not at all."

"I don't know about having children." She was scared to tell him, but he deserved to know. "There are so many bad people in the world, people that could hurt them."

"I understand, baby."

"Do you really?" She bit her lip. "I try so hard to see the

good in the world, but the bad stuff is always out there ready to scare me."

"If we have children, you and I will both need to spend a lot less time at work and a lot more time at home. You've got a whole world full of starving children that would benefit from you sticking with your consuming research."

"You really believe that?"

"I really believe it."

"Maybe . . . maybe after I've perfected the enzymes and I'm ready to cut back on my research we could think about adopting."

"Lots of kids need families."

"Right, some that are starving for love as much as the ones starving for food."

"You're going to want to Lojack them, aren't you?"

"Probably. Just like I'm going to Lojack you."

He laughed and kissed her. "I'll wear a watch, but no way am I getting my belly button pierced."

"What about a nipple?"

"Oh, shit, you are going to keep me on my toes."

"Always."

"Always. I love you Lana, in a way I honestly never thought I'd be capable of doing."

"I love you, Mykola. You are my one and only."

"I'll love you forever."

"Promise?"

"On my heart."